THE HUNTED

VAMPIRE NAVY SEAL

S.B. ALEXANDER

Cover designed by Hang Le
Cover copyright © 2022 by S.B. Alexander

The Hunted
Book one: Vampire Navy SEAL – Sam and Layla Series

First Edition: January 2022

E-book ISBN-13: 978-1-954888-03-6
Paperback Print ISBN-13: 978-1-954888-04-3
Large Print ISBN – 13: 978-1-954888-05-0
Audiobook ISBN – 13: 978-1-954888-07-4

1

SAM

The area was shrouded in darkness as vampires entered the seedy club. The music from inside was loud and obnoxious, the bass heavy, and the electric guitar was ear-piercing, making me want to cringe with my sharp vampire hearing. I hated grunge. My taste in music was more on the indie rock side. But I wasn't there to dissect music genres.

My team and I were on a mission to gather intel on a well-known vampire criminal, Roman Brown, who ran one of the largest syndicates of the Vampire Blood Cartel. We'd gotten word he was meeting that night with Jose Douglas, the owner of the club. Our orders were to watch and listen, not to engage, not to kill, and not to reveal who we were.

Ben was positioned inside, Kraft was guarding the back exit, and Olivia was about a block and a half away. I watched the front entrance from a secluded alcove in an abandoned building that had once been home to a textile company.

An old rusty Nissan, a shiny new red truck, and a Porsche sat in the gravel lot across the street. The foot traffic going inside the club was nil to light for a weeknight.

The wind kicked up as the clouds skated over the crescent moon. Thank fuck it wasn't a full moon, or shifters would be tearing up the streets, and I didn't care to tango with them. They were known to be quite restless leading up to a full moon.

Chewing on the inside of my cheek, I leaned against a cement wall. I was veiled in the shadows of the dimly lit street, in a perfect spot to monitor who went in and who came out.

"Ben, do you copy?" I asked into my comm.

"Ten-four. Nothing happening," he returned. "I count about ten vamps. Jose is on his phone by the bar. But no sign of our target."

We suspected, if our intel was correct, that Roman might slip in through the backdoor.

"Maybe we got bogus info," Kraft chimed in.

"Let's give it another thirty minutes, then we'll call it a night. Roman is probably waiting for the club to clear out. This shithole closes in an hour, anyway," I said.

"We've got a black four-door sedan heading your way." Olivia's voice came through loud and clear.

Within seconds, headlights bounced along the street before a sleek black car slowed to a stop in front of the entrance.

I straightened. Maybe we were about to get lucky. The bio we had on Roman indicated he had a penchant for expensive black cars. The Infiniti sedan was high-end, but not in the realm of the Mercedes Roman had been seen in by our scouts. He liked to live high on the hog and spared no expense when it came to building his empire. To me, he was foolish. If I were trying to stay under the radar of the Vampire Council of Elders, showing off would be the last thing I would do.

The sedan's back door opened, and a brunette emerged, followed by a shorter chick with lighter brown hair than her friend. Both had their hair up, exposing their smooth long necks, and both were dressed in tight black jeans, cut-off tops, and boots that traveled up over their knees.

Automatically, I sniffed the air. A hint of sweetness carried on the wind and knocked me back a step. Definitely human. Definitely stupid to be walking into a vamp club, and even more idiotic to expose those smooth necks. Every vampire inside would be lining up to get a taste.

Hell, my gums pounded with the need to release my fangs. I had a ton of restraint, but I wasn't perfect. Still, my pulse shot up ten notches, and not because of my thirst for delectable human blood. If I had to save a human, that would only compromise our mission.

The problem, though, was that as vampire soldiers—Navy SEALs to be exact—we protected our own, but also humans, both foreign and domestic. Not only was it our job to make sure vampires didn't kill humans, but we took down the lowest, dirtiest, and most lethal of vampires who broke our laws, and we had strict ones in our world.

A third woman climbed out. She was slender yet curvy and dressed in an outfit similar to her friends'. Her auburn hair was thick, long, and wavy, spilling down around her shoulders.

I sucked in air. Her emotions hit me like a Mack truck—fear, nervousness, and a dusting of excitement.

Fucking empath ability.

My twin sister could read minds, but I'd gotten stuck with feeling every damn emotion on humans and any supernatural. If I let them, those emotions could stop me in my tracks.

Red whipped around. Her blue gaze, a beacon in the night, darted in all directions as if she knew I were hiding in the shadows. Then she tapped the roof of the car, and the front passenger window lowered.

"Thank you. We don't need your services anymore tonight," she said to the driver. The sound of her voice slid up my arm like butter on warm toast.

I sniffed the air once again, and this time my fangs slid out of their own accord. Where her friends smelled like apple pie, Red's scent was chocolate and cherries. I dragged my tongue over one fang, staving off the need to taste her that instant.

Focus, man or your ass will be chum for the fish in the bay if you fuck up this basic mission.

With my fang embedded in my tongue, I sharpened my hearing.

Her two friends shimmied up to the bald bouncer.

The taller of the brunettes rubbed her hands up the beefy vampire's chest.

"Rianne," the shorter brunette said in a teasing tone. "I think we should show him a good time."

The two women giggled like schoolgirls flirting with the hot quarterback at a pep rally.

The humans were definitely either smoking crack or up to something. The bouncer wasn't just a regular guy. He stood two heads taller than the women and had arms like a sumo wrestler. He could sink his fangs into them before they could blink.

"Should we show him how we do a three-some?" Rianne asked her shorter companion.

The redhead joined her friends. "Ladies, we should take this inside."

The bouncer eagerly opened the door for them, his fangs front and center with an odd grin on his face as though he was drunk.

Red tossed a look over her shoulder, scanned the area once, and then went inside.

The hackles on my neck rose high as her fear tickled my senses.

As if the humans were leading the bouncer to slaughter, he followed on their heels.

"Ben, do you copy?"

"Go," he said.

"Three humans, women, are heading your way."

"Humans are not our problem tonight." Kraft's tone was placid. "But keep an eye on them, Ben."

Our orders were simple. "Don't blow your cover for anyone," Webb London, commander of the Navy SEAL team, my brother-in-law, and a vampire I didn't want to piss off, had made a point to tell the four of us not once, but twice.

"Something stinks of trouble," I said. "I can't help but think that Roman sent them in to do his dirty work." Humans mixed with vamps was never a good combination.

"Another bogie coming your way," Olivia announced.

I licked the blood off my lip as a black Mercedes pulled up to the entrance. I slinked back into the shadows, toying with my fangs with the tip of my tongue.

The back passenger door opened, and Roman Brown got out, combing a hand through his blond military cut. He waited a beat before a curvy woman who was all legs and tits took his hand.

He grinned like he was in love, his canines pointy and sharp.

The buxom blonde rose up on her toes and kissed him square on the mouth. "I love when you look at me like that."

The good news was that the woman wasn't

human but a shifter. They always had a distinct earthy dog odor. Nevertheless, I made a mental note to add her to our intel.

A sharply dressed vampire in a pinstriped suit that seemed too small for his broad chest got out of the front passenger side and scanned the area, staying close to Roman and his date.

Once they were inside and out of earshot, I alerted the team. "Our target is headed in. Remember to observe and don't engage."

Maybe our info was wrong, and Roman wasn't in the market for vampire blood but human blood, which was why the humans were there. While that was possible, I shrugged it off. Human blood was readily available at blood banks, and Roman could raid those without a second thought. Besides, he made his money from the vampires who had rare abilities similar to mine.

As natural-born vampires, we carried a gene that would give us two supernatural abilities when activated around our teenage years. If a vamp developed anything more than that, they were considered unique or elite. However, in our world, my sister, father, and I were the only vampires who had been gifted, or cursed in some respects, with several supernatural abilities. No other vampire could read minds like my father and sister, and for that very reason, we were considered powerful. So much so that we'd been hunted by our own kind for our DNA. Vampires like Roman, who were hungry for power and wanted to build armies of vampires, could only succeed if they turned humans into vampires. That was how Ben had become a half-breed. He'd been turned by a former enemy who was now dead.

Vampires began to run out of the club as if there was a fire.

I bolted into action and stopped a heavyset dude who had terror in his eyes. "What's going on?"

He bared his fangs. "It's chaos in there. Vamps are passing out."

I knitted my brow. "From what?"

He stabbed a fat finger at the entrance. "Three humans are shooting darts at vamps like they're target practice. I'm not hanging around to find out what's in those suckers, especially if it's some endotoxin. That shit might not be able to kill some of the elite military vamps, but I'm just a lowlife."

My slow vampire pulse ramped up to a hundred beats per minute in less than a second. I didn't have time to question him about how he knew of the endotoxin. That was top-secret government info, but we had our own dark web where info could be found.

If those darts were filled with the endotoxin, then the correct dose could kill any vampire. Even as one of the military elites he'd referred to, I wasn't immune. But I wasn't worried about myself. Ben was in more danger since he was part human.

I started to run towards the club when the heavyset dude caught my arm. "Don't go in there if you want to live."

"They're human," I said. "Surely, a vampire can take them out."

He laughed, walking away. "It's your life."

2

SAM

I was met with ghostly silence as I entered, almost tripping over the bouncer, who was out cold. I could still hear his heartbeat, so he wasn't dead.

"Olivia, Kraft, we have a problem," I said into my comm. "The humans are shooting darts filled with some type of drug. Kraft, stay put and detain whoever exits the building. Olivia, get down here and guard the front entrance."

Both returned with "copy that."

I pulled out a leather strap from the side pocket of my cargo pants and tied my black hair back into a low ponytail. Then I jogged down the long hallway. The smell of stale beer co-mingled with the humans' sweet fragrance. My gums throbbed. The thirst for blood was stronger than ever as adrenaline coursed through me at warp speed.

I slowed as I approached the doorway leading into the main part of the club.

"You don't know what you're getting into." Ben's voice trickled out into the hall, but I couldn't see him yet.

"Shut up, or I'll gut you like a fish," one of the female humans replied.

I stepped off to the side of the doorway to get a glimpse of what I was dealing with. Vampires were passed out on the floor or slumped over tables, and the shorter brunette was pointing a gun at the back of someone's head who I couldn't see from where I stood.

I opened up a telepathic connection. *Ben, what are we up against?*

The three women have dart guns filled with a drug that shuts down limbs and knocks you out. The two brunettes have Roman at gunpoint. He's not passing out like the other vamps. Not sure why. The redhead who seems to be the leader has a needle primed and ready to jab in my neck, Ben responded.

Is Roman the only vamp awake? I relayed to Ben.

Yep. The bartender is out behind the bar. The

owner of the club, Jose, is also slumped over at Roman's table.

What the fuck do they want?

You, man, Ben replied.

What the fuck do humans want with me? It was a rhetorical question, and the only answer that came to mind was that it had to do with the CIA.

Granted, there were a handful of top human officials high up in the chain of command who knew of our existence. The Council of Elders worked with the human government to keep chaos from erupting. I doubted those humans were behind this. They knew their lives were on the line as well as their families' if they so much as whispered the word "vampire" to anyone.

The CIA wasn't one of those groups. However, we'd had a run-in with two CIA agents who had teamed up with our enemy five years ago. But their knowledge of vampires had been erased from their memories.

A popping sound followed by a grunt severed my thoughts.

"Motherfucker. What's in these darts? Has to be cobalt because my skin is burning from the inside out." Roman sounded like he was in pain. That had to be him talking since he was the only vampire not comatose.

"Why isn't he passing out?" one of the women asked with panic evident in her tone.

Roman laughed, evil and murderous. "When I get out of this, you three ladies are dead meat," he grunted. "What the fuck do you want anyway?"

"Sam Mason," Red said, "who I suspect is listening to us." Her airy tone sounded like a siren's call luring me home on a foggy night.

My dick jerked in my cargo pants. What the actual fuck? No female in my existence as a human and now vampire had ever had that effect over my dick.

"You want Sam Mason?" Roman asked in a shocked tone. "The Sam Mason of the Mason family? Why the fuck would you take out a club of vamps to lure him out?"

That was the million-dollar question.

"Sam Mason," Red said, "we know you're close by. Might as well come out, or I'll gut your half-breed."

"You have no idea what you're up against," Roman said.

"Shut the fuck up, or else I'll pump more drugs into you. Then you won't be able to move for a year," the third human said.

"Go ahead," Roman chided, "but be warned:

you three are dead." His tone was sharp and jagged.

I had all sorts of powers to handle these humans, but none that would bode well for them. I wanted answers anyway, like who hired them.

Red raised her voice, "Mason, if you don't show yourself by the time I count to three, your comrade will die. We're not bound by vampire law."

Might as well get this comedy show over with. The scared vampires who had bolted might not have been inclined to stop these humans, but with my powers, I had no problem. In fact, they were in for a rude awakening.

"Olivia, Kraft, stay put until you receive my command." I didn't want to risk them getting shot with one of those darts. It was bad enough that Olivia had been a victim of the endotoxin a few years back and almost didn't make it.

Then I plastered on a grin and waltzed in with my hands raised. "So, what will it be, ladies? A threesome or a foursome?" I wasn't exactly digging the brunettes, but if they offered, I wasn't one to turn down a night of blissful sex.

I was five steps in when Roman laughed. "Let me guess. You're tailing me?"

I jerked my head to my left. The shorter brunette was standing at Roman's side, although a good distance from him, and had a gun aimed at his neck.

"Seems to me you're in a bind," I said to Roman.

Several darts were embedded in his chest, and his silk shirt had burn holes in it.

"Apparently, there's something in these darts that won't let me move my fucking limbs. You should try it, Mason," he said. "Ladies, what are you waiting for?"

Rianne, the taller brunette, trained her gun on me.

"I guess group sex is out of the question." Then I glared at Rianne, who had her brown eyes narrowed, her hands steady on the gun, and her nostrils flared. "I would think twice before you use that gun on me."

"What are you waiting for, Rianne? Do it," the short chick said.

"Shut up, Jordyn," Rianne said without taking her eyes off me. "Something tells me he's going to be a problem."

I roared with laughter even though the women were getting on my last nerve.

"Tell you what." I regarded Red, who had Ben pinned against the bar and was ready to plunge the needle into his neck. "Let Ben and Roman go.

Then you can shoot all the drugs you want into me."

Red gave me the most blinding grin as she rammed the needle into Ben.

Instantly, he collapsed to the floor with a thud.

Scorching anger gripped my throat. "If he dies, I have no problem killing humans."

"Amen," Roman said. "Maybe there's hope for you, Mason."

Rianne fired her gun, the dart on a collision course for my chest.

Quick as a flash, I slid to one side before I had my hand around her throat with vampire speed. My fangs dripped with venom, and on a blink, my eyes flashed from green to silver.

The gun dropped and boomed to the floor. Rianne's small hands gripped my wrist as she struggled for air. I let up just a tad, eager to find out why these women wanted me.

She sucked in air. "Let me go, or your sister's house will blow."

I tilted my head as though she was the most fascinating creature. The fuck she was. But just to be sure I heard her correctly, I demanded, "Repeat that."

"You heard me, bloodsucker," she snarled as spittle sprayed onto my face.

Brave human.

I squeezed tightly once again.

"I'll gut the half-breed alive if you so much as hurt her," Red bit out albeit nervously as she produced a dagger from the inside of her boot.

Roman mumbled something I couldn't make out.

My gut told me Red was all talk, but as much as I loved Ben like a brother, I had bigger fish to fry. This human had just threatened my blood, my twin.

I drilled my silver gaze into Rianne, chanting a series of numbers I used when I compelled someone. She was going to be toast when I was done with her.

The other chick, Jordyn, screeched, the sound adding fuel to my fire. I'd made a pact with myself a long time ago: the next person, human or vamp, who so much as whispered my family's name, especially my sister's, would die a slow death.

"I'll burn you alive." Fervent terror gushed from Red's tone.

Ignoring Red's threat, I continued my assault on the lowly human. Within seconds, Rianne went limp, and I threw her to the ground. In a flash, I had the dart gun in my hands and aimed at Red.

Roman guffawed as though he were enjoying

the show. I hated that I was allowing my target to see me in action. Hardly anyone did unless they were about to die.

Footsteps pounded as Jordyn ran to Rianne.

Red was squatting down with the dagger primed to slit Ben's throat.

"I wouldn't do that if I were you." My voice was deep and commanding.

Her eyes widened, her hand shaking around the hilt of the dagger. "Or what, vampire?"

I had to hand it to her. She had some female balls to continue to push my buttons. Grinning, I tossed the dart gun behind the bar and stalked closer to her. She was upright in a second, pointing the dagger at me.

"You know that won't hurt me."

Her stunning electric-blue eyes swirled with fear as her panic rammed me right in the chest.

While I hated to feel another's emotions, I welcomed hers. Fear had a way of driving me to kill or get what I want, and I wanted answers.

I clenched my fists at my sides as I summoned my elemental powers. The ground beneath me began to shake. Bottles and glasses behind the bar crashed to the floor.

Red's mouth dropped open.

"Do you need help?" Kraft asked through the comm.

"Not yet," I returned. "I can handle the humans. I don't want you or Olivia in harm's way." I inhaled deeply, glaring at the beautiful redhead. "This place will crumble if you don't start answering my questions." If she continued to piss me off, an earthquake was about to take down this building. "Is my sister's house ready to blow?"

Roman chuckled. "I would answer him if I were you."

"Sis," Jordyn said. "This job isn't worth it."

Sis? Interesting development.

Silence followed for a beat as Red pinned me with a glare.

I laughed. "Your fear is pathetic. Did you really think you could capture me? Kill me?"

She slowly stepped back, heaving a breath. "What did you do to Rianne?"

I let out a guttural growl, and the dagger in her hand fell. She fumbled to pick it up, and when she did, her cherry fragrance tickled my nostrils and made my dick jerk again.

"You first." I eased up on my elemental power, and the building stopped shaking. "Is my sister's home rigged with explosives?"

Her heartbeat raced for the finish line as she

lifted her chin, feigning confidence she didn't have. Nevertheless, she laughed.

"If you're going to use that weapon"—I opened my arms—"go ahead." In three strides, I was an inch from the blade.

I blatantly sized her up, not caring how she took my bluntness. Up close, she was stunning. A sprinkle of freckles around her nose. Blue eyes rimmed in black. Lashes long, and I would bet soft to the touch, and her mouth... I sucked in a quiet breath, imagining those plump lips around my cock.

She stuck out her tits, which would fit perfectly in my large hands. "Like what you see?" Her voice was steadier than it had been a second ago.

I was ready to sink my fangs into that smooth neck of hers while I fucked her from behind. "I'll ask for a third time. Is my sister's house rigged?"

"No!" Jordyn shouted. "It's not. Layla, we need to get out of here."

Depending on the dosage of the drugs in the vampires scattered around, they might be waking up soon.

"Layla." I rolled that name around on my tongue a few times. Pretty name and one I liked better than Red, the nickname I'd given her.

"I swear you women will pay for this," Roman piped up.

I should check on him, but that would mean I would have to look over my shoulder, and I was fascinated with Layla. Besides, if the drug had worn off, Roman would be following through on his threat.

"Rianne, wake up," Jordyn said.

"What did you do to Rianne?" Layla asked.

I ran my tongue over one fang. "One of my many lethal skills."

Layla pressed the tip of the dagger into my stomach without puncturing the skin. "You will let us go."

A grin emerged. "Baby doll, you are not going anywhere until I get answers."

"We already told you your sister's house isn't rigged," Layla said.

"You'll say anything to get out of here."

She jutted out her chin, defiant and strong. "Call her, then."

"I promise your sister's house is fine," Jordyn said in a trembling voice. "If we're lying, then you can kill me."

"I'll be more than happy to," Roman said as a chair scraped along the floor.

I quickly tossed a glance over my shoulder, and

Layla took that moment to ram the dagger into me.

Growling low, I removed the jagged blade as my bloodthirst became stronger than it had ever been in my existence.

She was about to run when I reached out and pulled her by the hair. Her back hit my chest. "Not so fast." With my arm around her waist, I spun us so I could keep an eye on Roman. The drug was beginning to wear off, and he struggled to stand.

I didn't have long before he would be feasting on any one of the women. I couldn't exactly blame him if he did, not because he wanted to kill them as much as I was certain he wanted to taste them.

Layla alone smelled like a hot fudge sundae, and I would be damned if she didn't smell like cherries too. I sniffed her hair. Yep, cherries.

I ran the blade along her smooth neck, stopping on her carotid artery. "Surely you didn't hold a vampire club hostage to lure me out for a quick fuck?"

She wiggled her ass into my groin. "While the thought of you sliding your dick into my tight pussy sounds enticing, I have other plans for you."

A lust-filled cloud hung over me as I pictured her doing just as she'd bragged. "What might those plans be?" Given their threat to blow Jo's house, I would bet my vamp ass that they wanted me dead. But I had to ask.

She reached around behind her, grabbed my cock, and squeezed. "The next time we meet, I'll be cutting off your dick."

I choked out a laugh as I pushed her away. "I highly suggest you take your sisters and get the fuck out before I decide to do something far worse to you than what I did to your sister." My tone was even but held a threat just the same.

She heaved a breath, snarling. "I'm not afraid of you."

"Baby doll, you're drenched in fear. I can taste it. But it's not only me you should worry about." I pointed to Roman. "He's about to come out of it." I marched toward her. "I'm giving you one chance to walk out now." There was no point in keeping them. Jordyn might sing like a canary, but Layla wouldn't, and I had to get them out before they became victims of Roman's wrath.

Layla scrambled to get her sisters as Roman and I watched them hurry out.

"Olivia, humans are coming your way. Let them pass," I said into my comm.

There was no sense in detaining them. I knew that within the next day or so, Layla would be on her knees, begging me for help.

3

LAYLA

I pressed the gas pedal down as far as it would go on the dilapidated Nissan we had dumped in the lot outside the club the night before. The car sputtered as I careened around the corner on a deserted street. I couldn't wait to knock back a stiff drink to calm my nerves.

But first, I had to put as much distance as possible between the club and the three of us. With our luck, that Roman vamp or even Sam was following us in the shadows. Although, with as many darts as we'd pumped into Roman, I doubted he would be able to do much for a while.

I quickly checked the rearview then over my shoulder. Rianne slid to one side, her head falling into Jordyn.

"Fuuuuuck!" I screamed. "What kind of compelling did he do?"

Rianne's brown eyes were hollow as if she'd had a lobotomy. I'd seen a victim of compelling, and they'd had a faraway look in their eyes, but nothing like the zombie state Rianne was in.

Argh! I wanted to scream.

Stupid. Stupid. Stupid.

I should never have agreed to take this job, but my sisters and I needed the money, and two hundred grand was hard to pass up.

Jordyn, the youngest, slapped Rianne on the cheek quite hard. "Sis." She snapped her fingers. "Come on. Wake up."

"You know we need Mason to help here." The only way Rianne was coming out of it was if Sam was dead or he removed the spell himself.

"Turn around and go back." Jordyn was on the verge of tears.

"No. It was a miracle he let us go." I suspected he had because he knew we would need his help with Rianne. "We need to wait until Mason calms down first." I doubted the sexy vamp would help us. We'd pissed him off, and when a vamp was enraged, there was no getting through to him. "Plus, I don't want to chance running into Roman."

"Then we need to call our uncles," Jordyn said.

"Oh, fuck no." The last people I wanted help from were my father's brothers. Uncle Jack would berate and belittle me until I had no soul. Even if we did call them, it would take them at least a day to get out here, and honestly, I would rather confront Sam than my uncles.

Besides, Uncle Jack didn't have a soft spot for me. I believed he would help me if I needed it, but in the process, he would make a point to tell me how idiotic I was and that I shouldn't be hunting. He thought a woman's place was in the home, not carrying weapons and chasing the undead.

But the need to rid the earth of bloodsuckers resided in our heritage. Some of our family members dating back a century had died at the hands of vampires, my father included. Still, my dad hadn't shared the same belief as Uncle Jack. Dad had wanted us girls to know how to protect ourselves. He'd taught my sisters and me everything we needed to know about how to kill a vampire—burn them, drive a cobalt blade through their hearts, or cut off their heads.

Jordyn snarled as our gazes collided in the rearview. "They're more skilled than we are."

That might be true. My uncles had been hunting vampires a lot longer than us, but my ego wasn't ready to give in just yet. "We need to lie low for the night and regroup. Let's figure out if we can salvage this job, still get paid, and get Rianne back." Our benefactor wanted Sam breathing, and I wanted to fuck his brains out, and then drive a cobalt blade through his heart.

I gripped the steering wheel even tighter. My dad would roll over in his grave if he knew I had salacious thoughts about a vampire. It had been years since I'd had a guy in my bed. Too long in my book, and my sex toys weren't cutting it anymore.

"Come on, sis. Snap out of it." Panic filled Jordyn's voice as she slapped Rianne again, even pulled on her hair. "Screw the money; we need to go kill Mason. Once he's dead, she'll come out of the trance." Fury and fear mingled in her tone.

"This is all my fault," I said with a heavy breath.

"We're all at fault. We agreed to take this job."

It was supposed to be simple. Our benefactor had everything set. He knew where Sam would be. He knew who Sam was meeting with and why. He seemed to know every move the vampire Navy SEALs were making. All we had to do was shoot a few drug-laden darts and take Sam Mason hostage. That was it.

The car jerked as I shifted gears as though I didn't know how to drive a stick shift. My hand trembled like a ten on the Richter Scale. As much as I loved to hunt, my nerves still took control. I couldn't remember a time where I was as nervous as I was at that moment. Scratch that. My first time hunting with our dad, I peed my pants when we captured a vampire.

I slammed on the gas pedal, which only made the car spit and sputter. Damn piece of shit. The first order of business when I had a chance was to buy a new car.

When I shifted again, the gears made an awful grinding noise, and I screamed.

"Can you not drive?" Jordyn shouted at the top of her lungs. "You're supposed to be the calm one. And didn't Rianne drink the potion I made to block compelling?"

"As far as I know, she did." But I hadn't been watching her. I didn't think I had to.

I downshifted, pumping the brakes, but not fast enough. We sailed over a hill, and the wheels came off the ground. And it wasn't just one hill; the street had several like a mogul run on a ski slope.

I hated this coastal city by the bay. We'd only been in Massachusetts for less than a month, and during that time, the weather had been brutally cold. The heating system in the house we were renting was on the brink, and we had a nosy neighbor.

"Watch out," Jordyn gasped.

I blinked just in time to miss a pedestrian. "Fu-uuuuck." I swerved, speeding through the stop sign before pumping the brakes again. Who the hell walks around at two in the morning?

I tried to regulate my breathing as I took the next turn down a quiet neighborhood street, my body shaking hard.

A wooded lot loomed ahead, and the moonlight guided me down the sleepy street lined with modest two-story homes that were dark with only a porch light on here and there. I eased into the dirt driveway of a house that appeared to be under construction.

I cut the engine then hopped out and ran up to the edge of the woods, bent over, and inhaled and exhaled. "Stupid. Stupid. Stupid."

"We're not safe out here." A soft tone replaced the anger Jordyn had held a moment ago.

I jumped a mile before I straightened. "I need a minute." Or more like a lifetime. "Why didn't Roman react to the drug?"

She scanned the area with mechanical precision. "He kind of did. He just didn't pass out. He's going to be a problem."

I opened and closed my hands, trying to stop the trembling.

Headlights lit up the street behind Jordyn.

I stiffened. "Don't move."

Quick as a spark, she pulled a gun from the back of her black jeans, ready to annihilate anyone who dared to threaten her.

My heart rammed against my ribs.

The car turned into a driveway halfway down the street, and once again the area was cloaked in darkness.

Jordyn and I let out a collective sigh.

I closed the distance between us and hugged her for dear life. "Again, I'm sorry. I fucked up royally tonight."

"Stop already. I told you. We all did. Now, let's get Rianne home." She held the gun with two hands, aiming it at the ground, ready to fire at a moment's notice.

I jogged up to the car and opened the back door. Drool dripped down off Rianne's chin. "Sis, are you in there?"

Rianne blinked as if to say yes.

I pushed out a relieved breath that at least my sister was in there.

Jordyn climbed in next to Rianne. "Layla." There was a bite to her tone. "Get behind the wheel, and let's get the fuck out of here. Vamps might not be on our ass, but one of the homeowners might call the cops. Not sure we want to bring any attention to us."

I kissed Rianne on the forehead. "I love you." Then I rushed around and slid into the driver's seat.

Once the car was moving, Jordyn and I let out another collective sigh.

I glanced at myself in the rearview. My auburn hair was frizzy. My blue eyes looked like death, and my skin was pale. If I wasn't human, I might pass for one of the undead.

Jordyn held Rianne's hand. "My twentieth birthday is next week, and I feel like I'm forty. Once we're in a good financial place, we need to give up this shit."

"Maybe, but do you want our kids living among vampires?" If I had kids. I had to find a man first, and that might be difficult given what I did for a living.

Still, I was pushing twenty-three, and I felt old as well. Rianne, the middle child at twenty-two, had so much more energy and courage than Jordyn and me.

Jordyn didn't answer. Instead, she gazed out the side window.

The city lights twinkled in the distance, and the farther we drove, the more my pulse slowed.

"Sam and Roman know our names," Jordyn said.

"They only know our first names."

"But Sam is a Navy SEAL. The military has ways of finding out who we are."

I didn't see how until something hit me, and my breath hitched.

"What is it?" Jordyn asked.

"It's nothing. Just shaking off nerves."

But as I passed a sign indicating that the highway was up ahead, I debated whether I should keep driving until the city and the state were in our rearview mirror.

4

SAM

A medicinal odor burned my nostrils as it always did when I walked into the infirmary, or lab, as Doc liked to refer to his home away from home. "Dr. Vieira," I called out.

The state-of-the-art facility had been upgraded in the last month with brand-new machines and lab equipment. A pristine white tiled floor punched a path down the middle, separating waist-high lab benches that traveled the length of the room on two sides. The soft whir of the overhead exhaust fan against a far wall hummed along with the three refrigerators that housed lab samples, medicine, and blood.

My bloodthirst reared its ugly head at the

34

traces of Layla's mouthwatering scent embedded in my nostrils.

Ben clung to me, his body practically limp. "Just drop me in one of the rooms."

I made a sharp right toward one of five patient rooms. "Man, you're dead weight." He had to be two hundred and fifty pounds of solid muscle.

"And you're a vampire with super strength. Are you getting pansy-ass on me?" He chuckled weakly. "Fucking stomach is on fire, and my limbs feel like saltwater taffy."

Whatever drug was in the dart, coupled with the cobalt, had to be doing a number on him as a half-human.

"Doc!" I shouted as we passed his empty office.

Ben coughed. "He's not here. Otherwise, he would be running to our rescue."

He was right about Doc. The man would run into battle to save any one of us, but especially Ben. Doc viewed Ben as an anomaly and made it his mission to study his DNA.

Doc was also studying another half-breed who had been a victim of an experiment gone wrong—an experiment to genetically manufacture vampires from humans by a former and now dead enemy, Edmund Rain. We also knew there were more half-breeds out there, but we didn't know where or if they were still alive. In the five years since we'd killed Edmund and demolished his research, we hadn't seen or heard of the other half-breeds.

I deposited Ben on the bed in the first room I came to.

He moaned. "Have you heard from Jo?"

I snatched my phone from my cargo pants. "Not yet." Before I could call Jo for the tenth time, my phone rang. "What?" I answered as I started to go in search for Doc.

"Is that how you address your lieutenant?" Tripp's tone held a slight hint of playfulness.

Tripp and I were tight, and I considered him one of my best buds. He'd just been promoted to lieutenant about six months prior, stepping into Webb's former shoes. Before then, he'd taught me everything I knew about being a vampire. He'd been assigned to Jo and me after we'd been forced to lose our humanity five years ago—a process that was unique. To activate the vampire gene, those born with it had to ingest their vampire father's blood. The process couldn't be done until one reached puberty or later. Even then, it was a choice. But Jo and I hadn't had a choice. In order to save me, she had given up her humanity. My father's blood hadn't been strong enough to turn me since, as a human, I'd been on my deathbed thanks to Edmund Rain. So Dr. Vieira had pumped Jo's vampire blood into me.

"Sorry. Did you get a hold of Dr. Vieira?" On the way back to base, Kraft had called Tripp to get Doc on standby.

"He's on his way, as am I," Tripp said before he hung up.

As I pocketed my phone, my bloodthirst hit me like a freight train. "Doc will be here shortly," I said to Ben as I left and beelined it to the fridge.

I snagged a sixteen-ounce bottle of blood, popped the top, and knocked back the irony drink like I was downing a cold brew. The throbbing in my gums dulled until Layla and her tits skipped through my brain. I got another bottle and didn't waste any time draining the contents, hoping I could get my hunger under control. But the more I thought of Layla, the need to taste her blood amped up. I tossed the empty bottles in the trash and collected another one. Maybe three was a charm, but somehow, I didn't think an ocean of blood would sate my hunger if she kept invading my thoughts.

"If you drink all that blood, Doc will have a cow," Tripp said behind me. "The blood bank can't deliver anymore for a week."

I whirled around. "A little warning you're here would be nice."

He laughed but quickly shifted his tune, his bronze eyes flashing to vampire black. "What's got you rattled? And why didn't you hear me?"

I was thinking of a curvy, auburn-haired woman who had my dick begging for freedom. "Where do I begin?" I took a swig of blood.

Leaning against a lab bench, he crossed bulky arms over his broad chest. The lights above served to enhance the shine in his sandy-blond hair.

Ben stumbled out of the room and practically fell into a computer and the table it was sitting on. "Did you get Jo yet?"

Tripp's forehead creased as he examined Ben from a distance. "I still don't get how a recon mission went awry. And how a half-breed like you allowed a human to best you."

Ben mumbled something under his breath as he managed to lower himself into a chair.

Tripp nailed me with his stern lieutenant glare and tight mouth. "And explain what went down in that club since Kraft and Olivia don't have all the details."

I'd only given them bits and pieces of what had happened, and they hadn't seen anything from outside the club.

"Please tell me Roman doesn't have a target on Jo?" he asked.

If I didn't know him or what Jo had been through with Edmund, I wouldn't have caught the hint of trepidation in his tone. That uneasiness was not only out of concern for Jo. None of us wanted to be around Webb if Jo's life was at stake.

Tripp prodded me with those black vampire eyes, waiting impatiently.

I smoothed a hand over my black hair and rested against a sink next to the fridge. "The humans were trying to flush me out into the open, but they also threatened Jo's life. I don't know why they want me either."

He scraped a hand along his unshaven jaw. "Humans want you?"

A printer came alive, warming up before it began to spit out sheets of paper.

"When will Doc get here?" Ben was hunched over with his head between his legs. "My insides are burning like a motherfucker."

"So, this drug," Tripp said, "knocks you out and freezes your limbs?"

I bobbed my head. Ben had only woken up a mile before we'd reached the base. "And it has cobalt in it." Cobalt was a vampire's kryptonite, and it could be deadly if a cobalt blade was driven through the heart. However, it would have to be embedded for a period of time to allow the metal to burn the heart to a crisp.

Tripp popped off the lab bench and paced like a madman. "Webb is going to have a field day."

Our new commander was going to blow his top for sure. My old man would too. Like me, he was tired of anyone and everyone hunting our family.

My fangs finally retreated, and my thirst was sated for the moment. "Please tell me Webb and Jo are at their house on base and not at the one in Maine," I said. Even though Jordyn had said they didn't rig Jo's house with explosives, a part of me needed one hundred percent confirmation. Regardless, Jo had been talking about going up to Maine for the weekend. Maybe she'd left midweek.

The double doors creaked open, and Dr. Vieira came in looking like he'd had a rough night already. His brown hair was disheveled, and he buttoned his lab coat, surveying each of us like he so often did when we showed up in the infirmary after a mission. "Where's the fire?"

"In my veins," Ben whined as he stumbled to stand.

Dr. Vieira regarded me. "You look like you're in one piece."

I grinned. "Don't worry about me. I'm a Mason."

He grabbed Ben's arm. "I worry about all you Sentinels. And may I remind you that the name means nothing. You can die just as well as the next—"

Tripp's phone rang, slicing off Dr. Vieira's words. "It's Webb." He tapped the speaker button and set the phone on the glossy black marble top. "I got Sam here."

Ben and Doc went into a patient room as Ben explained to him what had happened.

"Sam, is there something wrong?" Webb's exhaustion came through loud and clear. "You've been blowing up Jo's phone. We tried to call you but got your voice mail."

I shuffled closer to Tripp and his phone. "I had spotty coverage at the club."

"Sam," Jo said in a sleepy tone.

Hanging my head, I said a quick prayer of thanks that nothing had happened to her. "Sorry to wake you."

"What's so urgent?" she asked.

"Go back to bed. I'll talk to you in the morning." My voice cracked on the last word, a rush of emotion consuming me. I would stake my own heart if anything happened to her.

"It is morning," she teased.

"Go, angel," Webb said to her. "I'll be a few minutes." A rustling noise came through the line then faded before a door closed. "Now, did you get any intel on Roman?" he asked.

"You might want to hear this in person, and you should wake my dad." He'd returned earlier that day from his council meeting in Boston. My father had been promoted to serve on the Council of Elders. His job was to oversee the vampire military. In turn, Webb had stepped into the commander position, but my dad was heavily involved in what the SEAL team did. "I would rather not keep repeating myself. And it seems we have bigger problems than Roman."

"Fuck me." Webb growled before he hung up.

Tripp collected his phone. "I need to check on something in the control room. You and Ben head down to the war room in fifteen minutes."

I nodded to my superior officer and was about to check on Ben when my phone chirped. "Yeah," I answered without even looking at the screen to see who was calling.

"You're a hard vamp to track down." The man's voice was brusque and one that I knew.

"Roman. How did you get this number?"

He chuckled, the annoying sound grating on my every nerve. "I have my ways. So, who were the humans?"

I let out a roar of laughter.

"You find that funny?" Roman asked.

"What I find funny is you assuming I would tell you about the humans." I didn't know who they were, but I wouldn't tell him even if I did. All he'd kept talking about after the women had left was how he would hunt them down.

I had no recourse to stop him. Not yet, anyway.

"I'm curious. What did you do to piss off three gorgeous humans whom, I might add, I'm dying to taste?"

I growled low.

"You want a taste too. I saw it in your eyes."

I wanted more than to sample Layla's blood. Irritation scraped along my arms. "What do you really want, Roman? I don't have time for games."

What I knew of Roman had only been on paper. He was quite intelligent. He held several degrees in chemistry, law, and business. He'd worked for a pharmaceutical company that made one of the raw ingredients in some drug used in operating rooms. However, seeing him in the flesh gave me a newfound hunger to take him down. He reminded me so much of Edmund Rain that I was ready to snap his neck before ripping his head off.

"You realize they'll be calling you for your help, don't you?"

He was right. I was the only one who could bring Layla's sister out of the compelling spell. "I'm not telling you anything about them. Is that the main reason you called?" Surely he knew I wouldn't give him that info.

A horn sounded in the background.

"Did you know that your DNA is worth millions?"

I rolled my eyes. "So? Are you targeting me for your own scheming ways?" As head of a blood syndicate, his motives were money and power.

"Nah," he said casually. "I found someone who is worth more than you."

"Yeah? Who?" I knew he wouldn't tell me, but I had to ask anyway. However, if he named my sister, I wouldn't follow military protocol or the vampire government's edicts.

"Tsk. Tsk. Tsk, Mason." His tone held that you-know-better-than-to-ask attitude.

"Get to the fucking point already."

It was too late to trace the call. By the time I called down to the control room, Roman would be gone.

"I'm giving you forewarning," he said. "First one who gets to the humans gets to taste their sweet, savory human blood."

I pushed my fingers through my hair, and the strap fell out. "And what did I tell you about touching the humans?"

"Since you're tailing me, then you should know I don't follow the law."

"You called to goad me?"

"Just taking your temperature, Mason." Then he was gone.

I had to get to Layla before Roman did. Otherwise, I might not get the chance to find out why she wanted me or who she was working for. More importantly, her life was at stake.

5

SAM

By the time I entered the theater-style war room, Tripp and Webb were huddled near the long conference table at the bottom in front of a giant movie screen.

Ben grumbled as he lagged behind me at a slow pace. Luckily for Ben, he would make a full recovery thanks to his vampire side.

"Doc said to keep drinking water to flush your system," I tossed over my shoulder.

Doc didn't have a fast-acting remedy, but he'd taken Ben's blood to send to our lab in Boston to identify what substances the humans had used. The symptoms Ben had didn't align with the endotoxin that some of our team members had been victim to years back. It didn't exactly mimic the drug Edmund Rain had used to subdue vampires either.

Until we knew more, we had to be on high alert.

"The burning isn't as bad," Ben said, "but I feel like I could sleep for a week."

I chuckled, the sound echoing in the ample space and bouncing off the high ceilings. "I'm ready to kick back with a case of beer."

"Sounds like a plan," Ben returned.

Webb flicked his chin at me as I approached. He looked like death in his jeans and scrappy T-shirt. It was rare to find him in anything but his uniform or to see the dark circles beneath his vibrant blue eyes. Since his promotion to SEAL commander, he'd been busting his butt nonstop. It was a position he'd tried to get out of, but my old man had insisted he take it.

"You look like shit," I said to Webb.

"I can't believe you talk to him like that." Ben winced in pain.

I could because he was my brother-in-law, though I didn't get away with too much.

Webb gave me one of his deadpan expressions. He was the master at hiding his emotions, something I needed to learn, particularly when I was in a challenging situation. "And you look like you're ready to tear off some heads," he volleyed back. "What happened tonight? Tripp gave me the short version. I want to hear everything, but we'll wait for your father, who should be here shortly."

Ben stood at parade rest, hands behind his back, feet shoulder-width apart. "Sir." He bobbed his head at Webb then at Tripp, who stood next to Webb.

"Are you doing okay?" Webb asked Ben.

"I'm good, sir." Ben focused on the movie screen behind Webb and Tripp. "Nothing I can't handle."

Tripp raised one eyebrow, knowing full well Ben had been whining like a baby up in the infirmary.

The side door from the control room squeaked open. My old man stalked in, ready to take on an army or two. The man didn't sleep. His green eyes were bright. His black hair was perfectly combed, and he was sporting a close-shaven beard. Unlike Webb's casual attire, Steven Mason was dressed to impress—a sharp black suit, crisp white shirt, no tie, and black patent leather shoes that were shinier than the big-ass diamond my sister wore on her finger.

He unbuttoned his suit jacket. "Son, this better be good." His jaw was stiff.

"Love you too, Pops. And no disrespect, but you smell like you just dumped a bottle of cologne over your head. Hot date?"

Ben let out a quiet snort, but to vampire ears, it sounded like an explosion.

My dad's eyes flashed vampire—green to silver. "What's your problem, soldier?"

Ben snapped to attention, his eyes hollow as he looked past my father. "Nothing, sir."

My old man had been a hard-ass as a former military commander. Nothing had changed in his new role as a high-ranking official within the vampire government. Steven Mason didn't tolerate anything, even from his children. He was a military man who had been serving the vampire nation and protecting humans for eons. He expected his underlings to follow the chain of command, respect one another, and live by the moral code that said quitting wasn't an option.

I started in, trying to cut the tension. It was late, and all of us needed to take a breather. "Three human females interrupted our mission tonight."

Dad jerked his head at me. "Humans?"

Webb crossed his arms over his chest. "Start from the top."

Ben and I took them through the events. I gave them my side first.

Then Ben launched into what had happened before I'd gotten into the club. "The redhead, who seemed to be the one in charge, came up to me like she knew me. Before I could get a word out of my mouth, she put a syringe in my throat. Then her sisters used the remaining vamps in the room as target practice. One by one, they went down, except Roman Brown. Whatever was in the drug that shut down the ability to move was the only thing that had any effect on him. He was lucid the entire time."

"He had to have taken something to protect him from such a drug," I said. "Like the antidote we had to counteract the drug Edmund had used on us at one time."

"Do you think Roman and the humans have teamed up?" Dad asked.

I shrugged. "I don't think so. When he called me a few minutes ago, he was dead set on finding the humans."

Webb reared back. "He called you. Why?"

"Not sure. But if I had to guess, he wanted to find the humans. We need to get to them before Roman. Not only are their lives in danger now, but we'll never find out why they lured me out into the open or why they want me."

"You?" Dad removed his suit jacket and tossed

it on one of the seats in the front row. "You think this was a setup to lure you out to get your DNA?"

I nodded. It was becoming the norm for us to fight those who wanted the Masons' DNA or to sell our blood on the open market.

Tripp inhaled deeply. "If that's true, then we have another fucking mole. No one but our team knew you would be at the club."

We'd had two moles in the past. Webb's sister had been one, but she was now dead. The other mole had been a human doctor who had been employed by Dr. Vieira. Dr. Case had given top-secret info to the CIA. He was behind bars at a prison we had for those humans who had broken their silence about us. It was doubtful Case had anything to do with trying to abduct me.

Ben relaxed his stance. "Or someone has hacked into our computers."

"I'll get Sawyer on the case," Tripp announced. "He's our top computer analyst."

"We're right back where we were five years ago with Edmund and my brother," Dad muttered. "For fuck's sake."

"You're really not going to like this part then," I said. "Roman made a point to tell me that he's found someone other than me who is worth millions."

Webb's jaw hardened. "The only person worth more than any Mason is Abbey. At least to my knowledge, unless there's someone out there who we don't know about."

Abbey Rain, daughter of Edmund and Rachel Rain, both deceased, was an extraordinary human who was slowly changing into a vampire as she aged, which was unheard of among our kind. Her DNA had started shifting when she was just two years old, along with her ability to see into the future. She'd been living on the naval base and under our protection since she was a baby. We all had a soft spot for her, but when Rachel died at Edmund's hands, Jo and Webb stepped up to adopt her as their own.

It was imperative that we protected her at all costs. If the prophecy proved to be true, then Abbey would become the only female vampire in our existence to have kids. That alone would be worth millions to some sadistic vampire.

Dad scrubbed a hand down his face. "We can't assume anything here. We need to find out what is true and what isn't. Let's start in-house and check if we have a leak. I doubt we have a mole. They know Jo and I will read their minds like we did the last time we were faced with this situation, so I tend to agree with Ben. Someone has hacked into our computers. If we discover who, then we can unravel the rest. In the meantime, I want to know more about the humans. Did you get anything else from them? Names we can go on? Anything?"

"Layla, Jordyn, and Rianne. I compelled Rianne. I would guess they're in their early twenties like Ben and me." Hot as hell. Well, Layla was. I couldn't shake her tight, curvy body or the over-the-knee boots, and man, she had a nice rack. Suddenly, heat was traveling south to settle in my groin.

Dad gave me a sidelong glance. "Really?"

"Get out of my head," I snapped.

Other than my sister, my old man was the only other vampire who could read minds, and he was reading mine like a sex scene in a romance novel.

"We'll talk later," he said, sounding extremely perturbed.

I was ready to tell him fuck no. I didn't need his advice on sex, but we weren't there to argue about who I fucked. Instead, I removed the dagger from the side pocket of my cargo pants. "The one who seemed to be in charge, Layla, stuck this in my gut. Ever seen this crest before?" The dagger looked like it belonged in a museum. The letter A was carved into the black leather handle, but it wasn't just a plain letter. Two lions made up the sides of the letter, and a double-edged blade connected the two.

Suddenly, my dad paled. I mean he was white as a fucking ghost. Steven Mason never revealed his true emotions. I'd never seen my father frightened. His fear hit me like shrapnel from a roadside bomb.

Webb snagged the blade and examined it. "Old and expensive."

Tripp whistled low. "May I?" He took the ancient-looking weapon from Webb. "A family crest on the hilt. The Aberdeen family."

Webb pinched his eyebrows together. "You mean the family of vampire hunters?"

Dad tore the dagger out of Tripp's hand. "That's right."

I reared back. "You know them?"

Dad's jaw hardened as he sat down in the front row of the theater seats. "Man, we haven't seen activity from them in about two years if my memory serves me correctly. I thought they'd given up their fight." His gaze was glued to the dagger.

"Vampire hunters," I said more to myself, attempting to wrap my mind around the concept. My old man had never mentioned the threat of vampire hunters. In all fairness, though, since I'd turned five years ago, life had been nonstop fighting the enemy and training to become a Navy SEAL. Besides, the enemies I'd faced had all been vampires, not humans, although the CIA could've posed a problem when they showed up on our doorstep a few years back. I guessed, in essence, they could be called vampire hunters.

"This isn't good," Dad said.

I agreed. We didn't need another group or anyone getting in the way of our mission to take down a blood cartel.

"Mr. Mason, sir," Ben said. "I get the meaning of vampire hunter, but a family of humans seems like a non-issue. Surely, we can stop them."

I dropped down next to Dad and dug my elbows into my thighs. "Ben's right. But, Pops, you looked spooked over humans. I don't understand? I plucked the dagger from him. A small spec of my blood was crusted on the base of the blade near the cross-guard.

Dad pushed to his six-five height and began pacing. "Son, I'm not afraid of them. But if the Aberdeens have resurrected their family business, the vampire population is in jeopardy."

"They're that good?" Ben asked.

My father bobbed his head. "They're not a family you want to run into on a dark road in the middle of the night. Hell, we tried to get one of them to work for us, but shortly after I made the offer to Wayne Aberdeen, the youngest of the three brothers, the Aberdeens dropped off our radar. We sent out a team to find them and came up empty. We speculated that they went into hiding. Although rumor had it that one of the Aberdeens had been killed."

Tripp leaned against the table. "So you think they're making a comeback, sir?"

Dad practically wore a hole in the plaid carpet. "Fuck, I hope not. We don't need this shit. The council has enough problems with our kind."

"Sam's right. We need to find these humans, especially before Roman does," Webb said.

Dad came to an abrupt halt, shoved his fingers through his coal-black hair, and sighed. "Agreed, but I doubt they'll tell us anything."

Ben regarded Dad. "Elder Mason, sir. Can't you read their minds?"

I was still getting used to his title as an elder. Regardless, Dad still presided over the vampire SEAL team, which meant Webb reported to him. Not much had really changed in the chain of command. When we got right down to it, Dad still led the military.

He shook his head. "The Aberdeens have ways to protect themselves from our powers."

My eyebrows drew down. "But I compelled one of them."

"Something isn't adding up, then. If they are true Aberdeens, then you wouldn't be able to."

Quiet reigned for a beat.

I straightened in my seat. "Then let's start our search."

LAYLA

I cinched my robe and wound through the rickety old house we were renting on the outskirts of the city. Snow had begun to fall the minute we'd pulled into our driveway only hours before.

I hated to get snowed in with no way to run. I'd taken several detours on the way home and hadn't seen anyone behind us, yet the hackles on the back of my neck were keeping me on edge. Vampires had a way of hiding in the shadows without being seen. I was still trying to figure out what the fuck had happened at the nightclub and where we would go from there.

The muted light of dawn spilled in as I checked every window to make sure they were bolted shut. A nervous laugh broke out, echoing on the first floor. The house we were renting came with the bare minimum of furniture, empty walls, and thin curtains.

Despite our setup, a damn lock wouldn't keep Sam Mason or Roman or any vampire from blazing in like they owned the place—especially not Sam. Our benefactor had warned us his powers were strong, but I hadn't been prepared for just how strong they were. Aside from making the building shake, rattle, and roll, his compelling skills were unlike any vampire's we had come across in the years we'd been hunting. One of my cousins who'd been compelled by a vampire had that faraway look in his eyes but was still able to speak. Thankfully, his compelled state hadn't lasted that long. My uncle found the vampire and burned him over a fire pit.

My family had only spoken of the elder Mason and his mind-reading abilities that no other vampire had. That was the reason he was considered powerful among his kind.

I puffed out my cheeks as I settled at the window in the vacant living room. The only way to bring Rianne back lay in the hands of the mesmerizing green-eyed vampire, the one who had me in knots in more ways than one. The danger he exuded should've made me run in the opposite direction, yet all I'd wanted to do was run toward him.

My mom had warned my sisters and me to be careful around a vampire. "They will lure you in with their charm," she'd said.

Sam definitely had charm—an arrogant one. But he also oozed danger and mayhem. His swagger screamed that if I fucked with him, he would annihilate me in a second. That both thrilled me and freaked me out.

I had two choices to help Rianne: I could ask Sam for help or kill him. The latter would be a surefire way to remove the spell, but considering he lived on a heavily guarded military base, chances were slight that I could get past the guards.

The only option I saw was to barter with the gorgeous vampire. If I told him about our benefactor, maybe he would remove the spell in exchange.

The one tiny problem I had with that scenario was our benefactor. We didn't know much about him. We had a name and nothing more. His instructions came via email, we'd spoken a couple of times on the phone, and the drug he'd given us for the darts had been deposited in a locker at the city's private airport.

A chill skittered down my spine as I replayed the club scene. The plan had been going well until we'd encountered Roman. The irritating vamp hadn't passed out like the others. We'd gotten lucky that part of the drug had worked on him. Otherwise, I wouldn't be upright and breathing and leaning against the window watching the snowfall.

The storm outside was nothing in comparison to Sam Mason, though. He could've decimated us. I'd seen pictures of him in preparation for our job, but photos didn't do him justice. The vampire was imposing and formidable. I'd lost my breath when I'd laid eyes on him. But nothing had been more breathtaking than when I'd been inches away from him. His dimples gave him a softer look underneath his rugged and cocky personality. And then there was his dick. I didn't even want to think about how big or hard he was. Apparently, the vampire got off on exuding his powers.

I took a few deep inhales and stared out at the breaking dawn and wide-open fields. The house we'd rented sat on ten acres of land that butted up to a thickly wooded forest outback. We had neighbors on either side of us. From where I stood, the peak of the roof of our nosy human neighbor to my left poked out above the trees. The thirty-something man lived alone, as far as I knew. When we'd moved in, Gerald Becker had made a point to introduce himself and offer any help we might need. He seemed nice enough, but we couldn't afford to trust anyone in this city.

The wind picked up, causing the chimes hanging from the porch to sing, low and soothing. I hugged myself as the light musical notes sank in, reminding me of warm summer nights, family, and laughter. Mom had been an avid collector of wind chimes. She'd had several that on those windy days and nights, they sounded like a symphony orchestra.

I shivered at the mere thought of her as tears threatened. She'd been taken from this world way too early. As much as I wouldn't mind blaming her death on a vampire, I couldn't. Mom had battled breast cancer for far too long before the awful disease won out and claimed her life four years prior.

I blinked, and a tear slid down my cheek. I dashed it away as quickly as it fell. I didn't have time to reminisce or feel sorry for myself. I was the eldest. It was my job to protect my sisters. With one last big breath, I pushed off the window and then froze when something outside caught my eye. My pulse shot to the ten-foot-high ceiling as I went for the dagger beneath my robe. It wasn't my lucky dagger, which I made a mental note to get back from Sam Mason.

The wind whipped around as the snow came down heavier. I didn't see much past the flakes until something moved again. This time it was closer to the house. My heart rammed against my rib cage as I went over our escape route in my mind. My gaze darted back and forth when a deer came into view.

The air in my lungs rushed out as my shoulders sagged and my muscles loosened. *Goddamn.* We definitely needed to get out of town or go deeper into hiding once we had Rianne back. Then again, we knew how to lure vampires out and pick them off one by one. In order to do just that, we needed more than two people. I hated to think that Jordyn was right about us needing to call our uncles, but like wolves, we were stronger in packs.

Before I did anything, I needed a jolt of coffee —or a pot of it. I had hardly slept in the last forty-eight hours, and if I was going to tango with a vampire, I needed to have my wits about me.

The coffee machine beeped just as I entered the kitchen, and I flinched. Maybe I should trade the caffeine for a shot of whiskey. But I had a better idea.

I poured two cups of coffee then snatched the bottle of whiskey from the counter next to the fridge and added a shot to my cup. The first sip always burned, but man, it was a welcome relief as my nerves settled a smidge.

I took another swig for good measure then headed upstairs. Jordyn lounged against the headboard as Rianne lay sleeping like she was one of the undead. If her chest weren't rising and falling, I would swear she was dead.

The blue carpet muffled my footsteps as I ambled in. I was about to set one cup down on the glass nightstand when Jordyn opened her eyes.

"I smell something wonderful," she said, taking a cup from me. "Did you put whiskey in mine?"

She knew me too well. "I didn't."

Bringing the mug to her mouth, she inhaled the pungent aroma. "You make strong coffee, so I shouldn't need the added jolt."

I sank down on the edge of the mattress, cradled my cup in my hands, and glanced at the poster of Tom Cruise in *Top Gun*. Rianne carried that damn poster with her wherever she went. Not because of Tom Cruise; she loved the movie.

Jordyn sipped her coffee. "We need to contact Sam."

"I know," I said low. "You don't want to call the uncles, though?"

She shook her head. "I thought a lot about it. They've all but disowned us since Dad died. And I don't care to hear Uncle Jack berate us."

Uncle Jack was the ass of assholes.

"Damn it, Layla. This was supposed to be the easiest job ever. Shoot a few darts and take a vampire hostage."

I laughed, expelling some nervous energy. "Dad would be laughing, too, if he heard you say that. But Sam isn't an ordinary vampire. I doubt the drug would've had any effect on him."

She pulled in a deep breath and smiled. "I miss Dad so much."

I rubbed her denim-clad leg. "I do too."

She blinked away a tear. "Roman is going to be a problem. I still don't understand why that drug didn't knock him out."

Again, my eyes were drawn back to Tom Cruise. Rianne loved that movie, but she also loved fighter jets. Her dream had been to fly jets one day for the military. "We can't worry about him right now. We need to help Rianne."

"What about our benefactor?" She glanced at me with tired brown eyes over the rim of her cup.

"We'll deal with him later. Besides, if I can get close to Sam, then maybe I can finish the job."

"Sam is into you."

I snorted, almost spitting out my coffee. "He wants to kill me. Nothing more."

Jordyn scoffed. "He wants to fuck you then maybe kill you."

"I would go for the former. I did grab his dick, by the way."

Her eyes bugged out. "And?"

I sighed. "Huge. Hard."

"He was hard?" She shivered. "Our family would shit their pants if they knew our fantasies."

As teenagers, the three of us had wondered what it would be like to date a vampire, but none of us had gone down that road. Every time we'd returned from a hunt, that fantasy had become a nightmare. As handsome as some of them had been, they were evil, pure and simple.

"I won't be slipping in between the sheets with Sam, although if that's what it takes to get Rianne out of her comatose state, I'll screw him in a heartbeat."

"He'll help without you having to strip naked."

My eyebrows hiked up to my hairline. "Oh? Do you have psychic abilities now?"

Jordyn rolled her big brown eyes. "Of course

not. But the way I see it, we could threaten to expose him. We could blast their existence over social media. We could even stage it, so we get him to show his true colors. Vampires don't want to be exposed to the human population."

"Threats won't work. Look at what he did to Rianne. Sam will want to know why we were at the club to kidnap him."

Jordyn took another sip of her coffee. "Then we tell him. We don't have much on our benefactor except his name."

"I would bet Dowell isn't his real name." I nursed my coffee. "Or we could kill Sam. That would bring Rianne back."

"Too difficult. He's a vampire Navy SEAL and on a heavily guarded naval base. Plus, the element of surprise is blown."

"And he has my dagger. The one with the family crest on it."

She pursed her lips. "Layla Aberdeen." Her chiding tone reminded me of our mother's when we'd done something wrong.

I hung my head. "I'm sorry. You know I'm superstitious. That dagger brings me good luck. Well, it did until last night."

She set her cup on the nightstand. "It doesn't matter anyway. I'm sure the vampire military has a way of finding out who we are without a dagger." She got up. "I need to use the bathroom."

I'd expected her to scream and shout at me for leaving my dagger behind. Rianne sure would have. If either of my sisters was a stickler for detail and making sure we covered our tracks, it was Rianne. She was the tactical one. I was the strategist, and Jordyn had a knack for computers and research.

I slipped into Jordyn's spot next to Rianne and swiped my hand over her hair. "We'll get you back. And when we do, you can beat Sam Mason to your heart's content." I could picture her doing just that. She wasn't afraid to tango with the enemy. None of us were.

But we had never come face-to-face with a Mason. As much as I didn't want to beg a vampire for his help, I had no choice. It was time to confront the vamp who'd made me want to ride his dick until the sun came up.

7

LAYLA

I threw on a pair of black jeans that fit like leggings, a long-sleeve T-shirt, a sweater, boots, and a soft knitted scarf that had a cashmere feel to it.

Jordyn rested her shoulder against the door-jamb of my room. "I'm going to make some breakfast before we head out."

I opened the blinds. "I'm not sure if our car will make it to the navy base in this weather."

"We can't sit here all day," she said before she left.

She was right. We needed to keep moving, although walking onto a military base full of vampires wasn't exactly the greatest idea to keep moving.

After a few swipes of a brush through my hair, I secured it up with a band. Then I tucked a dagger inside my boot. The suede fur-lined ankle boots weren't as accommodating as the over-the-knee ones we'd worn the night before. We'd been able to hide several weapons in that style of footwear.

Once I had my phone, I checked myself in the small mirror tacked to the wall. Dark circles marred the undersides of my eyes, making the blue of my irises stand out. My skin was paler than usual, and the corners of my lips were chapped. Damn cold weather made humans look like something out of *The Walking Dead*.

I snagged some Chapstick I had in a dish on the dresser then made my way downstairs. I'd barely reached the landing when I heard glass shatter.

"Jordyn!" I shouted as I bent down and pulled out my dagger.

I heard no response.

I climbed down each step with caution as I called out her name again. Cold air and snow swept in through the open front door.

Son of a bitch.

I flew down the remaining steps. Once at the bottom, I skidded to a stop at the front door. My heart punched my ribs like a boxer ramming his fists into a heavy-weight bag. I quickly checked the driveway and didn't see any cars or tire tracks, but when my gaze landed on the footprints on the walkway leading up the porch steps, my blood gelled.

The first person who came to mind was our neighbor. I'd never liked the way he looked at my sisters and me. I might be jumping the gun, though. After all, I did piss off a vampire Navy SEAL—one who didn't have any problem showing us how powerful he was. One last pass of the front yard, and I came up empty. If Jordyn had been taken, then they'd gone out the back.

I rushed through the house and once again skidded to a halt, as did my heart. Jordyn was pinned against the pantry door by a monster of a woman. Sasquatch had her claws around Jordyn's neck. By claws, I meant animal claws. No doubt the tall, beefy woman who had to be six feet in height with arms bigger than Sam Mason's was a shifter. Which kind, I wasn't sure. The more I came into contact with supernaturals, the more I found that I shouldn't be surprised by anything in this world.

Jordyn shook her head as if to tell me not to react or try something stupid. I wasn't planning on it, not with Sasquatch's lethal canines showing.

But when I followed her line of sight to the blond man sitting at the small island, I was ready to launch my dagger at him.

Roman definitely was not Sam or our neighbor. He was reading on his phone with a coffee cup in front of him as though he lived there.

"You can put the dagger away," Roman said without looking at me.

I squeezed the pummel with every ounce of strength I had. "I don't think so."

"Humans," Roman muttered. "So defiant and stupid."

I couldn't argue with him on that. I *felt* stupid. I felt as though I'd never hunted vampires before, given how this job was turning out. Dad would be so disappointed. He'd always put me up on a pedestal for my expertise when it came to killing the undead.

"Have a seat, Layla." Roman was still absorbed in his phone. "I have a proposition for you."

My jaw slammed to the wood floor. "You want to make a deal with me? Then let Jordyn go."

Sasquatch jerked her head at me, her high black ponytail whipping from one side to the other.

"Layla." Roman's voice was deep and commanding. "You're in no position to bargain."

I couldn't argue with him. Sasquatch was ready to tear off Jordyn's head. "So talk."

He chuckled as though I'd said the funniest thing. Then he set his phone down and gave me his undivided attention, raking his blue eyes up then down my body.

Suddenly, I felt like I needed to take a shower to wash off the slime.

He licked his lips. "I see why Mason is into you."

All Sam Mason was into was sinking his fangs into me, much like Roman seemed to want to do as well.

I raised an eyebrow. "What's your proposition?" He wasn't there so we could talk about Sam Mason and how much he liked me.

He waved his hand to a stool at the head of the island. "Sit."

"I would rather stand." My nerves were singing, and I wouldn't be able to keep still.

He lost his grin. "If you don't sit, my friend Vera will slit your sister's throat." His tone brooked no argument.

The name "Vera" did not fit Sasquatch, but concerns about her name paled when she dragged a sharp claw underneath Jordyn's chin. Blood oozed out, and before I could take a breath,

Roman was pushing Vera off Jordyn. Vera sailed through the air and crashed into the back door. The glass pane shattered, and a whoosh of cold air blew in.

Roman bared his fangs at Vera. "Why the fuck would you do that? I told you not to do anything until I say so."

Vera climbed to her feet, growling like the animal she was. "Touch me again, vampire, and I'll rip out your intestines and eat them as a snack."

I couldn't breathe. Jordyn appeared to be holding her breath as well.

My vision blurred when Roman lowered his head, ready to sink his fangs into my sister. I screamed at the top of my lungs. "No! I'll sit, for fuck's sake."

Roman froze for a beat before he swiped the blood off Jordyn's neck, stuck his finger in his mouth, and moaned. "Delicious." Then he shoved Jordyn at Vera. "Get her out of here, or else I will drain her, and we need her."

I pinched my eyebrows together so hard they hurt. "Need her?"

Vera snarled at Roman as she dug her claws into Jordyn's arm and dragged her out of the room.

I thought about blocking Vera as she passed, but I couldn't take on a shifter and a vampire.

Retracting his fangs, Roman licked his lips. "You look confused." He sauntered over to me with a sense of purpose and hunger in his eyes that had changed from vampire black to blue. "Let me un-confuse you." He quickly took the dagger from me then grasped my hand and guided me to a barstool.

I had no choice but to sit. "What do you want?"

He refreshed his coffee, and as soon as he returned to his seat, his phone vibrated on the island, and I flinched. After he read the text, he flipped his phone so the screen was facing down.

I looked up at the ceiling, hoping it would give me a clue or an idea of how to get out of the mess we were in.

Roman followed my line of sight, and the corners of his mouth curled upward. "Vera won't hurt her yet, but she *is* looking forward to getting revenge."

"For what!" Sure, we'd knocked out a few vampires, but we didn't harm them, and I hadn't been aware of any shifters at the club.

"Jordyn killed her sister."

I reared back. "Come again?"

He gulped down coffee as though we were having a friendly convo. Quite the opposite. The air dripped with tension, although I was the only one with my muscles locked tight and my hands twined together in my lap.

"Apparently, the sedative plus whatever other drug was in those darts killed my girlfriend, who happened to be Vera's sister."

My voice rose as I exclaimed, "A vampire dating a shifter?" Usually, supernaturals stuck to their own kind, as far as I knew.

"I was." He emphasized the last word. "That's not the point. I've made a deal with Vera. She'll leave Jordyn alone until I get something from you."

"What could I possibly have that you want?" Other than my blood, which was the only thing that came to mind.

"You're going to do something for me."

I laughed loud and free, and it felt fucking good to relieve an ounce of tension. Still, this vampire had to be smoking dope.

"You find that funny?" His tone was unpleasant.

I crossed my arms, holding myself tightly as if that would protect me. "What could I possibly do to help you? And please don't say you want my blood."

"I want you to get in bed with Sam Mason."

I choked out a laugh that time. "Literally?"

He shrugged his broad shoulders. "That's up to you. But I want you to get me information. I need to know if the vampire military is protecting a human girl, age ten, with black hair and blue eyes. My source tells me her name is Abbey."

I knitted my eyebrows. "What do you want with her?" Nothing good, I suspected.

"That's none of your business. The job is simple. Get close to Mason. Find out if my intel is correct."

"You just want me to get you information?" Somehow, I didn't think he would make it that simple. "And if I do, no harm will come to my sisters or me. Right?"

He glanced past me and into the living room. "Tell me why you were there for Mason. And why make such a big production of it? Seems to me there were easier and better ways to snag him."

In a perfect world, we could've hidden in the shadows and completed our job, but getting close to Sam was impossible. He'd never gone out alone. He was always with his team, and we had to be careful since he was powerful. We also knew a surefire way to get him out in the open was to dangle someone he cared about over his head. SEALs stuck together like glue, and they would never let one of their own die. What we didn't know or expect was Roman, and now a shifter was dead. More shit to pile in our laps.

"He's a hard vamp to get close to," I said. "And if you must know, someone hired us to kidnap him."

Roman belted out a laugh. "He is worth a million or more for his DNA alone."

My jaw hit my lap. No one in my family had mentioned that critical piece of info. Powerful, yes. Worth millions, no. Maybe I needed to renegotiate with our benefactor. "He does have some strong powers," I mumbled.

"His blood also has some kick to it."

"Why aren't you hunting him, then?" I asked. "Oh, wait. Abbey is worth more?" Dowell had informed us that Roman was head of a blood cartel. Therefore, he was in the business to make money —lots of it.

"You're as smart as I thought," he said as though he was proud of me.

"A ten-year-old human doesn't have vampire powers, not even a natural-born one." From my knowledge of the undead population, they lost their humanity around their teenage years or older.

A smug grin played across his lips. "My source says otherwise."

Impossible. But if he was right, then he wanted to profit off her. *Unbelievable.* I wasn't about to turn over an innocent human, let alone a child, to a crazy money-hungry vampire.

On the other hand, I would gladly take a second shot at kidnapping Sam if Roman wanted to make me a higher offer than our benefactor. However, I doubted Roman would entertain an offer for Sam since he had his sights on Abbey.

I bounced my knee. "I'm not getting in the middle of your scheme to use a ten-year-old child so you can profit off her."

"You will." Vera's voice made me jump off the stool as she dragged Jordyn in, bound and gagged.

"What the fuck?" I snarled at Roman. "This is your idea of not hurting her?" Then something dark and twisted hit me.

"I see the lightbulb brightening in that brain of yours," Roman said. "Jordyn will be our prisoner until you get me what I want."

Fear was stamped on Jordyn's face.

"Take the gag off her." My tone was shaky but firm.

Roman nodded to Vera, who in turn removed what looked to be a ripped pillowcase.

Jordyn sucked in air. "Don't take the job, sis. We're dead anyway."

"I'll figure a way out of this," I said.

Jordyn's chest heaved. "Don't, Layla. You do one thing, and he'll want more."

I knew that, but I wasn't about to let her die, nor could I use a child as a bargaining chip. I squeezed her tightly. "I love you." The minute I stepped away, the weight of the world dropped on my shoulders like a boulder had fallen from the sky and crushed me.

"What's it going to be, Layla?" Roman's casual attitude was grating on my nerves.

What a fucked-up situation. Maybe if I told them about my benefactor and how it was his idea to take a club of vamps, Vera would change her tune. Then again, Roman knew he had me by the neck. He knew I had to see Sam. He also knew I wouldn't let my sister die.

"You never answered my question. If I do this for you, no harm will come to me or my sisters?" Whether I agreed or not, I had no doubt Vera was ready to snap Jordyn's neck. As for me, Roman wanted revenge. At the club, he'd even said we would pay for what we'd done to him. Therefore, Jordyn was right. We were dead either way.

"Let's just agree to one step at a time." Roman shoved Jordyn toward me. "Say your goodbyes now."

I caught Jordyn before she fell. "Stay alive." I wrapped my arms around her.

"Call the uncles," she whispered in my ear. "You need help."

What I needed was a miracle, because the way I saw it playing out only led to death with or without my uncles' help.

SAM

I danced on the balls of my feet as Tripp and I sparred in the gym. I was too amped up to sleep. After our meeting in the war room, I'd spent a couple of hours with Sawyer and the tech team. We had one tech searching rental properties in the name of Aberdeen in the city and surrounding towns. If they were smart, they didn't use their real name.

We were also checking transportation companies since Layla and her sisters had driven up in a black sedan. I'd been kicking myself for not getting the license plate of that vehicle. Still, any transportation company like Uber or Lyft would have a record of who the driver had been.

The other problem was trying to figure out if

our computer system had been hacked. Sawyer had his tech team scrubbing the database for any malware and trojans that might leave a trail.

Plus, we had a team returning to the club to question the owner. I would've taken that job if it weren't for my gut telling me Layla would seek me out. She wouldn't let her sister suffer too long. Rianne wasn't in any pain, though. She just couldn't talk.

"I taught you better than that. Stay focused," Tripp barked as he came at me with a roundhouse kick.

I ducked, but the heel of his foot grazed my head and knocked me off my game as I faltered. "Fuck."

Tripp wiped sweat from his brow with his forearm. "Where are you? You have not paid an ounce of attention. Is it the vampire hunters?"

It was my whole fucking life that was distracting me, not just a ball-squeezing redhead who I wanted to fuck and taste in more ways than just her blood. I was tired of always looking over my shoulder for the next moron who wanted my DNA so he could use me or my sister, Jo, like lab rats locked in a cage to benefit from some twisted plot to build armies of vampires out of humans.

Frankly, I was ready to decimate every vampire

or human who dared to kidnap us to do as they pleased with our DNA.

I crossed the room. "I'm trying to figure out who Roman thinks is worth more than me. Abbey? And then there are the Aberdeen women."

"Given the lust wafting off you, I would guess you're thinking of screwing one of them too?"

My jaw came unhinged. "Empath isn't your only ability now. Do you read minds too?"

"Dude, you gave yourself away in the war room when you were talking about... what's her name? Layla? Her name alone is giving *me* a hard-on."

I dropped down on the slatted-wood bench adjacent to a closet door. "Wait until you see her." My mind switched on a dime to her gorgeous body and those huge-ass tits. I shook my head, willing my dick to take a breather.

Tripp snagged a towel from the cabinet on the opposite side of the padded room. "I want to caution you, dude." He wiped the sweat from his neck and face before joining me.

I ruffled my hands through my sweat-soaked hair. "For what? Wanting to screw a human?"

"Exactly. Your father will skin you alive."

I snorted. "He's tried a few times for other stuff. I can handle him."

My father and I hadn't had the best relationship. It didn't help that he had put the military before his own children or that after my mother had died, Jo and I ended up in the foster care system with no sign of dear old Dad for years. In fact, we'd only reconnected with him five years before, which was the first time I'd been kidnapped for my DNA.

Regardless, after my father had explained his reasoning for why Jo and I had grown up in foster care, it had taken me a while to warm up to him. To make a long story short, Jo and I had been in danger with Edmund hunting us as humans. Dad couldn't and wouldn't tempt fate to pull us out of the foster system. He'd been afraid Edmund would find us, and he had.

After my ordeal with Edmund, in which he'd left me on my deathbed as a human, I'd understood Dad's reasons. Since then, we were definitely in a better place in our relationship. To be fair, my old man was also one of my superior officers, so I understood Tripp's warning.

I braced my elbows on my knees. "Let's not forget our mothers were human." The science was mind-boggling. A female had to have a blood type of Vel negative to get pregnant by a vampire.

Which meant we needed humans if we wanted to have kids. The problem in our world was that those unique humans with that particular blood type were becoming extinct, at least according to the vampire government. They had been tracking human women for centuries.

Tripp laughed, deep and hardy. "Our mothers weren't vampire hunters."

The sound of a door opening and closing in the distance filtered into my ears.

"Have you ever been with a human?" I asked.

Tripp rarely talked about his personal relationships. As far as I knew, he didn't have a special lady.

"Once, when I was a teenager and a newborn vamp, which didn't go well. If my father hadn't walked in, she would be dead."

"Christ," I mumbled.

"Take my advice," Tripp said. "Stick with lady vamps."

I wasn't planning on pursuing Layla, but I wasn't sure if I had the willpower to stay away. Her blood was tempting. I could smell cherries as if she were right next to me. Her tits were imprinted on my brain, and so was her hair. I wanted to wrap it around my hands while I sucked on her delicious essence.

Tripp grabbed a water bottle out of his bag at his feet. "And what happened to Harley, by the way?"

I lifted a shoulder, recalling the blond vamp and some of our sexcapades. "We're just having a good time. Friends with benefits." We'd both agreed not to get serious. Besides, I wasn't the type to settle down like Jo. If my sister had any say in my love life, I would be on blind dates every week, which wasn't my cup of tea. I didn't see any value in a relationship. The foster homes I'd been in had been toxic. The couples were constantly at each other's throats or didn't speak to one another. I also didn't see myself spending my immortal life with the same person. *Not happening.*

"Speaking of Harley, she says Webb has been on edge since before I relayed Roman's message about someone worth more than me." Harley was Webb's assistant and Sawyer's sister. He'd hired her recently to handle all the admin paperwork the military was famous for, something my dad should've done when he'd been the commander. Then he wouldn't have been so stressed.

"Yeah, Abbey is having nightmares," Tripp said. "And she won't talk to Jo or Webb about them. Webb thinks Abbey is getting glimpses of something terrible that's about to happen."

I could almost feel the wind changing and the tides turning. The last year had been somewhat quiet with missions until a month ago when Roman had surfaced. We'd heard rumblings that someone was trying to follow in Edmund Rain's footsteps by fabricating a serum to build an army of vampires. We weren't surprised. We knew it was only a matter of time.

"I wonder if she's seeing her own fate," I said.

At the age of ten, Abbey's abilities were growing. She was able to see more of the future either by touching someone or dreaming.

"If Roman is targeting Abbey, then he's a dead man," Tripp said. "Webb will stop at nothing to kill him, and he'll have the approval of the Council of Elders, including your father. But that doesn't mean you're off the hook, or Jo for that matter. We still have to ensure no one gets their hands on either of you."

"Fuck, they can certainly try. I will definitely go on a beheading spree." I would entertain doing the same to mere humans if they tried to fuck with my family and me.

"Speaking of threats, what did you do to that Aberdeen sister?"

I grinned. "Made it so she couldn't speak."

"Christ, Mason. I know what you're capable of, but I'm always amazed at what you can do."

"Alia Costner taught me well." She had been a math teacher at the human high school where Jo and I attended when we'd been in foster care. At the time, little had we known vampire DNA ran in her blood, although she'd never opted to turn vampire. She wanted kids, so she chose to stay human.

In our world, those who carried the vampire gene were given a choice at the age of sixteen—vampire or human. Most usually chose to turn, but some, like Alia, didn't.

If I'd been given the choice, I couldn't say what path I would've taken. I credited Alia for teaching me how to temper and use my powers, which had been out of control as a new vampire. My father had hired her as a private tutor for Jo and me. Even though she'd chosen to keep her humanity, Alia knew how to wield magic. Apparently, she had a line of witches in her family on her mother's side. Thanks to her, my compelling abilities were not the standard for a vampire.

Tripp stood to his full height of six-four. "I have to see where Sawyer and the tech team are in finding the Aberdeens and if our system has been hacked." He threw the towel into a basket near the bench and strutted out as my old man came in. They exchanged a few words about progress on the mole before Tripp's footsteps faded.

My father went over to our stash of practice weapons strewn on the floor and picked up a sword. He'd changed out of his tailored suit for a casual look of black pants and a blue button-down shirt. His black hair was pulled back into a low ponytail, and he looked like he could use some blood, given the veiny red lines in the whites of his green eyes. "It's been a long time since I used one of these." He ran the tip of his finger over the blade.

Yeah, we fought with the real thing. The blade wasn't cobalt, and we healed quickly. No big deal.

"Sounds to me like you miss your commander role," I said. "Is being an elder on the council not cutting it?"

"I love my role as head of the vampire military, but being peacekeeper between us and the human government isn't a fun job."

I picked my T-shirt up off my bag and threw it over my head. "Why did you take it, then?"

"Someone has to if we're going to keep anarchy and chaos at bay in this world."

"Are the humans not playing nice?"

"They're an odd bunch." He set down the sword. "I'll get right to the point, son. Under no circumstances should you engage in any kind of personal encounter with the vampire hunters. Are we clear?"

"Are you telling me who I can and can't fuck?" I knew he would try to give me advice after being in my head when we were in the war room.

Within a second, my old man and I were nose to nose. "I'm warning you. Nothing good can come out of getting involved with an Aberdeen. Trust me on this."

"I'm down for sparring with you, Pops. Seems to me you need to get rid of some anger."

He flared his nostrils. "Did you not hear me?"

"Loud and clear. But do you think I'm stupid? Just because I feel the urge to screw someone doesn't mean I will. What's really got you spooked?" He wasn't telling me something. "Really. Talk to me."

He scraped a hand over his chin. "I'm worried what will happen if you let your dick drive you into a situation that will start a war. With the combination of sex and the need to taste her blood, you won't be able to control yourself. Your hunger for both is extremely strong, and it will blind you."

"But Pops, it's not like I can get her pregnant,

and I'm good at controlling my bloodlust." I'd never said I was good at controlling my sexual appetite.

He studied me like I had ten heads. "Well, let's see how strong you really are."

"Come again?"

"Layla Aberdeen is here."

I grinned like an ass. "Told you." I started for the door, eager to see the vivacious redhead.

Dad blocked me, ramming a hand into my chest. "Not so fast. And wipe that smirk off your face."

"I can handle this." Or maybe not. Maybe he was right, and I would start a war.

"I have no problems overstepping Webb's authority here and throwing you in the brig until we find out what the Aberdeens are up to. After all, I am your father."

Anger bubbled to the surface, and I clenched my jaw. "I think I can handle a human." The operative word was *think* because the thought of being close to Layla was sending heat to grip my balls.

He pierced me with his dagger-like gaze. "Son, you have no clue the power of a human woman with blood so fucking sweet. She will drive you so insane you won't be able to stop yourself."

"Sounds to me like you speak from experience."

"Samuel, I'm warning you."

As I walked out, the hairs on the back of my neck shot to attention, and not from my father's warning.

9

LAYLA

B ile sloshed in my throat, and nerves poked my skin like a thousand tiny blades as a badass female Navy SEAL by the name of Brock, as indicated on her uniform, frisked me for weapons just inside the main gate of the naval base. She was pretty too, with her dark hair braided and twisted in a bun on the back of her head. Her brown eyes were bright and had a glint of eagerness floating in them. I hadn't been aware of a woman Navy SEAL before. Then again, she was a vampire, and they had their own rules and regulations.

I raised my arms over my head, eyeing the daggers strapped to her legs and the gun holstered to her hip. Thoughts of snagging one came to mind, but I quickly discarded it. If I wanted Sam's help, I had to play nice.

"Turn," she ordered in a tone that sent a chill down my spine.

I obeyed, glancing at Rianne, who was watching me intently from the backseat of the car.

When Brock finished patting me down, she spoke into the radio tacked to her shoulder. "Sir, coming in now." Then she flicked her chin at my car. "Follow me." She jumped into the Hummer that was parked behind the guard shack.

I slid behind the wheel as knots formed in my stomach. "Here we go." I pressed the gas pedal as I checked on Rianne. "We'll get you out of that trance soon."

She smiled, seemingly alert, but still unable to speak. I imagined she was thinking of all the ways to chop Sam Mason into a gazillion pieces. I knew I was.

The windshield wipers squeaked as they cleared the big fat snowflakes. The announcer on the radio indicated that it would snow for the next several days. I was surprised I'd gotten as far as I had in this old piece of junk.

Still, all that snow didn't give me a warm and fuzzy feeling. With our luck, Rianne and I would be stranded on base. My plan was to get in and out as fast as I could, provided I could confirm that the vampire military was protecting a little girl by the name of Abbey. I was sick to my stomach that I had to involve a child in my desperation to save Jordyn. But if Roman was right that Abbey was under the protection of the vampire military, then nothing could happen to her. Roman would have a difficult time getting his hands on her.

I focused on the road, gripping the steering wheel and taking in deep breaths. My stomach was knotted into one big ball of nerves. Dad or my uncles would think I'd lost my mind. None of them would enter into a deal with a vampire, but I didn't have any backup. Maybe I should put my pride aside and reach out to Uncle Jack. Even if I did, I wasn't sure he or Uncle Ray would come to my rescue.

I loosened my grip on the steering wheel as we passed camouflage-painted buildings that looked like small homes tucked away among the assortment of snow-covered evergreens and deciduous trees that towered over them.

As I rounded the last curve, a four-story brick building emerged, looking ominous against the sunless sky. To hell with trying to relax. Strong tension snapped my spine into a perfectly straight line, and grew tauter when I spotted guards on the rooftops of not just the main building but also the brick ones flanking it.

The Hummer stopped under the portico, and I debated whether to follow suit or gun the engine and get the hell out.

I had to keep telling myself I could do this. The problem was I felt naked without my dagger or any weapon.

I pumped the brakes with a shaky foot, my courage nonexistent. No sooner than I threw the Nissan in park, my phone rang. A number I didn't recognize flashed across the screen. Roman was probably checking up on me. His final words to me before he and Sasquatch dragged Jordyn out of the house kicking and fighting were that he would be in touch. He hadn't given me a time limit, but I knew I didn't have long if I wanted Jordyn to remain unharmed.

"What?" I answered in a harsh tone, ready to scream at Roman.

"Where's my package?" The man, who wasn't Roman, sounded angry.

It took me a second to realize the person on the other line was our benefactor. "I can't talk."

"You were supposed to check in an hour ago." His tone was full of anger.

Brock got out of the Hummer and waved at me.

I raised my finger then pointed to my phone, hoping she would give me a second.

"I have to call you later. I'm right in the middle of something." I should come clean and tell him what I was up against. He might be able to help.

He knew every detail about the Mason family, and Sam in particular. Which meant he probably knew about Abbey, but I didn't have time to pepper him with questions. Brock was staring me down from the tail end of her vehicle.

"Do not hang up on me." His tone could cut ice. "I've paid you a shit ton of money, and I expect an update."

Money he would never see again. Regardless, we knew three things about our benefactor: he had tons of money, his name was Dowell, and he wanted Sam Mason alive. What we didn't know was why he wanted Sam, which didn't matter to me. My sisters and I had a job to do, the payout was great, and it resulted in one less vampire on earth.

I swallowed the sharp tacks stuck in my throat. "Did you know Sam Mason is worth at least a million? So I think we're getting screwed."

Silence stretched over the line.

"The job is off," I continued. "We can't help you. And if you want to threaten us, then get in line." If he did, it couldn't be worse than dealing with some pissed off vampires and a shifter.

"The fuck it is!" he shouted. "You promised me Sam Mason."

I chewed on my lip. "Well, I don't have him."

His heavy breathing blared in my ear. "It was an easy job. I set the whole thing up for you. Walk into the club, shoot the sedative into the vamps, draw Sam Mason out, and do the same to him. What was so fucking hard about that? You're vampire hunters. That's your specialty, and capturing one who is down for the count isn't as difficult as catching a live one."

Well, when he put it that way, I couldn't argue with him, but Sam Mason wasn't an ordinary vampire.

"Did you know Roman was immune to the sedative part of that drug you gave us?" The way I saw things, that was our first problem. If we'd taken out Roman, Jordyn would be with me. I might be able to handle one vampire, but two and a shifter was more than I bargained for.

"Nonsense," he said. "Every vampire goes down with the amount of shit that's in that drug."

"Why would I lie? And another tidbit of info—

that drug kills shifters. The way I see it, you're the murderer here. Now the shifter's family wants revenge on Jordyn. Who, by the way, has been taken by Roman and his shifter partner. So, until I get her back, you don't get squat." My family came first.

"Don't go into that building." His anger morphed into trepidation, almost like he cared. "If you do, you won't remember a thing when you come out."

I jerked my head in all directions. "Are you following me?"

Brock marched over and opened my door. "Ma'am, my boss is waiting."

Scrunching my face, I hung up on Dowell. "I'm here to talk to Sam Mason. Is he your boss?"

She deadpanned.

The hairs on my arms fired to attention. "I should leave."

She glanced in the backseat. "You're welcome to leave. But if you want our help with your sister, I suggest you come with me." I guessed she was well informed of what Sam had done to Rianne. I wondered if he'd bragged about it.

"While you're speaking with my superior, I'll have your sister taken up to our infirmary." Her tone was soft, and she gave me the sense I could trust her.

As much as my intuition urged me to leave, I couldn't until Sam removed the spell. So I eased out of the car.

Brock's radio crackled. "Petty Officer Brock, where is she?" The familiar-sounding voice was similar to Sam's but older.

"We're bringing her in now, sir."

"Good. Settle her in the viewing room."

I laughed nervously. "Viewing room?" An image of an auditorium of vampires came to mind, all of them watching me behind a one-way mirror while they auctioned me off to the highest bidder.

"I promise you're safe." Brock could no doubt hear how fast my heart was beating and see the terror on my face. "We don't harm humans."

One of my eyebrows shot up to my hairline. "Really? Tell my sister that."

"This way." Her tone propelled me to move my legs.

Reluctantly, I left Rianne as Brock escorted me past the sentries and into the lobby of the lion's den. As soon as we were inside, a whoosh of cold air slapped me in the face, and I shivered. Something felt off to me as I stood in the spacious room with high ceilings and a circular desk ahead of me.

I was about to turn and run, but the steel doors closed with a thud.

As if Brock could sense my anxiety, she said, "No one here will hurt you."

"Are you sure about that?" I whispered more to myself than to her.

I was sure she'd heard me, but she didn't react. Instead, she walked up to the petite blonde who was absorbed in something on her computer screen behind a round desk. "Ruth, is the viewing room unlocked?"

"It is," Ruth said.

Brock nodded then ushered me along the left wall adorned with pictures of naval ships and other military scenes. As we approached the viewing room near the elevators, a plaque caught my eye.

Jupiter Sentinels
A SEAL Team Community
We protect the Superior World from all enemies, human and non-human, and uphold the laws of our existence. We strive to shield and protect the Inferior World from those who seek harm upon them.

"That plaque." I stabbed a finger at it. "By inferior, do you mean humans?"

"Yes," Brock said. "We do our best to make sure humans are protected."

"Does Sam Mason know that?" Heavy sarcasm drenched my tone.

She gave me a cold smile and waved her arm toward the room. "My superior will be here shortly."

Once I was inside the ten-by-ten room with no furniture, not even a chair, she closed the door.

Knowing full well Brock could hear, I said loudly, "Please take care of Rianne."

I shuddered at the thought that my sister was in the hands of the enemy. A crazy laugh broke free. Both of my sisters were in the hands of our enemies. I shook my head, hoping I could get some clarity through the nerves and anger and every other emotion barreling through my veins like an F-5 tornado before I had to deal with Sam Mason.

10

———

LAYLA

Brock had been gone roughly ten minutes according to the time on my phone. I couldn't believe it was only ten in the morning. It felt like days had passed since I'd locked horns with Sam Mason, when in fact, it had been only eight hours earlier.

I turned my phone over and over in my hand and walked up and down the room in short strides. I hated waiting for anything, but especially when my sisters' lives were on the line. I tore off my scarf and shoved it into my coat pocket. Then I practiced my yoga breathing as worry for more than just my sisters sat heavily in my stomach. A bad feeling was seeping into my veins. I couldn't exactly pinpoint anything specific, but the weird tingling in my legs was always an indication that the road ahead was dark and dangerous.

I mumbled a quick prayer. "Whoever is listening, please keep my sisters safe."

I checked my phone as I slowed my pace. No calls. No missed texts.

Heaving a sigh, I twisted the knob on the door, and the blood drained down to my boots. Brock had locked me in. A fire built in my veins, spreading and snaking out before giving way to anger.

I screamed as I banged on the door. "Hello!" Every muscle in my body locked in place as I continued to pound my fists, shouting again. "Brock!"

Dead silence greeted me.

I gritted my teeth, staving off the need to bawl my eyes out. I hadn't cried since Dad's funeral two years ago, but for fuck's sake, I was ready to unleash all my pent-up emotions. I was so screwed if the vampires kept me prisoner.

"Always follow your intuition," Mom had said too many times for me to count. "Your subconscious can see the future. Never ignore that."

I'd hardly listened to her wisdom when I was a teenager, but I wasn't in my teens anymore. I knew better than to walk into a coven of vampires.

You had no choice.

I did, though. I should've left before I'd gotten out of the car. I should've put my stupid pride aside and called the uncles. They couldn't remove the compelling spell, but they sure could help me kill.

Think, Layla. What would your dad do?

He would definitely not feel sorry for himself. As I absently scanned the room, a red light caught my eye. A tiny camera hung from the ceiling in the corner. Then the red light blinked to green.

I hurried over to it. "Unlock the door. You have no reason to keep me here." I stuck my hands on my hips. "I swear if you don't let me out, I will make sure the world knows about you fuckers." Not that anyone would believe me.

I was met with nothing.

I ground my back teeth together. "Are you afraid to confront me, Sam Mason?" I pictured him on the other end, smirking and sizing me up, so I stuck out my chest. My tits had gotten his attention at the club. I hoped that my D cups would again. "Don't be. I won't kill you yet."

Fisting my hands at my sides, I spun on my heel and back to the door. "Open up." I glared at the camera. My idle threat of ousting them wasn't working.

I only knew one way to get Sam's attention at

lightning speed. It might cost me a limb or my psyche, but my sisters were depending on me.

I returned to the camera, setting my jaw. "If you don't let me out, Roman will take matters into his own hands with your sister." Sweat began to bead on my neck. Probably a stupid move, considering what he'd done to Rianne when she'd made the idle threat about his sister.

Sam blew through the door, fangs down, his silver eyes like high beams lasering me where I stood.

My fight-or-flight instinct kicked in, but I didn't have to think too hard about which to choose. I wasn't afraid. I should be, but I was ready to do whatever it took to get what I wanted, even if it cost me my life.

I inhaled deeply, and my chest rose, drawing his attention to my tits.

I rolled my eyes, snapping my fingers. "Up here, vampire."

His head jerked, and strands of his black hair fell loose from his low ponytail. "How many times are you going to threaten to hurt my sister? Have you not learned your lesson?" His voice was gruff and gravelly, and it sent delicious shock waves to settle between my legs.

Stupid body.

I flipped him off again. "Suck it." Poor choice of words with a vampire.

One side of his mouth curled as he backed me into the wall underneath the camera. "I should've ended you at the club." The seriousness in his tone made the hairs on my arms stand at attention.

Despite the fact that I didn't have any weapons and he could end me in a flat second, I wasn't one to back down. So I kneed him in the balls.

His face reddened. If he was in pain, he sure as shit wasn't showing it as he threw his head back and laughed. "You're going to be hellfire when I'm inside you."

I snorted. "Sorry to disappoint, vampire, but that will never happen."

"Wanna bet?" he singsonged.

I wanted to punch that cocky smirk off his gorgeous face, but as hard as his jaw looked, I would probably break my hand. Instead, I pushed him, but he didn't budge.

He leaned in. "Careful, Red. I like a fighter." Then his hot breath breezed over my ear as he whispered, "Instead of stopping that racing heart of yours, I might fuck you right here."

My brain suddenly fogged, thick and soupy. I was well aware that he was a vampire, that he could drain me of my life's essence, that he could end me in a nanosecond. But I didn't care. I suddenly wanted to slide my hands down his body until I was gripping his dick again. I wanted to feel what it was like to be on the brink of death just as he sank his fangs into my neck. *Would it hurt? Or would it send me over the edge to the point that I was freefalling into the abyss?*

I tilted my neck to one side as my heart rammed against my rib cage.

He stepped away and began pacing, seemingly trying to get himself under control.

That lust-filled cloud in my brain vanished as I brushed my hands down my legs, straightening my spine.

A Sam look-alike came in. His black hair was just as dark. His green eyes were vibrant but held a world of experience in them. Given the way he carried himself and the faint lines around his eyes, I imagined he'd been around a long, long time. Age wise, I couldn't tell how old he was. My guess —he'd turned vampire in his mid-twenties.

He regarded Sam then me. "I'm Steven Mason. You must be Layla Aberdeen." His tone matched the scowl on his face.

"You know my last name?" I shouldn't be surprised. I knew any government had the means to find out who anyone was.

He tucked his hands in the pockets of his black pants. "I knew your father."

I lost the ability to breathe. "You did?" Dad had never mentioned he knew a Mason personally.

Steven nodded. "I won't get into that now, but how is he?"

I ground my back molars. "One of your kind murdered him."

Sam widened his stance like he was digging his heels into the carpeted floor and preparing himself for an onslaught of punches. "Well, that's what you get for hunting vampires." He cupped his hands in front of him and gave me a smirk that was equal parts hateful and sarcastic.

My fists itched to wipe any emotion off his handsome face.

Steven growled at Sam. "Knock it off."

I held back a grin as Sam clamped his mouth shut.

"I'll cut straight to the point," Steven said. "What do you want with my son?"

That was a loaded question. In the space of one breath, I wanted to feel what it was like to screw his brains out, and in another, I wanted to drive a cobalt blade into his heart until it burned into ash.

I glared at Sam, not knowing if I should spill my guts about Dowell. I decided why not? I had worse problems with the shifter and Roman. If Dowell wanted to hurt us, then he had to get in line.

I stuck my chin out at the elder Mason. He seemed just as powerful if not more so than Sam, but I had nothing to lose at that point, and frankly, I needed help. If I could get rid of Dowell, then that was one less problem to deal with.

"I'll tell you after Sam helps Rianne." I was among enemies, so I shouldn't be so bold, but I had to try.

Steven scrutinized me, sending eerie shivers down my spine.

Sam, on the other hand, glowered, his silver eyes now a deep green, reminding me of a lush forest after a hard rain. I couldn't decide if I liked the silver or the green better on him. It didn't matter at the moment.

"Samuel, wait outside." Steven kept a keen focus on me.

Sam hesitated before he did as he was told.

Once Steven and I were alone, he shut the door.

I would bet Sam ran to the room where he could watch every move I made and hear every word I spoke. To my surprise, Steven motioned with a hand in front of the camera, giving whoever was on the other end the sign to turn it off.

I had no doubt he could hear my pulse beating fast and smell the sweat beading on my neck. I was ready to pee my pants. Sam I could handle. Steven I wasn't sure about. Needless to say, nausea swirled deep in my gut.

"Are you in charge of the SEAL team?" I asked for nothing more than to break the tension strung between us. I understood a father wanting answers about why I was at the club to kidnap his son and threaten his daughter. But he wasn't dressed in a uniform, so I wasn't sure if he was here in a more official capacity.

"Yes and no. I oversee the vampire military as a top official, but I'm not Sam's immediate boss. I'm here as his father. I'm also here because I have the most knowledge of your family." He rubbed his strong angular jaw as he pierced me with a hard look. "Layla, I can tell you're an intelligent woman. I would think long and hard before you answer my question."

A bead of sweat trickled down my neck and kept sliding further as he continued to pierce me with his green gaze. At any moment, he would probably show me the real him if he didn't believe what I was about to say. Then I remembered something that made my hands tremble. The vampire could read minds.

I inhaled, digging deep for what Dad had told us to do if ever confronted by the elder Mason. The problem was that I couldn't think straight with him glaring at me. *Oh crap. He's probably reading my mind now.*

I swallowed thickly, thinking of anything other than the second reason I was on base.

"Before I get to my question," he said, "I want you to know we are not the enemy. Roman, the name you dropped earlier, is an extremely cunning and lethal vampire who wants nothing more than to profit off others. If you're working for him, I'm sorry to tell you, but you won't be able to leave unless you tell me everything you know about him."

"You would hold me prisoner?" Duh, I was already a prisoner.

"I will do what I have to do to protect those in harm's way, especially my family."

I was tired of being threatened. "I don't care how powerful you are. I came here for help, not to be interrogated. If you want an apology, I can't give you one. I didn't do anything wrong." At least not in the eyes of human law. And since I was human, I didn't conform to or follow vampire law.

Fury poured off him as he raised his chin. I got the feeling no one crossed Steven Mason.

Too bad. I had had enough. The only way out of there was to lie to him. If I told him the second reason I was there and what Roman wanted, Jordyn was dead—yet if I didn't give him something, I would never see the light of day again.

He sucked up all the air in the small space, and the walls seemed to close in. I wasn't claustrophobic like Jordyn, but I was beginning to understand how she felt when locked in or cornered, especially alone in a room with an extremely powerful vampire. I had no clue of the magnitude of what Steven Mason was capable of.

He waggled a finger at me. "You have some female balls, you know that? I'm beginning to see why my son likes you."

My dad had always praised me for being tough. Despite Steven's compliment, I didn't know whether to laugh, roll my eyes, or snort. I chose to go with none of those, and instead slipped my hands into my coat pockets and ignored his comments. "Does that mean you'll help my sister?"

He and I were roughly ten feet apart. The door

was behind him. If I wanted to run, I had to go around him, and that was a tall order. He was fast, strong, and deadly. I had to find common ground—a win-win for both of us. My dad had taught me that.

"Mr. Mason, I'm not working with Roman." I was being threatened, and that was much different than doing a job.

"Layla, one thing you'll learn about me and my children is our ability to get to the truth. Therefore, all I have to do is touch you to read your mind. If I find you're lying to me, I can guarantee you will not walk off this naval base."

Well, there went my human existence unless I could remember what Dad had told me about how to block Steven from reading my mind. "I know you can read minds."

He startled. "Your father told you?"

"We know vampire history. We know which of you are more powerful than others." That was partly a lie. I didn't know the magnitude of what Sam was capable of. I was slowly finding out, though.

"Mm. So you know what my children are capable of too?"

"My dad didn't talk about your children, but I saw how Sam made the nightclub shake and what he's done to Rianne." Steven's grin told me he was pleased with his son.

I wondered for a moment if Sam could read minds. *Holy shit!* If he could, then he knew my innermost thoughts about him. *Sam doesn't need to read your thoughts, girl. He can smell your lust.*

I held out my hand. "Then read my mind." Holy hell. I had a way of shielding myself from being compelled, but when it came to reading my mind, I had nothing.

Steven didn't hesitate.

Once my small hand was in his large one, I felt a warm feeling travel up my arm. Then on a blink, his eyes were liquid silver. As we stood bound to one another, thoughts of Sam skipped through my head. Sexy thoughts too. Not just the one where I was driving a dagger through his heart, but the one where I envisioned us naked and sweaty.

My cheeks burned with embarrassment, but it was either that or... I didn't want to finish that thought.

Steven dropped my hand. "Mmm."

"I'm sorry. What does that mean?" Maybe he felt awkward when he found I had been imagining Sam and me naked.

He smoothed a hand over his hair. "What do you want with my son?"

I pushed out my shoulders. "I'm confused. You just read my mind, didn't you?"

"Somehow, I don't think you were at the club to drive a dagger through Sam's heart. You were blocking me. I'm not surprised. But, Layla, my patience is wearing thin." His voice dropped several octaves. "Answer my question."

I blew out a breath. It was best to come clean. Again, one less thing I had to deal with if I enlisted Steven's help to get Rianne out of her comatose state. "Fine. My sisters and I took a job to capture Sam. Some guy named Dowell paid us a lot of money. He didn't say why, and I did ask." The tension whooshed out of me as though a ten-ton brick had been lifted off my shoulders.

He studied me with a calculating glare. "How do you know this man? And is he a vampire?"

"I don't know him. He contacted us. He didn't share much except his name. He knew Sam would be at the club, and that Roman would be too. And our clients are all human."

He scraped a hand along his angular jaw. "Are you sure he's human?"

I nodded. "He told us he was."

"Are your uncles helping you on this job?"

I felt as though I had whiplash with him firing one question after another. "You know them too?"

He chewed on the inside of his cheek. "I tried to recruit your father. I never met your uncles, but I know of them."

My mouth fell open. "Come again?" Dad had never shared that with me or my sisters. "Do my uncles know that?" If they did, they hadn't told us.

"Not sure. I never approached your uncles. I wanted your father to work for the vampire government."

Silence stretched between us as I processed this newfound news and wondered why Dad had never shared it with me. But I wasn't there to reminisce. "Why would you want my father to work for you?"

"That's a story for another time. Layla, we want the same thing. We want my kind to stop killing your kind and vice versa. We want a peaceful existence."

"That may be true on your part, but I don't see it. What I see is a world that's growing darker and darker every day. My sisters and I are frightened to start a family. We don't want our children to grow up in a world where monsters need them to survive."

He gave me a warm smile as his features relaxed. "I'll have my son remove the spell from your sister, but I need your help with this Dowell person. Can you do that?"

He'd just given me an opening to stay longer, which meant I could possibly glean some inside info on Abbey and if she was living on the naval base. Maybe things were looking up.

11

SAM

I waited by the elevator not far from the viewing room for Layla and my dad to come out. I'd tried like hell not to blow my top or tear off Layla's clothes before my old man came in. His words echoed in my head: "Son, you have no clue the power of a human woman with blood so fucking sweet, she will drive you so insane you won't be able to stop yourself."

I'd been ready to go madman style in that room. Not only had she threatened Jo again, but her cherry aroma clouded my brain. Her big tits blinded me, and the lust pouring off her had my dick hard as stone.

It took all the restraint I had to step away from her or even walk out of that room on my father's order. I was beginning to agree with him that a human woman like Layla had power, but I wasn't admitting that out loud.

I watched Ruth, our receptionist, collate a stack of papers as I tuned in to listen to Layla and my father. I didn't need to be in the room to hear them, but I sure wanted to see her reactions as my father interrogated her.

"Layla, one thing you'll learn about me and my children is our ability to get to the truth. Therefore, all I have to do is touch you to read your mind. If I find you're lying to me, I can guarantee you will not walk off this naval base."

I grinned as I imagined Layla stiffen.

"I know you can read minds," she said confidently.

Maybe my old man was right, and the Aberdeens had a way of blocking our powers.

"Your father told you?" Dad asked.

"We know vampire history about those of you who are more powerful than others," Layla replied.

She lied. She had no clue what I could do. That had been evident at the club when both she and her sister were shocked at what I'd done to Rianne.

The phone rang at the reception desk, jarring me away from the conversation.

Ruth's usually soft voice boomed through the vast space.

I stretched my neck one way then the other and resumed listening.

"Then read my mind," Layla said to my dad in her siren voice that was gripping my dick like she had her lips around it. Her pulse slowed to a crawl.

Yep, my old man knew this family. But what had me confused was how she could block him. We had a mind-blocking potion that on occasion was a staple for the SEAL team. With my father and Jo able to read minds, we didn't want them in our heads. I hadn't taken any recently. I wasn't around Jo all that much, and my father spent a good amount of time in Boston at the Council of Elders' headquarters.

Several silent moments passed as I homed in on Layla's heartbeat. I would love to be a fly on the wall to see the look on her face. In order to read their mind, my father had to be touching the person unless it was Jo or me. He didn't need to with us. It had something to do with being related. Jo, on the other hand, was stronger than our dad. She didn't have to touch anyone to read minds. I felt sorry for Webb, who continually had to block her out.

It seemed like an eternity before my father said, "Mmm." With his even tone, I couldn't gauge what that meant.

The elevator dinged, and Harley called my name. "Sam?" She sounded distraught as the strawberry blonde sashayed toward me, all wide hips and pretty smile. "Do you not answer your phone?"

My phone hadn't gone off. "Bad signal down here."

"Your sister is looking for you." Harley batted dark-blue eyes at me. "She's up in the infirmary with Abbey. Call her."

"She had you track me down?" It must be extremely important. After Layla's sister threatened Jo's life, my sister probably wanted to find out more.

"I told her I was on my way down to the lobby. I have to fill in for Ruth while she goes to lunch. By the way, why are you out here and not in there?" Her lips twisted. "Oh, the human is with your father? Poor thing."

"She should be more afraid of me," I mumbled.

"Sam," Harley warned, "be careful."

I closed the distance between us. "I can feel your jealousy."

She brushed me off with a swat of her hand. "Pfft. We've had this convo. We're just friends with the occasional hookup. Besides, I have a date tonight."

My brow creased. "Who's the lucky guy?"

"None of your business."

I moved an errant strand of hair off her face. "He better treat you right or else."

"You know I can handle myself."

As a vampire, she could. "It's not your physical strength I worry about."

She rubbed her hand up my chest before raising up on her toes and kissing me on the cheek. "You're a great friend, Sam. Don't let anyone tell you you're not." She started for the lobby desk. "I'll let you know how my date goes. And make sure you don't hurt that human in there."

Heat traveled to my groin at the thought of Layla. "I can't promise."

She giggled as she traded places with Ruth.

The door finally opened, and Layla glided out, smiling, until she laid eyes on me. Then her expression soured.

I smirked. "Feeling's mutual, babe."

She narrowed her blue eyes. "Don't call me that. I'm no one's babe."

My father came out a second later, reading something on his phone. "Sam." His warning tone went in one ear and out the other.

"It's okay, Steven," Layla said in a downright sexy voice. "I can handle Sam."

Not on your life. "After what I did to Rianne, are you sure about that, Red?"

My father looked at her like she was insane. "Have you forgotten I was in your head?"

His interesting reaction made me tilt my head at my old man.

She blushed, shy and sweet, sending my stomach into a whirlwind of butterflies. *What the fuck?* I didn't do butterflies. I'd never had that reaction to a chick.

She addressed my father. "Can I see my sister now, please?"

My father nodded. "Layla, wait here." He stabbed a finger toward the entrance to the lobby. "A word, Samuel."

Once we were on the other side of the room where Layla couldn't hear us, he said, "I see why you like her. She's a beautiful woman."

I reared back. "What happened to 'I'm warning you. Nothing good can come out of getting involved with an Aberdeen.'? Or 'I'm worried what will happen if you let your dick drive you into a situation that will start a war.'?"

He sighed. "I'm still cautioning you. She likes you, but she wants you dead, and I'm not surprised, given her background. Still, I don't want a war between us and her family."

I didn't either. "Is that what you read in her mind?" Not that her wanting me dead was a surprise. Nor was the fact that she liked me—or rather lusted for me.

"I didn't get far. She kept blocking me, much like you and Jo do when you don't want me to know something."

"So she's hiding something?"

He regarded Layla, who was talking to Harley, then stepped closer to me. "I believe she is, and my gut is telling me it's big. But she did come clean on something. She was hired by a human named Dowell. He wants you."

"Never heard of the dude." That didn't mean anything. My DNA and the money one could get for it was becoming common knowledge. "Well, what now?"

"Take her up to the infirmary and remove the spell from her sister. Jo is up there. I'll text her to see if she can read Layla's mind better than me. Afterward, she'll be our guest and help us flush out who this Dowell character is. But son, tread lightly around her."

I wasn't about to promise him anything. I'd learned my lesson quickly after being in that room with her. "I'll try."

His phone rang. "I have to take this. The Council of Elders is breathing down my neck about the Aberdeens. I'll alert Webb and Tripp about Dowell." With his phone to his ear, he walked out of the main entrance.

"Where are you from?" Harley asked Layla.

I sauntered over to the reception desk, racking my brain about Dowell, but the minute I was ogling Layla from behind, I lost all thought.

I felt such a strong pull toward the redheaded goddess. Maybe it was her essence or the fact that I wanted to taste her blood, and fuck her until the sun went down, came up, and went down again.

Layla shrugged. "Montana."

"Cowboys and ranches," Harley tittered excitedly. "Any good-looking ones you know?"

Layla giggled. "Many."

Maybe I should just keep walking and have Harley take Layla up to the infirmary. Then again, Harley couldn't leave the reception desk with Ruth gone.

Harley smiled. "What brings you here, aside from targeting my good friend Sam?" Harley emphasized the word *good* with a warning in her tone.

My leg brushed Layla's as I sidled up to her, and an electrical charge zapped me. "Some guy named Dowell?"

She huffed before sliding away from me, snarling, "Take me to Rianne."

Harley's eyes went wide, no doubt from the sudden change in Layla's attitude. "I can take her if you want to answer phones, Sam."

I snorted. "You want me to answer phones? I can't. I have to help her sister."

"I'll be fine," Layla assured Harley. "I'm in a place that brags about protecting humans." Layla pointed to the plaque on the wall behind the reception desk.

We did protect humans, but I wasn't sure about vampire hunters. "Come on, Layla. Let's get this show started." I was ready to hit the gym to blow off some pent-up energy. Maybe I should do that before I even entertained getting into an elevator with her.

She followed, her footsteps resounding in the quiet room, blood pumping through her veins at warp speed. Stabbing the elevator button, I held back a laugh. My own blood was doing the same if I were being honest.

She sighed, puffing out her cheeks.

"Are you worried about getting in the elevator with me?"

"Not at all," she said as the doors slid open.

"Liar." I swung my arm out. "Ladies first." I might be an ass, but I would like to think I had some redeeming qualities.

Layla stiffened. "Maybe we should take the stairs."

"This is the only way up." That wasn't exactly true. We had a back way into the infirmary, but that was through the building next door and the long way around. The faster we got up to the fourth floor, the better for both of us. My old man might have slightly changed his tune about easing up on me when it came to Layla, but if I drained her of blood, he would definitely go ballistic on me.

Regardless, my gums throbbed at the thought of her and me alone with no distractions. Maybe it was wise if we took the stairs. Either way, it didn't matter. My thirst for her blood wasn't going away anytime soon.

"If you so much as touch me, I will cut off your balls."

I belted out a laugh. "Seems like you're all talk. At the club, I recall you saying, 'the next time we meet, I'll be cutting off your dick.' Yet my cock is still alive and well."

She stomped into the car and found a spot in the corner, hugging herself.

Following her in, I couldn't help but smirk as my throat burned like an inferno.

12

SAM

Layla's lovely scent wafted around as I stabbed the number four button. After a few seconds, the doors closed with a thud, and Layla winced. She fixated on the floor numbers lighting up as the car hit level two. When we reached level three, I pushed the stop button, and the car jerked to a halt.

Horror etched her pretty features. "What are you doing?"

I leaned against the wall adjacent to her. "It's time to chat. Tell me why this Dowell dude wants me."

"I already told your father. Ask him."

She motioned to get the elevator moving, but I

131

jumped in front of her. "Not so fast. We have some business to take care of."

She pressed her small hands into my chest and pushed.

I didn't budge except to protect my balls with my hands. I could take a ton of pain, but when she'd kneed me in the groin, I'd seen angry red stars. I might not die easily, but I could still feel pain.

She tightened her jaw as she stared me down.

In a quick second, I pounced, pinning her against the cold steel wall.

She lost her breath as her nostrils flared. "You're an ass."

I trailed my fingers over her flushed cheeks, taking in every freckle she had smattered around and across her nose. "So I've been told."

She slumped, giving in. "Do your worst. I'm tired, I'm hungry, and I want to see my sister."

I swiped the pad of my thumb over her plump bottom lip, and a noise squeaked out of her as her breathing increased.

Lust consumed her, weaving a tight web around us.

Fire burned through me as my fangs dropped. I couldn't quite understand the magnitude of my own emotions, except one—the need to devour her. "Tell me you want me as badly as I want you." I nuzzled my nose into her hair and sniffed. Her sweet cherry scent traveled through my veins, igniting my senses.

"I hate you." Her tone was weak at best.

My fangs grazed the sensitive spot behind her ear. "Your body says otherwise."

She mashed her tits into my chest, seating her hands on the waistband of my gym shorts. "You have me under a spell."

"Layla," I whispered as I captured her earlobe between my teeth. "If I did, you would be naked."

She angled her neck, exposing her carotid artery, supercharging my bloodlust. Growling, I licked her earlobe then tugged lightly. She tasted of heaven and home. She mewled, hauling me to her until my cock pulsed against her stomach.

My body hummed, my gums throbbed, and my brain shut down.

I fisted my hands at the nape of her neck, ready to sink my fangs into her when she squirmed, turning her jaw until her lips were on mine. Her tongue dipped into the cavern of my mouth, teasing and taking.

I froze until she bit down, willing me to engage, to fight back, or do anything but act like I'd never been kissed before. "Are you afraid, vampire?"

Blood—my blood—exploded on my taste buds and kicked my thirst into gear. I pulled the band from her hair and her long red locks tumbled free. I grabbed a handful, the silky strands slipping through my fingers, and yanked, forcing her to look up at me. Her eyes were full of want and need and were insanely blue.

"Never." That fire burning through me turned to an inferno as hot embers singed my willpower into ash, and I became a madman. I glued my mouth to hers, taking what I needed to ease the desire drenching me as more of my blood dribbled from her bite.

She giggled as though she'd won, but this prelude to whatever was happening between us was not a competition—it was the beginning of a mating ritual.

Human or not, Layla Aberdeen was mine, and I dared anyone to tell me otherwise or get in my way.

I grasped her hips, lifting her up and anchoring her to the wall. She wrapped her legs around me, locking her ankles, her heels digging into my lower back. She thrust her hands into my hair, her mouth begging me to take her places she'd never been before.

I explored her sweetness as it mixed with the iron tang of my blood. "Fuck," I mumbled.

She moaned loudly, her breaths coming in short bursts.

I broke the kiss, pulling on her bottom lip, and when I did, one of my fangs caught, and the scent of her blood knocked me back a step. Suddenly, my throat burned, hot and dry.

She stiffened as fear permeated the air.

My tongue snaked out. Just one little taste.

As if she knew the war raging inside me, she licked away her blood, but it was too late. My resolve vanished. I captured her lips in between my teeth and sucked. My eyes rolled back in my head as the tiniest droplet of her sweet blood awakened a part of me I didn't know existed. Lust took the wheel as I crashed my mouth to hers, shoving my dick into her stomach as hard as I could to get friction. The need to bite down on the softness of her thighs made my cock harder than granite.

"Sam," she whimpered. "No." It was her turn to yank on my hair. "Sam."

I heard her, but the vampire in me couldn't stop. Sweat slid down my spine as I nuzzled my nose against her ear. "Layla, you need to kick me in the balls like you did earlier."

Laughter bubbled free from her sweet mouth. The sound, glorious and airy, only made my bloodlust stronger.

"If you don't, I'm going to sink my fangs into you." I was hanging on by a thread and suddenly afraid that I was a second away from ending her life. As much as she wanted to kill me, the feeling wasn't mutual.

Just as I licked the spot on her neck, readying myself to feast, she threw her head forward and clamped down on my bare arm, her teeth breaking skin and drawing blood.

The sting of her bite threw me backward, but the act alone snapped my spine upright. "That's not my balls."

She gave me a brilliant self-satisfied smile. "It worked, didn't it?"

I licked my own blood off her mouth to rid myself of the taste of hers.

She ducked under my arm and walked around once then twice, brushing her wavy auburn hair with her fingers. "What just happened?"

I tried to retract my fangs, but they weren't moving. So I thought of war and death, anything but her. *Fuck.* It was impossible with that cherry fragrance clouding my brain and controlling my actions. "Seems you can't keep your hands off me."

She closed her coat and hugged herself. "You're the one who attacked me."

"Mmm. You're the one who kissed me."

She puffed out her cheeks. "That will be the last time I do that."

I sighed. "I doubt it."

She clenched her teeth. "You're so sure of yourself. Such an ass. You think you can take what you want."

Once again, we were practically mouth to mouth. "I can't take from the willing, Freckles." That should be my new name for her.

Her cheeks became almost as red as her hair as shyness enveloped her. It was quite sexy to see a different side of her. I grasped her wrists. "Don't hide your beauty."

Her mouth parted. "You are a walking enigma."

My fangs finally retracted, then a momentary flash of darkness hit before my eyes shifted from silver back to green. "I aim to please," I teased.

She shrugged out of my hold. "Stay away from me."

I chuckled.

"What? Can you read minds like your father?"

It would be fun to mess with her, but I had something better that would ring true. "No, but I am good at predictions."

That tension she'd been harboring ebbed. "This I have to hear."

I feathered my lips over hers. "You won't be able to stay away from me. In fact, you'll be in my bed in two days, tops."

Flustered, she skirted around me to engage the elevator. Little did she know, I was an empath and could read every emotion she was desperately trying to hide and failing miserably.

The car began to move.

"You're so wrong, Sam Mason. The way I see it, you'll be the one in my bed first."

"Want to throw down a wager?" I loved a good game of cat and mouse.

She lifted a casual shoulder. "Why not?"

"If you're not in my bed in two days, then you can do as you please with me.

"You mean I can kill you?"

"If that's your pleasure."

Her lips parted. "You're that sure you'll win."

"I never lose. And if I win, I get to have my way with you."

She pursed her lips. "I never lose either. And

I'm looking forward to carving you into tiny pieces."

It was becoming clear to me that I didn't want anything as badly as I wanted her.

"Oh, and Layla, when I finally win, I warn you now. This place right here"—I rubbed a spot along her inner thigh—"is where I'll take my first bite."

She quivered, seemingly turned on by the idea.

Outwardly, Layla Aberdeen might be tough and strong and despise vampires, but inwardly, her desire to be with a vampire was more powerful than she would ever admit.

13

LAYLA

The minute the elevator doors opened, I raced out like a runner sprinting to the finish line. I was an idiot. Stupid. It wasn't natural for me to like a vampire. I killed them for a living. But Sam had an incredible pull, as if we were polar opposites coming together like magnets.

I stopped short when the long and narrow hall blurred in front of me. Suddenly, dizziness made my head spin like I was riding a fast-moving merry-go-round.

Sam's hand landed on my back, strong, hot, and urgent. "Something wrong? Still reeling from our bet?" His voice held too much excitement for my taste.

He was smoking some serious dope if he

thought I would slip under the covers with him. Us naked was a recipe for one of us to die. Yet the thought of him biting me in that spot he marked on my thigh was sending riveting chills down my spine. Maybe that was the reason I felt dizzy and suddenly a tad queasy.

I inhaled and exhaled, wanting nothing more than to knee him in the nuts again. "I'm fine."

We began our trek down the hall from hell. No doors. No people. No way out. Again, I wasn't claustrophobic, but I felt like I wanted to puke as panic began to overtake my psyche.

Sam Mason was the very essence of what I hated about the world I lived in, yet I couldn't get enough of how he was making me feel. In that elevator, I'd gotten lost in a world where the sun shone, the mountains soared, and evil was a thing of the past. There was no other place I'd wanted to be.

I scolded myself for wanting to feel what he offered, and guilt punched me square in the stomach for thinking I could defy my family's belief that vampires didn't belong on Earth. I'd allowed a vampire to play me like a puppet. I was the one who'd kissed him, but he hadn't made it easy for me to walk away. Hell, I'd had no means of escape in that elevator and no weapons to boot.

Don't blame your actions on the elevator.

He took one long stride to my two, and I was having a difficult time keeping up—then another wave of dizziness washed over me, and I listed to one side.

"Layla." Sam sounded extremely concerned, which was a sharp contrast to his arrogance. "Are you okay?"

I stopped and bent over, inhaling and exhaling. "I don't know." I stared at the bright white floor that seemed blinding and hurt my eyes. "I'm dizzy all of a sudden." After another breath, I straightened, and when I did, the floor rose up fast.

Sam caught me before I face-planted. "You said you didn't eat. Maybe that's it. Doc should have something for you to nibble on in the lab."

"Sam." His name slurred from my lips. "I think I might pass out."

He felt my forehead with his long fingers. "You are warm."

"It's not hunger." I knew what the effects of not eating felt like. "It might be the flu." Although the flu wouldn't come out of nowhere. I closed my eyes. Suddenly, an image of Rianne beating the shit out of Sam played out behind my eyelids.

I felt Sam's calloused hand scraping my cheek. "Layla?"

Blinking several times, I oriented my vision, and his handsome face sharpened before me. "I think I'm hallucinating. You did something to me."

A deep crease settled between his eyebrows. "I did not bite you. Even if I had, you wouldn't get lightheaded and dizzy." He curled one arm underneath my legs and the other around my waist, then lifted me. "Your blood sugar is probably low."

"I can walk." My protest was weak.

"You're white as snow. Doc will check you out." He hurried down the hall, and the small act of bouncing in his arms soured my stomach.

I covered my mouth with my hand, feeling like I was on a ship in rough seas. Maybe it was the whiskey that I'd put in my coffee coupled with an empty stomach. I blew out a breath, willing the dizziness and the queasiness to go away.

"It's okay if you need to puke."

"On you? No. Put me down." I was all for making Sam suffer and sweat, but throwing up on him wasn't what I had in mind. Still, I allowed a weak smile to emerge, knowing he didn't care about puke but he seemingly cared about me. As quickly as that thought danced in my brain, I erased it. Sam didn't come across as someone who cared about anyone but himself. Oh, and I couldn't forget his sister.

"No. I can feel something isn't right."

If he were human, I would have thought he was nuts to be able to feel what I was feeling. "You're scaring me." Nevertheless, I willed my stomach not to lose the coffee and whiskey as I rested my head on his shoulder and closed my eyes.

Suddenly, the movie starring Rianne played out as a doctor with light-brown hair I didn't recognize stabbed a needle in my sister's arm. My breath hitched and my eyes flew open.

Double doors loomed ahead with the word "Infirmary" stamped on them. Sam stopped at a panel just outside and stared into it until the doors opened.

Once we were inside the massive medical complex, Sam shouted, "Doc, where are you?"

A woman with black hair and purple highlights hurried toward us. "Sam? What happened?"

"Not sure. She was fine one minute, and the next she was about to pass out. She hasn't eaten."

The gorgeous lady with the brightest silver eyes scrutinized me. "So, this is the other human?"

"Where's Doc, sis?" Sam asked.

"Please put me down. I'm okay." Despite feeling a tiny bit better, I didn't want to be in his arms. The longer he held me, the more I wanted to kiss him again.

His eyes flickered from green to silver.

"Your scent is all over her," his sister said, smiling. "You kissed her."

"Get out of my head," Sam bit out.

My blood gelled before I was clawing my way to get down. *Another Mason who could read minds and didn't have to touch Sam to read his. Holy mother of all shitstorms.*

I needed to get Rianne and leave as quickly as possible. I still didn't know if Steven found anything when he'd been in my head. Regardless, I couldn't take the chance of them finding out about.... I switched my thoughts to Sam. He seemed to be the safest person to think about. After all, he had a way of clouding my mind.

He finally set me on my feet. I gripped a tall bench that spanned the length of the room. *Inhale. Exhale.* The blinding lights overhead were doing a number on my eyes, and my vision blurred. "Where's Rianne?" I blinked several times then darted my gaze to the rooms that lined one wall. "Is she in one of those rooms?" I skirted past Sam's sister and bumped into a young girl. "I'm so sorry." I felt like I was drunk.

"Layla," Sam called. The sound of his footsteps

was loud and obnoxious. "You should sit down. Jo, where is Doc?" His fingers circled my upper arm, and images of fire and brimstone flashed before me. I shook off the flames, and when I did, Sam and I were tangled together with me sinking my teeth into his neck.

Oh, for all that was holy, I was turning into the undead. No freaking way. I'd only had a few drops of his blood. Blood that was giving me visions. Impossible.

The room spun. The lights above darkened, and my body felt as though I'd been dipped into a vat of hot oil.

"Layla." Sam's smooth and husky tone penetrated through the hell that was playing out in my head.

"I want to see Rianne." My voice didn't sound like my own.

Sam was about to lift me up again, but I shoved him off.

He chuckled then whispered in my ear. "Fight me in bed. Right now, you need help."

His arrogance was disarming, which didn't make sense. Minutes before, I wanted to cut off his balls. "You've done something to me, Sam."

"Where's her sister?" Sam tossed over his shoulder to Jo.

"She's in the last room," the young girl, who had to be about ten years old, said. "I'll take you." She batted her blue eyes that reminded me of the ocean off the deep waters of South America.

I managed to get away from Sam, or maybe he let me go. "I'm Layla. And thank you." She just became my new best friend.

"I'm Abbey." Her long shiny black hair fell to her waist, and she tucked thick strands of it behind her ear.

I froze as though someone had stopped time. *Abbey.* I said her name a few times in my head. Then I thought of Sam as quickly as I could. If Jo could read minds, I had to clear my thoughts.

Abbey tugged on my hand. "Layla, are you okay?"

Not in the freaking least. But I nodded just the same. "Sorry. I'm not feeling well."

"My mom can examine you," Abbey said.

Mom? I didn't know female vampires could conceive.

Abbey led the way as I shook off my shock. Jo, Sam, and I followed Abbey as if she was our queen and we were her subjects. I got the feeling she was a special little girl. She seemed like she was loved and well taken care of. She wore a cute pink fleece sweater that hung over navy-blue leggings. Her suede ankle-length boots were rimmed with fur at the top.

Abbey banked right at the end of the aisle. Jo and Sam chatted. I tried to stay upright even though the vertigo feeling hung on strongly.

"Dad isn't going to like you falling for a human," Jo said to Sam behind me.

I choked. "It's his bloodlust, nothing more." Sam wasn't falling. His actions toward me were driven by his dick and arrogance and the need for human blood.

"She's right," Sam agreed.

Jo mumbled something just as Abbey approached the doorway. "She's sleeping," Abbey said. "Mom gave her something to relax."

I pivoted on my heel so quickly that I lost my balance.

Sam's arms were around me before my body hit the floor.

14

LAYLA

Someone tapped on my face. "Layla." Her voice reminded me of Mom's. "Layla, it's Jo. Wake up."

My eyelids fluttered open, and I bolted forward. "What happened?"

Jo placed a gentle hand on my back. "You passed out. I'm not sure why. I took your blood pressure, and it was normal. I would like to run some tests if you don't mind."

She didn't need to run any tests. Sam's blood was making me feel like I'd consumed a half bottle of whiskey in one go. That was the only thing that made sense. It wouldn't hurt to know for sure.

I relaxed back against the pillow. "Where's Sam?"

Jo ambled over to a rolling cart that was packed with medical supplies. "He went to get Dr. Vieira."

"Are you a doctor?" I asked.

"I'm close to finishing my studies. I'm not sure about a residency gig yet."

The beautiful lady with glossy black hair and diamond-colored eyes had an elegant way about her. The exquisite square diamond surrounded by amethyst stones on her ring finger sparkled in the bright lights of the room. Her face had a touch of blush coloring her high cheekbones, and her long lashes were lightly coated with mascara. But it wasn't her physical appearance that gave me the sense she was graceful. She carried herself like she knew who she was and was proud of it and happy.

I wanted to be her. Up until that moment, I always thought I knew who I was and what I wanted. But I'd walked into what seemed like an alternate universe, seeing vampires who loved each other and would die for each other. I wanted that. I missed the feeling of being loved.

My sisters and I were tight and would protect one another, but since our parents passed, I'd lost that feeling of belonging. For far too long, I'd been roaming around in a haze, trying to take care of my sisters and make sure we had what we needed.

I'd always thought of college, a profession—detective came to mind. I loved to solve puzzles and mysteries of any type, including people.

Jo rolled the cart up to the bed. "Do I have your consent to run some tests?"

I let out more air, feeling less panicked than I had before. My gut was telling me I could trust her. My instincts had always been spot-on, so I nodded. "It's fine."

"Good. Let's get you out of that coat."

After I shrugged off my winter parka, she set it on the chair by the window. Then she readied the equipment necessary to take my blood.

"What part of the medical field are you interested in?" I asked.

"I've been studying genetics and hematology."

"An interesting choice." If I wasn't mistaken, hematology was the study of blood, which struck me as comical, given that she was a vampire.

She tore open an alcohol wipe. "My mom died of leukemia, which is one reason I've chosen that route."

"I'm sorry." I thought of my own mom. "Mine died of breast cancer."

She gave me a sad smile. "My sincere condolences."

"I can't lose Rianne. She'll be okay, right?"

She opened the drawers on the rolling cart, looking for something. "She will."

"I've never seen a vampire compel someone like Sam."

She sighed in frustration as she continued to search for something. "Sam and I have several unique powers that no one else among our kind has."

"My parents and family never mentioned anything about you or Sam or your abilities." I had no clue why I was telling her that.

"Not many humans know about us," she said as she checked the medical cabinet.

"Is Abbey your daughter?" I hadn't been aware that female vampires could get pregnant.

"You're correct. We can't get pregnant."

"You're reading my mind? Who else around here can do that other than you and your father?"

Jo kept searching inside the medical cabinet. "Just me and him. But I don't have to touch anyone to hear or read their thoughts."

I was screwed. "What have you learned so far from reading mine?"

That wave of dizziness was slowly rearing its ugly head. I had a feeling I would be locked up in a dungeon after Jo took a hike down my memory lane.

She returned to my bedside empty-handed. Whatever she was looking for, she didn't find it. "Why? Are you hiding something?" Her silver eyes morphed into a deep violet color as she gave me a steely look.

I thought of Sam and me in the elevator, but I was having a difficult time not focusing on the reason I was there. "You know my sisters and I were at the club to capture Sam. You probably know Rianne used you as a way to threaten him. And I would go out on a limb and say your father already told you a guy by the name of Dowell hired us." I told her all that to keep my mind from conjuring up any other thoughts I didn't want her to know.

She studied me as if I was an expensive piece of artwork. "I also know you're into my brother. Seems odd to me, given your profession."

It was official. She would know my deepest, most intimate thoughts on vampires, and I would die of embarrassment.

She smiled. "I don't want to dive into your most intimate thoughts. I hate reading minds, by the way. But I want to be frank with you, Layla. My brother's heart isn't something to mess around with."

I laughed through a snort. "I am not into him." *Liar.* "I only just met him."

She bobbed her head in a patronizing gesture. "You are. You're just fighting it because you hate vampires. And love can happen instantly. Who says there's a timeline on how you feel about someone?"

She was so wrong about my feelings for Sam, yet she was so right about how someone could fall hard and fast. My dad had known the minute he'd laid eyes on my mom that he would marry her someday. He'd known he didn't want to be with anyone else. But what I was feeling for Sam was lust, nothing more.

"Why is your father so against a vampire and a human being together?" I asked wondering if it was me her father hated. After all, a vampire hunter and a vampire weren't exactly marriage material. Regardless, I wanted her thoughts on the topic. "Isn't that how you were born? Your mom was human?"

"It takes a special human female with a certain blood type, but let's face it, your family has been hunting and killing vampires for centuries. So, you and Sam are not exactly a match made in heaven. Plus, he doesn't want a war with humans. We have enough enemies among our kind."

My phone rang and startled me.

"I need to get a band to wrap around your arm, which I can't find in here." She zipped out as I fumbled to get my phone out of the back pocket of my jeans.

The caller ID showed the same number that Dowell had called me from. "I told you we were through."

"I'm worried about you." If not for the concern in his tone, I wouldn't have believed him.

The room spun. *What is happening? One minute I'm fine, and the next I'm passing out.* "I can't talk." I swung my legs over the bed.

"Get out of th—"

As soon as my feet touched the floor, the phone dropped from my hands. Claws of panic clutched at my neck and gripped my chest.

A tall figure came in.

"Sam?" I wasn't one to cry, but tears shot out. I closed my eyes, breathing in. I winced as I stood then keeled over.

Large hands landed on my arms. "Layla." Sam's baritone voice was soothing.

I puffed out my cheeks, blowing out a breath. "Something is wrong."

He swiped a hand over my hair. "Doc is on his way."

I felt like I was on some powerful drug like mushrooms, or maybe I was becoming the very creature I hated. But that was impossible. Humans who weren't born with the vampire gene couldn't become a vampire. Unless... no way. My family was not descended from vampires. Besides, it was impossible for me to turn into one. If my vampire history was correct, and if I had the vampire gene, then the only way for me to lose my humanity was by drinking my father's blood. Since he was dead that was out, and he was no vampire, anyway.

Sam helped me into bed. "Why are you being nice to me?" He didn't strike me as the type to coddle anyone.

"I'll take it from here," a voice I didn't recognize said.

A man came into view. He was the same man with light-brown hair, the doctor, who I'd had a vision of while Sam had been carrying me down the hall earlier. Panic stole the air from my lungs. No freaking way. *How was it possible for me to see the future?*

My breathing became labored, the room spun, and as the man drew closer, blackness overtook the light.

15

SAM

My sister looked at me like I was a stranger, angling her head one way then another. "Are you okay?"

I combed my fingers through my hair as I moved to the foot of the bed to get out of Dr. Vieira's way. "Of course. Why?" But I wasn't really. In the span of ten hours since I'd met Layla, my head was one big confusing mess.

"I've never seen you so concerned over a human, and one you hardly know," she said.

I couldn't explain it. I'd felt Layla's pain the minute I'd walked into the infirmary. "You know I can feel what others feel." I couldn't put my finger on why I was drawn to this woman, a human no less.

"Of course," Jo said. "But it's more than your empath ability."

I concurred, but I wasn't ready to admit that to her or anyone yet.

Dr. Vieira readied his stethoscope. "Jo, can you take her blood pressure?" Then he listened to Layla's heart while my sister did as he asked.

I stood at the bottom of the bed, admiring Sleeping Beauty. She really was a gorgeous creature. Waves of auburn hair fell around her teardrop chin. Her heart-shaped lips were pouty. Her freckles blended in with the color of her hair, and her long smooth neck had my name written all over it.

I shook my head like a dog shaking off water.

Doc cleared his throat. "Sam, are you okay?"

"Never better, Doc," I lied through my teeth. "What's wrong with her?" I gripped the plastic footboard, and if I kept squeezing, I would crush it.

"I don't know yet," Dr. Vieira said. "She seems normal. But when I walked in, she had a panicked look on her face as though she was frightened of me. Odd."

"Her blood pressure is fine," Jo added. "She gave me consent to take some blood samples. Should we?" she asked Doc.

Doc nodded at Jo as he wrapped his stethoscope around his neck and addressed me. "I agree with your sister. You seem to be quite taken with her."

I chuckled. *Got to love how vampires can see right through people.* "Look at her. Wouldn't you be? And let's not forget that if something happens to her, my father will behead me." That wasn't a lie. I'd tried like hell to restrain myself in that elevator. I swallowed the dryness in my throat as I thought about how fucking delicious only one drop of her blood had been. I wanted more. I wanted her blood running through my veins.

"Tell me what happened," Doc ordered.

I erected a mental shield around my brain so Jo wouldn't go digging. First chance I had, though, I needed to down a bottle of Alia's mind-blocking potion. I could still lie, but Layla's life could be at stake. "She bit me."

Jo didn't react, leading me to conclude she already knew. She had probably sifted through Layla's thoughts.

Doc's brow creased. "Why? What would ever possess a human to bite a vampire?"

"I told her to. That's all I'll say for now," I said in a frustrated sigh. "Is my blood making her pass out? She was dizzy and queasy earlier."

"Possibly," Doc said with a nod. "Your blood is potent, and she is human. Not a good combination. Humans can't tolerate ingesting blood to begin with, let alone vampire blood as strong as yours. How much did she take in?"

"Not much. A few drops. She bit me on the arm." Which had already healed.

Doc tucked his hands in the pockets of his lab coat. "We'll send a sample of her blood to our Boston lab." He glanced out the window. "Although with the blizzard bearing down, that might not happen right away."

I turned to leave. It was imperative to see if Sawyer could unlock her phone and find out who she'd been talking to before she passed out.

"Can I have a word before you go?" Jo asked, batting her pretty silver eyes my way.

Why not? I imagined she was about to give me advice on women. Not that I had time for a sisterly talk about settling down with the right woman or putting myself out there to find a bride, but I was curious if she'd dived into Layla's memories.

Once we were out in the lab area and near the exit doors, she gave me a blinding smile. "You're falling for her."

"Sis, I just met her like ten hours ago. It's impossible to have any deeper feelings other than lust. And let's not forget that she wants me dead."

She curled strands of her purple-streaked black hair behind her ear. "No. She was at the club to kidnap you."

"Semantics. Were you able to read her mind? Pops said she was blocking him."

"Me too. All she kept thinking about was you."

I cocked a brow. "Oh?"

"I got nothing other than seeing her bite you. Dad's right. She's hiding something that she doesn't want us to know."

Maybe whatever it was had something to do with the caller. "I need to go. Can you let me know when she wakes up?"

"Considering she has your blood in her system, she might be out for a while."

"She didn't take that much." Then again, when it came to the vampire world, anything was possible.

"Don't try to figure it out," Jo said. "And let's not forget, Tripp's blood can put people to sleep too."

She had a point. When Webb's plane had gone down over the Alaskan mountains five years ago with no sign of him for months, Jo wanted to drink Tripp's blood so she could stay asleep for longer than three hours and dream. My sister could see glimpses of the future when she dreamed.

She grabbed my hand. "Sam, I want what's best for you, and I get it. Layla is a beautiful woman, and I want you to find a soulmate. It's not that she's human as much as her family is a problem we don't need."

All the talk about Layla made my hunger for blood rear up. I was surprised that I hadn't gulped down a case of it after being in an enclosed space with a human, and one who was settling into my psyche at that. Layla was taking up too much of my headspace. I couldn't think straight.

Time to change the subject. "Harley mentioned you were looking for me earlier."

Jo produced a hair clip from her lab coat pocket and twisted her hair up on top of her head. Since we'd become vampires, my sister had grown into a stunning woman. She was smart, caring, intelligent, confident, and the best sister a brother could have. Gone were the high school days when I'd had to fight off foster dads or bullies. Jo Mason could fight her own battles. She didn't need me anymore. I would still massacre anyone who dared to hurt her.

"Yeah. I've been tracing our DNA and doing

some extensive research on Mom's side. But it can wait."

Jo was fascinated with genetics, how the human body functioned, and our vampire DNA. Her penchant for the sciences ran in the family. Our dead uncle Patrick had been a well-known geneticist, but he'd used his expertise against us, extracting our DNA to develop a serum to alter the DNA of humans into vampires. Case in point: that was how Ben had become a half-breed.

Dr. Vieira stuck his head out of Layla's room. "Jo, can I see you for a minute?"

"Be right there," Jo returned. "We'll talk later."

I pushed through the double doors, and after two flights of stairs, I was walking into Webb's cluttered office. Stacks of books, folders, and papers were scattered around on tables, his desk, and even on a loveseat in a lounging area of sorts, tucked into one corner adjacent to the door.

Webb looked up from his laptop while Tripp lowered his phone to his lap.

I sat in the chair next to Tripp in front of Webb's metal desk. "I think she was talking to Dowell." I held up her phone. "I'll get Sawyer to break into it. Maybe he can pinpoint a location on Dowell."

"Or Roman," Webb said.

"Maybe, but I caught the tail end of the man's voice as I walked into her room. It wasn't Roman," I said.

Tripp crossed one leg over the other. "Sawyer found that our computer system was hacked. He traced the location of the hacker. We have Ben checking it out now."

Webb sat back in his leather captain's chair and studied me. "What's happened to Layla?"

"The better question is what did you do to her?" Tripp asked.

I let out an exasperated sigh. "Why does everyone think I did something to her?"

"Did you?" Webb asked.

My problem wasn't Webb and Tripp but with my father. He would have a cow when he learned Layla had bitten me. I could block him, but it was no use. He would smell her on me.

I understood the magnitude of what Layla's family could bring down on us—war and anarchy. Yet I wasn't sure I could stay away from her. I had a dire need to protect her all of a sudden, and it wasn't my libido at play but a strong metaphysical force.

The minute I was in the same room with her, nothing mattered around me. No one could pry me from her. My brain shut down cold. I felt like an invisible rope was binding us together. Maybe it was the empath in me feeling what she was feeling, and she wanted me. That had to be it.

Layla's phone trilled, pulling me from my thoughts.

The three of us looked at the phone like it was a bomb about to go off.

I tapped on the answer button, then speaker, and set it on the edge of the desk.

"Layla." The voice was male but not Roman's. "Hello?" The caller sounded panicked.

"Who's this?" I asked.

"Who are you?" His voice bordered on a growl.

"Depends," I replied.

"Where's my niece?"

I said the first thing that came to me. "Indisposed."

"Let me speak to Steven Mason. I know he's there," her uncle stated.

Tripp, Webb, and I exchanged a surprised look.

Then Webb's voice was in my head. *I think your father called him.*

"This is his son Sam," I said. "Who am I speaking to?"

"Jack Aberdeen, and if you so much as hurt any of my nieces, you will burn over a fire pit like the pigs I roast and the many other vampires who have died by my hand. Now put Layla or one of my other nieces on." I didn't know what the man looked like, but I imagined his face was as red as a tomato.

"Sir, I'm sorry." My tone was even. "Layla left her phone in this office and forgot to take it with her. I'll find her and let her know you called."

"Bullshit. You vampires are up to something. If she doesn't call me back within the hour, I'm sending out a hunting party." The call ended before the screen returned to a picture of Layla and her sisters.

"That went well," I mumbled.

"What went well?" My father sauntered in, wearing a suit jacket over his black pants and blue shirt. His black hair was combed back and damp, and his jaw clean-shaven.

"Did you call Layla's uncle Jack?" I braced myself, erecting my shields in preparation that he would read my mind.

He settled on the side of Webb's desk. "No. We have a scout in Montana on our payroll not far from the Aberdeen ranch. I had him relay a message to Jack Aberdeen. Did he call her?"

Tripp went over to a small fridge along the wall of military pictures. "Jack Aberdeen is pissed."

My dad unbuttoned his suit jacket. "Not surprised. Jack is a hothead, but I don't blame him for being mad. I'm curious what Layla is up to without her family. It's unlike them to hunt solo, which was the main reason why I called him."

Tripp popped the top off a bottle of blood. "You told them where we are?"

It was unlike my old man to give up our location and to a family of vampire hunters.

"Not yet, but he probably has the means to track her on her phone. Plus, I'm sure Jack will be calling me next. I made sure to pass along my number. I want to head off the Aberdeens before Jack gets a wild hair up his ass to come blazing in with an army. We have too much going on with our own kind to deal with humans. The sooner we take care of the Aberdeens, the sooner we can get back to Roman and whoever the person he's referring to is who's worth more than Sam."

Webb leaned back in his leather desk chair. "Steven, do you honestly think the Aberdeens will walk away once they have their nieces back? Don't get me wrong—I agree we need to nip this in the bud before we're in a fight with humans. But the Aberdeens won't bargain with us. Anyone in our community who knows of them is aware of that."

My father loosened his royal-blue tie. "We need to try." There was alarm and unease underneath my old man's tough exterior. He was hiding something about the Aberdeens.

"Pops, what aren't you telling us?" I joined Tripp at the fridge and got my own supply of blood.

Creases lined the underside of my father's eyes as they changed from green to silver. "Nothing to worry about. Is Layla with her sister? Did you remove the compelling spell, son?"

Webb and Tripp stared at me.

I guessed no one had filled him in. I built a mental steel wall around my brain, took a deep breath, and explained what had happened in the elevator between Layla and me, focusing more on my bloodlust and not my sexual lust. After I was finished, deadly silence hung in the room with tension so strong that, if it snapped, it would sever our limbs one by one.

"I'm sorry, Pops. You were right. Her scent, blood—everything about her is hard to resist, but I did. I told her to kick me in the balls, but she bit me instead."

My father was expressionless. "So, you're telling me she ingested your blood, and now she's passed out?"

All I could do was nod.

"The Mason blood does have some strong effects," Webb said. "I know firsthand. Your sister's blood gives me a high like no other. My system can handle it. I suspect since she's human, her system can't. It's almost like an overdose of a drug, which is one of the reasons we deal with people like Roman who sell blood like ours."

My father loosened his tie even more as he tried to hold in his rage. "What about her sister?"

"I haven't removed the spell yet," I said. "We should wait until Layla is awake." If Rianne woke up before Layla, I imagined the feisty Aberdeen would go apeshit when she saw her sister in a hospital bed.

"You're right." My dad pinned each of us with a stern look. "I need to get to Boston. I've set up a meeting with the Council of Elders. We need to have our ducks in a row in the event the Aberdeens agree to meet. Do you know where the third sister is?"

We all shook our heads.

Webb rose. "Steven, go. We'll locate the other sister. Ben should have some intel on the hacker. Maybe by then Layla will be awake, and we can get the answers we need."

"Son, walk me out." My father marched to the door.

Tripp's voice entered my head. *Good luck.*

I was tempted to flip him off but refrained. The fact that my father wasn't yelling or throwing me in the brig was shocking. I wanted to keep it that way.

I downed the rest of the blood and tossed the bottle in the trash when Webb's desk phone chirped.

Webb answered on speaker. "What is it?"

"Ben trailed the hacker to an apartment in the city. Do you want him to engage?" Sawyer asked.

"Have Ben hold tight and keep an eye on him. We'll be right down." Webb clicked off.

I regarded my father. "Can we chat when you get back? This is important." Getting my ass chewed wasn't.

"I'll check in later." Then my dad was gone.

I slumped my shoulders, relieved that I'd averted my father's wrath.

16

SAM

An hour later, the bell on the glass door dinged as Tripp and I walked into a coffee shop in the downtown area of the city. The aroma of coffee mixed with sugary pastries wafted through the air.

Except for Ben and the blond barista behind the glass-top pastry case, the place was empty. With the falling snow making some roads impassable, people were hibernating. That was better for us, since there would be fewer witnesses in case things went awry with the human.

Ben sat at a table by the window, his body too big for the small chair he was in.

"Coffee, gentlemen?" the barista asked,

beaming at us as though she was grateful for customers.

"No, thank you. Not staying." I stood alongside Tripp at the edge of the table.

We didn't have time to kick back. I wanted to nail that fucker as quickly as we could. Layla might be waking up soon.

Tripp glanced out at the brick building across the street. "Any movement?"

Ben dragged fingers through his reddish-brown hair. "No. He went in about an hour ago. What's the plan?"

"Sam and I will pay him a visit. I want you positioned at the front entrance. Olivia is already stationed at the back exit, and Kraft will pull the van into the alley once I give him the signal. Any questions?"

Ben kept his voice low. "Are you sure this dude is former CIA?"

Ben had sent us a picture of the hacker, and the moment Tripp, Webb, and I saw it, we thought our eyes were deceiving us—but we had no doubt our hacker was none other than Agent Wyman. He'd played a role in helping our dead former enemy, Edmund Rain. The million-dollar questions were: did Wyman remember anything from five years ago? And if he did, what did he remember?

Erase his memories of everything he's seen with Patrick's research. Then compel him to get out of town with his family and not to speak to anyone within the CIA or Edmund's organization. Those had been Webb's orders back then.

I snagged a napkin and toyed with it, needing to do something with my hands. "The pic you sent us confirms it." I couldn't wait to find out how Agent Wyman got his memory back. Come to think of it, he could very well remember me. I'd never erased his knowledge of me, Webb, Tripp, or even my dad.

"Anyone else with him?" Tripp asked.

We were worried that Wyman was working with his former partner, Thomas, whose memories I'd also taken parts of. Man, it was going to be a shitshow if they remembered what had gone down. I wasn't so worried about Thomas or Wyman remembering vampires, but I was concerned they would recall that Edmund had a daughter. If so, then Abbey could be in danger. It was bad enough we had to keep her well protected from anyone within our world. Case in point: individuals like Roman. Fuck, if he somehow found out about Abbey, he would stop at nothing to get his greasy criminal hands on her just to make a profit. The CIA wouldn't be any different.

"Not to my knowledge," Ben replied.

Tripp tipped his head at the door. "Time to get this show started."

"I'll meet you outside." I glanced at the barista.

She beamed at me as I ambled up. "Change your mind on that coffee?"

I leaned over. "Actually...."

She met me halfway, curious to hear what I had to say.

I stared into her big brown eyes and erased any knowledge that she'd seen Ben, Tripp, and me. With that out of the way, the three of us dove into action.

Just before we entered the building, Tripp checked in with Olivia and Kraft and confirmed all was clear. Once inside the dingy hallway, Tripp and I sniffed and listened. It smelled like a family of cats had taken a piss in every corner.

I scrunched my nose to stave off the smell as Tripp raised two fingers to indicate two heartbeats. I looked around the staircase. A red exit sign flickered, and a set of mailboxes were built into the wall. I pointed up.

Once we were at the top of the landing, I sharpened my hearing.

"Layla, why aren't you answering? I guess I'll have to do the job myself." Keys jangled.

Tripp and I grinned at one another as adrenaline surged through me. It was going to be fun to confront an old enemy.

We made our way around the banister to apartment three. No sooner than we approached, a short man came out, and suddenly the past hit me—Edmund Rain, my uncle Patrick, and the days on end when I'd been holed up in a cold, sterile lab while my uncle poked and prodded me.

I fisted my hands at my sides, ready to annihilate Agent Wyman. The lines denting the area around his dark eyes would only multiply when I got done with him.

Tripp forced him to retreat into his apartment. "Agent Wyman, right?"

The man stumbled backward, raising his hands, his skin turning white as the snow outside. "No. It's Dowell. I don't want any trouble." He reeked of fear.

I closed us into the shithole he lived in—chipped paint on the walls, torn fabric on the couch, scratched coffee table, and trash that smelled like dead rats was piled high in the bin beside a small island.

Tripp backed him into one of three barstools, his fangs clicking into place. "Do you think we're idiots? We know who you are. What the fuck do you want with Sam? Is this about revenge, or are you working for someone?" Tripp's voice boomed. "Speak."

He dropped his phone and keys. A sheen of sweat coated the man's forehead as terror dripped off him. "What have you done with Layla?" Wyman stammered as his beady eyes darted from Tripp to me. "You better not have hurt her."

My fangs shot out as I growled. "Layla isn't your concern. Now start talking." One bottle of blood earlier had not done the trick, though I wouldn't be sinking my fangs into this human. His putrid odor burned the hairs in my nostrils and soured my stomach. "I compelled you to leave the city, yet you're here and you remember me. How?" My elemental powers were teetering on the edge.

Tripp stepped an inch away from Wyman, scrutinizing him as we both waited for the man to speak.

Wyman's Adam's apple bounced as he swallowed. "Two years ago—" He cleared his throat and took a deep breath. "—I overheard the name Mason in a conversation about vampires in this farm town in Montana. At first, I couldn't place the name until I saw a picture of your father, who looks just like you. Then I remembered you staring at me in a conference room."

"What else?" I asked.

He pressed his hands into the counter behind him, his pulse soaring into outer space. "Vampires exist. I'm not a CIA agent anymore. Not sure why. My wife had asked me why I moved the family to her sister's house in Montana. I couldn't give her an answer except it was time to live a quieter life. That's it. I swear." Ten more strands of his dark hair turned gray. I was exaggerating, but the dude was ready to piss his pants.

Tripp probed further. "Nothing else?"

Wyman's heart rate began to slow. "Look, I've lost blocks of time. If you're looking for something specific, I can't help you."

The knot in my stomach that had formed when I laid eyes on Wyman's picture loosened. I'd been worried I'd fucked up. Before we left the base, Webb and Tripp speculated that my powers hadn't been as strong five years before, given how I'd been learning and developing them.

I didn't compel like normal vampires. Alia Costner had taught Jo and me how to cast magic spells made up of a series of numbers to compel someone. With the right combinations of numbers, we could spark different spells to get a person to do what we wanted or take away their voice like I'd done with Rianne. Regardless of my strengths or lack thereof, the spells could be reversed by someone who practiced magic, like Alia Costner.

I quietly exhaled, studying Wyman like a science project. I didn't get any vibes that he was lying as his pulse ramped down. Or he was good at telling lies. "So you mentioned two years ago. Have you been watching me that long? And what were you planning on doing with me?" I clenched my teeth.

He puffed out his chest, a smug grin emerging as though he was growing some balls. "To turn you into the CIA." Okay, he grew some balls in a matter of minutes, and I had to hand it to him. He was honest.

I laughed so hard, the floor shook beneath my booted feet. "And you thought you would send three vampire hunters to capture me."

"The Aberdeen family is the best out there to do just that," he said.

"Obviously not," I returned.

Tripp skirted around me and into the kitchen, eyeing the pile of folders on the island that separated Tripp from Wyman. "Why target Sam when you know other vampires exist?"

Wyman tracked Tripp with a keen eye as though he didn't want Tripp to find something. "I understand that Sam is one of the most powerful of your kind."

I clenched my teeth. "Who told you that?"

Tripp began to pick through papers and folders, and when his hand landed on a leather-bound notebook, Wyman gulped.

"Leave that alone." Wyman's voice hitched.

"Mmm," Tripp muttered as he flipped through the pages of the journal. "He's detailed every place you've been, Sam, and Layla too. It says here that he was at the club last night. Listen to this. 'I dropped the ladies off in front of the club, each of them clueless to who I was, but I had to keep it that way in case they fell into the hands of the vampires. I couldn't let them know my identity until the time was right.'" He waved the journal at Wyman. "If you're trying to stay in the shadows, why are you detailing your actions in a journal?"

Wyman paled more than he had earlier. "I keep forgetting things."

Maybe erasing parts of his memory was having a domino effect, which boded well for us. The less he remembered, the better.

Tripp tucked the notebook into the back of his waistband.

"You can't take that," Wyman cried, ready to

launch over the counter at Tripp. Instead, he ran by me, but I blocked him.

He pushed me. "Get out of my way."

I didn't budge as I glared down at the short man. "You dare to tell me what to do?" I gripped his throat.

His face glowed red as he narrowed his eyes. As much as I would like to toss him through the film-covered window, we needed more answers from him. Not to mention, he'd just threatened me with the CIA. They were the last organization we wanted in our business.

I loosened my grip. "Now answer my question. Who told you I was the most powerful?"

"Layla's dad," he squeaked out.

I unleashed him from my grasp. That clarified how Wyman knew Layla.

He gagged, inhaling the stale air as he made a run for the door.

I laughed. "Humans."

Tripp collected the laptop and files. "Bring the van," he said into his earpiece.

I could chase Wyman, but Ben was at the front entrance, and Olivia was guarding the back.

"Ben," I said into my comm. "The target is coming your way."

"Check the bedroom," Tripp ordered. "Let's make sure we don't leave anything behind."

"You know he probably has a backup of that laptop," I said as I went into the bedroom.

"If he's smart, then he does, but we'll flush all that out back on base," Tripp said.

A sleeping bag, a pillow, and a blanket were strewn across the carpeted floor. I ducked into the tiny bathroom and came up empty. Then I returned to the living room. "Nothing in there."

Tripp pocketed his phone. "Let's go. Webb texted that Layla's awake."

I grinned as my stomach flipped and my balls tightened at the mention of her name.

Tripp cocked an eyebrow. "You really have it bad for her."

I was about to flip him off when Ben's voice blared in our ears. "Lieutenant, the target didn't come out."

Olivia chimed in. "Nothing here."

Which meant one of two things. He was hiding in one of the apartments or fleeing down a fire escape.

"Kraft, come in," I said.

"No sign of him on any of the fire escapes," Kraft said.

"Check the roof," Tripp ordered me.

He couldn't have gone up. I bolted out into the hall and listened.

Boom. Boom. Boom. Someone's heart was racing faster than a horse running around a racetrack.

"Apartment one," I muttered.

The other heartbeat we'd heard earlier was slow and steady and in apartment two.

"I have eyes on our target now. He's climbing out the window, or trying to," Kraft announced.

I kicked in the door, and at vampire speed, I had him by the throat once again. "Are you an idiot?"

Wyman gagged, clawing at me.

I squeezed his neck. "You're former CIA. Surely, you know we have the place surrounded."

"I can help you." His voice was strained. "I have something you want."

"I doubt that." But I loosened my grip, curious to know what he could possibly give us.

He struggled for air. "R-R-Roman."

"Roman Brown?"

"He's working with Layla," he squeaked out.

My old man had said she was hiding something.

I dropped my hand. "How do you know that?"

He bent over, gagging as he rubbed his throat.

"Answer the question." My tone bordered on a growl.

"He will later," Tripp said at my back. "We have to move."

Layla is freaking out about something and asking for you. Doc wants you back ASAP, Tripp said telepathically.

If Layla was conspiring with Roman, I would do much worse to her than I'd done to Rianne.

17

LAYLA

I repeated the word "murder" in my head a thousand times as I thrashed around like a fish out of water. The asshole vampire doctor had strapped me to the bed like an animal.

"Let me out of this!" My heart rate was off the charts as I screamed at the top of my lungs.

Dr. Vieira waltzed in, hands in his lab-coat pockets, his light-brown hair mussed as though he'd just been through a windstorm. "You must calm down, Layla. You're going to pass out if you don't." He kept his distance.

I bared my teeth, and for a split second, I had to question if I was still human. "Get me out of these."

"I will when I'm comfortable that you won't attack me again. And I can't have you running out of here. Otherwise, the guards will act accordingly."

In all fairness to him, he was trying to help. Hell, I didn't know how long ago I'd passed out. It seemed like years had gone by. Still, when I'd woken up thirty minutes ago and laid eyes on him again, I'd gone batshit crazy. Dr. Vieira was the same man who I'd seen in my visions, the one who had jabbed a needle into Rianne. I swore I was dreaming. I had to be. I was human. I didn't have visions.

"Where is Sam? I want to see him." I wanted to murder him then feed his body parts to a bear. He was responsible for whatever was happening to me.

"I'm not going to hurt you," Dr. Vieira said in a tempered tone.

"Maybe not, but I don't trust you."

"You trust Sam?" An undercurrent of shock resided in his tone.

A wild laugh burst free. "Hell no. But I would feel better kicking his ass than yours. Where's Jo, then?" I did trust Jo.

He looked over his shoulder as though he'd heard something. "Jo had to step out." Then he spun on his heel and left, not bothering to close the door.

Rather than expend my energy, I took in several calming breaths. I wanted to save my fury for Sam.

Voices hummed outside the room. I listened intently, trying to discern if one of them was Sam's, But I had something else on my mind. I searched around for my phone but came up empty. For all I knew, it had been days since Dowell had called.

Daylight filtered through the blinds as flakes of snow fluttered by. It had been snowing when I'd arrived. Maybe only hours had passed. Regardless, I had to get off this base. If I stayed any longer, I would be a nutcase, and no way was I spending the night surrounded by vampires.

I tugged on the restraints, swearing like a sailor and conjuring up a plan to carve up Sam like a pumpkin. I was in this predicament because of him.

It's your fault, my subconscious returned.

I snarled as the leather restraints dug into my skin. I inhaled deeply, staving off the need to cry or panic even more than I already had.

I listened again to the voices outside the room, and this time, I detected Sam's voice.

"Sam Mason." I sneered. "I know you're out there. You better get your ass in here."

I blew out a breath, forcing my heartbeat to

slow. Rianne and Jordyn needed me. I couldn't pass out again. I had to play nice.

But nice went out the window when Sam swaggered in wearing a sinful grin, seemingly thrilled to see me tied down. "Mmm." He swept his gaze over me, and my freaking body tingled. "This is giving me all kinds of ideas."

I popped forward, ignoring the butterflies in my stomach and the pulsing need pounding between my legs. "Take. These. Off. Me." I delivered each word with venom.

He crossed massive arms over an impressively muscled chest, looking all stealthy in his black uniform with daggers strapped to his legs, his black-as-night hair tied in a low ponytail, and those freaking forest-green eyes sparkling like he was having too much fun. "Now, Layla. That's not how to get what you want."

I eyed one of the daggers, remembering he had my family heirloom. "What I want is to use one of those weapons you have strapped to you to slice every limb off your body and feed it to the crows."

That smugness he exuded multiplied. "You could try."

Arrogant asshole. "You know, I just realized something. I'm going to enjoy killing you when you lose that bet you so confidently slapped on the table. I mean, if you keep me chained, I win. Right?"

He quickly lost his cocksure attitude.

I'd hit a nerve. Giddiness made me smirk until he ambled up to the bed and leaned over so his mouth ghosted over mine. My pulse shot off the charts. My breathing increased, and I wanted nothing more than to have his lips on mine, his tongue in my mouth, and to taste his blood once again.

Oh my word. My brain cells are fried. What is wrong with me?

His eyes flickered from green to silver then back to green.

I shuddered under his scrutiny. He was unnerving, yet there was no place I would rather be than this close to him. I was losing my humanity. That was the only reason I could think of for feeling the way I did.

He licked his top lip, and I swallowed a moan.

"Asshole," I squeaked. "What did you do to me?"

His nostrils flared. "Why do you keep insisting I've done something to you?"

I pushed out an exasperated sigh. "Look, just take these restraints off. Please. I would like to see Rianne and then leave."

My plan was to run as far away as possible. If I stayed, I couldn't promise myself I would not crawl into his bed. Then again, I didn't know where Sam lived, and I needed to keep it that way.

He finally straightened to his full height, shoving a hand through his thick black strands and pulling the leather strap out of his hair.

I'd never been that girl who drooled over men with hair below their ears or longer. Jordyn had a thing for men with that particular style. Rianne loved the military cut. My tastes fell somewhere in between, but I couldn't deny the way the waves of black framing his face only enhanced his beauty—strong jaw, thick lips, long lashes, and dimples that softened his hard exterior.

He snapped his fingers. "Did you hear me?"

I oriented my vision with a blink and shook my head. "You said something snarky, I imagine."

He ignored me and removed the restraints.

Once my wrists were free, I rubbed one then the other. "Thank you. How long was I out?"

"A few hours," he said.

Again, it felt like days. *Time to blow this joint.* I was about to swing my legs over the bed, but Sam had other plans.

"Not so fast." Gone was the cocky tone, and in its place was something far scarier than I'd heard before from Sam Mason. "Here's what's going to happen next, Layla. I'll take care of Rianne, then you can spend a few minutes with her. After that, you're all mine. You will come clean on why you're here."

"I told you why I was here. Your father wants my help with Dowell, but I really don't have anything else to say about him." I tried to stand. "Now get out of my way. It's time you bring Rianne back." *I hope she kicks the shit out of him.*

He placed a finger under my chin. The lightest of his touches sent an electrical current straight to my clit. "Like I said, you will come clean on why you're really here. If you don't, I will tie you up in a prison cell then tell your uncle Jack that you left the city. Your family will never see you again."

I reared back. "Come again? My uncle?" As quick as the shock hit, it vanished. Steven knew my family. "Did your father call him?" I prayed not. A fight between my family and the Masons would not be pretty. My uncles, cousins, and whoever else they had recruited would not stand a chance against the Masons or the vampire SEAL team.

"You're afraid of your uncles."

I pushed him, but he didn't budge. "You should be too."

"Interesting," he said. "I detect some animosity within your family."

"It's none of your business. Now, I suggest you take me to Rianne." My sisters and I hadn't had contact with Uncle Jack in over a year, but if I needed his help, I wanted to believe he would come running. The last conversation I'd had with my uncle had ended in a big fight.

"I'm in charge. It's my job to protect you now that your father is dead," Uncle Jack had said. "So you will do as I say. You will not be hunting anymore." The bottom line was that Uncle Jack wanted to control us like he did everyone else in the family. I hated to be told how to live my life, as did my sisters. So we'd packed up one night and hadn't looked back.

My family wasn't the issue, though; not even Sam or his father or Dowell was, either. Roman and the shifter were the elephants weighing me down. I envisioned Vera, torturing Jordyn.

Maybe I should tell Sam about Roman. The SEALs stood a better chance in helping me rescue Jordyn.

Sam's hot breath tickled my ear. "You spaced on me."

I pressed my hands to his chest and pushed

hard again. That time, I caught him off guard, and he moved, or maybe he was being nice.

"Rianne." I stumbled out into the infirmary. "Argh." I had to get my shit together despite the cloudiness still consuming my brain. Otherwise, Jordyn would die, and Rianne would live in a zombie state.

18

LAYLA

My legs felt like saltwater taffy as I staggered like I'd polished off a bottle of whiskey and then some. I was grateful for the wall and the lab tables and desks on either side of me.

Sam's footsteps plodded behind me. "Layla, you're in no shape to walk."

I hated that he was right. I seriously felt like I had a hangover. I spotted Dr. Vieira as he looked up from his microscope before rushing toward me.

My hands fought for purchase before I grabbed hold of his arms. "What did you give me?"

"Nothing," Dr. Vieira said.

Sam's hot breath breezed over my neck. "I got her, Doc." Sam gripped my hips, holding me upright.

"I want to see my sister." My protest was weak as I tried to punch out every word with force.

Dr. Vieira stabbed a finger behind him. "There's a chair in Rianne's room. Take her in there."

I leaned my back into Sam's front. "What's wrong with me?"

Dr. Vieira gave Sam a knowing look. "We've packaged your blood sample for the lab, but with the blizzard, it might be a few days. I suspect, though, that you're reacting to Sam's blood. I understand you bit him."

I craned my neck up and angled it to glare at Sam. "You told him?" My cheeks flamed as if someone had pressed a hot coal to my skin. Talk about embarrassment.

"I don't kiss and tell," he said so sweetly. "I just told him what you did. Nothing more."

The tension in my shoulders eased as Sam guided me toward Rianne's room.

She was sleeping when Sam and I walked in. The room had the same setup as the one I'd been in—standard hospital equipment and furniture, a window carved into the tan-painted wall, and the necessary medical supplies scattered around.

My sister's hands were cupped and resting on her stomach. She still wore her black jeans, black leather boots, and the black top that she'd worn to the club.

I smoothed a hand over her wavy brown hair. She reminded me so much of our mother that it was uncanny. Where she and Jordyn had Mom's features, I took after our dad with the blue eyes and auburn hair.

Sam joined me on the other side of the bed. "She's probably going to be quite upset when I pull her out."

"Ya think?" My sarcasm wasn't as strong as I would've liked it to be.

Dr. Vieira came in with a syringe in his hands, and I was quickly reminded of that vision that seemed to have taken a home in the forefront of my brain.

I clenched my teeth.

"This is not for you. I need to give Rianne an adrenaline boost so she'll open her eyes. That's the only way Sam can pull her out."

"She doesn't need that. Just wake her up." I tapped on her face. "Rianne."

"She probably won't wake up," Dr. Vieira said. "I gave her something to relax. Her heart was racing too hard earlier."

I narrowed my eyes at him even though I couldn't fault him for trying to keep her calm.

Dr. Vieira regarded me with warm brown eyes. "Layla, I take care of people—humans, vampires, and whoever needs my help. I'm a doctor first and foremost. I know strapping you to the bed wasn't a way to build your trust. I'm sorry about that, but I felt it was necessary. It was more to protect you than me."

He seemed sincere, and I wanted to trust him, but actions spoke louder than words.

The minute he injected the contents of the syringe into Rianne, she gasped, and her eyelids opened.

Sam got up close to her and morphed into vampire mode—fangs down and eyes bright silver. Then he stared at her, doing whatever it was he did to remove the spell.

In a matter of seconds, Rianne blinked several times.

I squeezed her hand. "Hey, sis."

She screamed bloody murder as she went for Sam's throat.

Sam darted away, but Rianne wasn't letting him off the hook. She vaulted off the bed like a wild woman and flung herself at the massive vampire. He caught her, but Rianne wielded her fists at Sam's jaw, punch after punch. "You son of a bitch!"

Sam allowed her to unleash her anger as bone

hit bone. Dr. Vieira was about to stop her when Sam shook his head. "Let her."

Rianne wasn't hurting him, but she would break her hand if she kept up her assault, so I tried to pull her off just as she swung her arm back, and her fist connected with my nose. Stars dotted my vision. "For fuck's sake, sis."

She was so far gone with fury that she didn't even notice what she'd done.

Wincing, I held my nose. "Stop her, Sam. She's going to hurt herself."

Then two things happened at once. Dr. Vieira produced a long needle from his lab coat, and Sam stomped his foot. It sounded as though a bomb went off as the building shook.

Dr. Vieira took that split second and plunged the needle in Rianne's arm. Instantly, she switched her rage to Dr. Vieira until her body relaxed. Then Sam set her down on the bed.

I watched in horror as that vision I'd had outside the elevator played out before me. My mind scrambled to figure out why I would see something like that before it even happened.

Letting go of my nose, I blew out a breath and then another. My pulse pounded in my ears, and it was all I could do to stay on my feet. I was human. Humans didn't see the future.

Sam's husky voice was in my ear. "Layla, are you going to pass out again?"

I continued to fixate on my sister and Dr. Vieira. "I think so."

Sam wiped the blood from my nose with his fingers and made a deep, throaty sound, causing me to switch my attention to him.

He quickly cleaned his fingers on his pants as pain seemed to wash over him. "Let's get you in that chair."

With Rianne settled in bed, Dr. Vieira came over with a tissue. "Use this." He handed it to me. "Human blood in this place will be the death of you."

After I sat, Sam ducked out of the room without so much as a word, as did Dr. Vieira.

Rianne and I stared at one another as her eyelids started to droop.

Well, that went well. "Are you okay?" I asked her.

She looked at her hand. Her knuckles were dotted with blood. "I will be. I'm sorry, sis. I didn't mean to hit you."

I brushed her off. "No apology necessary." I couldn't blame her for unleashing her fury on Sam. I would've done the same thing.

Dr. Vieira returned with bandages and made quick work of cleaning Rianne's hand.

"Is she going to be okay?" I asked him.

"She'll be fine. I gave her a very mild sedative."

Sam ambled in, his bloody nose and lip healed. He examined me, no doubt making sure my blood was no longer tempting him.

Once Dr. Vieira finished tending to Rianne's bruised hand, he left again without a word.

I had one burning question for Rianne. "Sis, did you take the compelling elixir before we left for the club last night?"

A crease formed on her smooth forehead. "I did." She regarded Sam. "How was he able to compel me?"

"You have a way to block a vampire from compelling you? No shit?" It was the first time I'd seen Sam shocked.

"So why were you able to compel Rianne?" I asked.

He studied me, debating whether to share his secret. Granted, he was powerful, which led me to believe the strength of his abilities was the reason.

"I don't compel people like other vampires," he said. "I use—"

Abbey ran in, her black ponytail swinging in the wind. "Uncle Sam, you made the building shake. Didn't you?" She beamed up at him as though he'd hung the moon for her.

He picked her up. "I did. And maybe you will too, someday."

"You know Grandpa doesn't like when you do that on base," she said sweetly.

"It will be our secret." His tone had more sugar in it than hers, and I was flabbergasted that Sam had a sweet bone in his vampire body.

She wiggled her way out of Sam's arms then ran over to Rianne. "You're awake."

Rianne gave her a sluggish smile. "Hi. Who are you?"

"I'm Abbey. I watched over you while you were asleep."

"Thank you," Rianne said. "I need to be protected from your uncle." Rianne glared at Sam.

Inwardly, I smiled. I had my sister back. For a moment, I'd thought she would have some detrimental aftereffects from Sam's powers.

"He's just a big teddy bear," Abbey said, as sure of that as the fact that snow was coming down outside the window.

I hadn't really looked outside, but I would guess that Rianne and I weren't leaving anytime soon. The roads were probably impassible.

Rianne swung her legs over the side of the bed. "Are you my protector?" she asked Abbey.

Abbey nestled in between Rianne's legs. "I am." She proceeded to flatten her small hands on Rianne's face.

What an odd gesture.

Abbey stared into Rianne's eyes.

"Please tell me she isn't compelling my sister," I mumbled to Sam, who stood beside me.

Sam didn't respond but kept watch on Abbey.

Rianne frowned. "What's wrong, Abbey?"

"What do you see?" Sam asked Abbey.

My gaze bounced from Abbey to Sam. "She can read minds too?" Horror careened through my veins. "She's human?" I knew the answer but wanted to confirm just the same.

"She carries the vampire gene, but she's still human until she becomes a teenager. And Abbey doesn't exactly read minds. She sees the future." Sam kept his focus on his niece.

So do I, I wanted to say, but that would sound like I'd lost a brain cell or five. Regardless, I could see why Roman wanted Abbey. She was a special little girl.

The room was deathly quiet until Abbey withdrew her hand and shuffled over to me.

I sucked in a sharp breath. No way did I want anyone to read my future. I preferred to live each day as best I could and not worry about the next year or the next decade. But I couldn't move even if I wanted to because deep down, I was fascinated by Abbey.

She touched my face, her hand soft and warm.

In a second, I was swimming in a sea of darkness. I felt as though I was blind until Abbey removed her hand, and the light came on.

Confusion and frustration churned in her big blue eyes.

Sam crouched down and took Abbey's hand. "You didn't see anything in Layla's future, did you?"

She shook her head. "Something is off."

"Does any of this relate to the nightmares you've been having?" Sam asked her.

Abbey shrugged. "Maybe. I'm not sure."

My voice trembled. "But you saw something in Rianne's future?"

If I'd never met Sam Mason, I would have never believed Abbey could see the future. Then again, I'd seen Dr. Vieira before I'd even met the man, but my visions were attributed to me ingesting Sam's blood.

"I only saw one thing, and I can't tell you why or when," Abbey said. "Usually, I can."

Sam kissed her hand. "It's okay. You can't carry the weight of the world on your shoulders."

She frowned. "I have to." She sounded tired and old.

My heart broke for her. She was way too young to be worried about the future. She should be at school, making friends, going to birthday parties, and enjoying all the fun stuff that kids did.

"What was the one thing you saw?" Rianne asked, appearing to be more alert now.

Abbey looked to Sam for help.

"You can tell us," he said.

She tangled her fingers together, worrying her bottom lip, and kept her focus on Sam. "Rianne is going to kill Layla."

Nonsense went through my head while Rianne laughed nervously.

"How?" I asked. "Don't answer that." I didn't want to know.

A phone rang, zapping the tension that had filled the room to the ceiling.

Rising, Sam plucked his phone out of his cargo pants. "Yeah. Ten-four. We'll be right down." He set his green eyes on me. "Layla, I need you to come with me. Abbey, can you get Dr. Vieira?"

She left without answering him.

I was still in shock from her revelation.

"Is she always right?" Rianne asked Sam.

He shrugged. "Things have been off with her lately."

"Can I have a moment alone with my sister?" I wasn't exactly asking.

He gave me a somewhat sad smile, as though he'd been affected by Abbey's prediction of my impending doom. "I'll be out there."

Once Rianne and I were alone, I went to my sister and hugged her.

She squeezed the hell out of me. "I'd never been so scared in all my life."

I dropped down next to her. "I'm so glad you're back." I swiped a hand over her hair.

"Do you believe Abbey?" She sounded scared.

I didn't want to, and I wasn't ready to discuss something that would or could happen. We had bigger issues at play. "No. Besides, we would never hurt each other. You should get some rest."

She frowned. "You're right." She eyed the door. "Where's Jordyn?"

Tension snapped my shoulders straight. I couldn't tell her about Roman and the shifter. Not there. Sam and Dr. Vieira were outside in the lab area, and I had a feeling they were listening. I hated to do it, but for both our sake's, I had to lie.

I schooled my features. "Waiting for us at the

house." I was going to hell. "Look, I had to tell these vampires about Dowell. Otherwise, they weren't going to let me leave. Now I need to answer some questions and try to help them figure out who our benefactor really is."

"We don't know much about him."

"I know. I shouldn't be long."

She yawned. "Fine. But hurry up. I'm hungry, I need a shower, and I don't want to be hanging out with vampires."

Not my idea of fun either but with the blizzard bearing down, I didn't think we would be leaving anytime soon.

19

SAM

I lifted Abbey up onto the lab bench next to Dr. Vieira, who was examining a slide under the microscope while Layla's voice tickled my ears. Hell, her sultry tone was doing more than that.

I tried to tune her out. "Where's your mom?" I asked Abbey, who was watching Doc intently. She was as fascinated with science as Jo.

Doc changed out the slide on the microscope. "Jo went to get some supplies from Alia. Hopefully, she won't have a problem, given the snow."

"Mind-blocking potion I hope." I had a couple of bottles left, but I needed to replenish if I couldn't get Layla out of my psyche. "The plows seem to be keeping up with clearing the main streets."

"Uncle Sam, you need to be careful with Layla."

"Where did that come from?" She didn't read minds, and she wasn't touching my face to see anything in my future.

Doc straightened. "Please tell me you haven't developed a new power." He sounded frustrated.

She shook her head as her gaze found Doc's. "No. But Sam is falling for her, and if my vision comes true, I don't want to see him get hurt."

I tucked an errant strand of her hair behind her ear. "You think I'm falling for her?"

Her serious expression sent a wave of nerves churning in my stomach. "I know so."

Dr. Vieira's eyes went wide. I imagined he was worried that Layla was a vampire hunter, or maybe he thought I would end up draining her blood. The latter was more of a possibility than falling for her.

I understood how vampires could sense shit like that, but Abbey wasn't a vampire yet. I couldn't exactly discount her conviction on my feelings for Layla. Abbey was an extraordinary human who was slowly acquiring more abilities than Jo and me combined, and her visions were rarely wrong. She scared even me.

But her predications at that moment weren't

the issue. If Roman was in fact targeting Abbey, we had to do everything in our power to stop him. Not only that, Tripp had the tech team searching for Wyman's former partner, Thomas. Given what Wyman had told us, we didn't think he remembered anything from Patrick's research or Edmund's organization. Regardless, we had to be one hundred and fifty percent sure of that if we wanted to keep Abbey safe.

"What vision?" Doc asked her.

"That Rianne will kill Layla," Abbey said as if she was talking about the weather.

Sensing Layla's presence, my head jerked up.

She gasped, stopping in her tracks. "Hearing that again still sends a chill down my spine."

Doc removed his nitrile gloves. "Sometimes Abbey's visions are wrong." Leave it to Doc to want to ease Layla's worry. He was always trying to make sure people didn't hurt, physically or emotionally. "How are you feeling, Layla? I suspect you might feel a little out of sorts until Sam's blood filters through your system."

"I feel okay," she said. "Maybe a little light-headed, but a lot has happened." She eyed Abbey, who was fiddling with Doc's microscope.

My phone pinged with a text from Tripp: *Get your ass down to the interrogation room.*

I kissed Abbey on the forehead. "Be good. I have to run." Then I strode over to Layla and cupped her elbow. "We need to go."

She puffed out her pale cheeks. "Can you make it quick? I want to try to leave before the snow gets any worse."

I didn't answer her. I didn't know whether Tripp and Webb would let her and her sister leave before my father had spoken to her uncle or located Jordyn's whereabouts. I hadn't heard if Webb had done just that.

Once out of the lab, Layla and I wound our way down an empty hall. It wasn't the same route we'd taken to get up to the infirmary from the lobby. The elevator might have been quicker, but it was best if Layla and I weren't in a closed space with no way out. As much as I would like to think I had willpower, I was finding with Layla that I didn't.

"Where's Jordyn, by the way?" I asked.

"At the house," she said as her mind wandered and her pulse increased.

"You're lying."

The sound of our footsteps bounced off the bare walls.

"I hate you," she muttered.

"We both know that's a lie too."

She created some distance but still walked alongside me. "Have you always been this arrogant?"

I slipped my hands into my pockets to keep from combing my fingers through her thick locks. "Ever since I was human."

She huffed out a breath. "You sound proud of that."

"When you have people fucking with your life since you were a child, you learn not to roll over for anyone."

"Sounds like you had a tough childhood." Her tone was even.

It wasn't the time to dive into my past, so I shrugged.

Silence dangled over us as the red exit sign up ahead drew closer.

"No elevator?" Her pulse quickened more as a wave of lust oozed off her.

I couldn't help but chuckle. "Sounds to me like you want to go for round two." Just the thought of us in an enclosed space made my cock jerk.

She gathered her long auburn hair from behind and draped it over her shoulder. "I don't think so." She didn't sound all that convincing.

A wave of scented cherries permeated the air, snuck into my veins, and made me fist my hands together. My self-control in not taking her right there was about to burst into flames.

"Do Abbey's visions always come true?" Her voice wobbled as she asked me that for a second time.

I couldn't blame her for freaking out. If someone told me Jo would kill me, I would have a hard time believing it. My earlier response hadn't exactly been a firm answer, and Abbey's visions had always been spot-on in the past. I hadn't lied about how Abbey was struggling lately, but that was only with her dreams. "Ninety-nine point nine percent of the time."

Instantly, her anxiety hit me like a Mack truck speeding down the road at a hundred miles an hour. I almost faltered.

What the fuck?

I cursed the ability to feel others' emotions, and Layla's were tearing my insides to shreds suddenly.

Put up your shields, man.

No matter how hard I attempted to shut my brain down and think of something off-the-wall, like a dog cuddling with a cat, I couldn't shake the desire to wrap Layla in my arms and tell her everything would be okay. I was beginning to believe that our little tryst in the elevator had something to do with whatever was happening to both of us.

"Sam." Layla said my name with so much emotion, I stopped mid-stride while she kept walking.

It took her a second to realize I wasn't beside her. Then she pivoted on her heel like a graceful ballerina, and waves and waves of auburn hair flew behind her.

I groaned as my fangs locked into place. My throat burned at the desperate need to taste one tiny drop of her blood, and my cock was pushing at my zipper, ready to feel her pussy gripping me tightly.

I clamped down on my lip as she sashayed up to me with a smile that knocked me backward a step.

Damn. She was gorgeous. Her electric-blue eyes had a softness to them, those plump lips promised a night of pure pleasure, and her shapely legs would fit perfectly around my waist as I rammed my dick so far into her that both of us would get lost for eternity.

She reached up and tucked my hair behind my ear. "Are you okay?" Her voice was breathy.

I grasped her wrist just as she was lowering her hand. Her pulse was even as it beat against my fingers. I found it odd that her heart wasn't galloping like it had been moments ago.

She eyed my hand and shuddered.

"What's happening?" I asked.

Her tongue darted out to lick her lips, and my dick jerked once again. "I'm not sure. All I know is that I feel you." She knitted her pretty eyebrows. "You're hurting."

I was in pain—my gums, my balls, and my gut. But nothing hurt more than the pain in my chest at that moment. I wasn't sure why. My guess was her—I needed to soothe her pain. If I did, then mine would go away too.

I ran my fingers through her silky strands, feeling the need to kiss her, tell her the world was good, tell her vampires had souls, tell her I would protect her with my life. "And how do you know that?"

She shrugged. "Not sure." She seated one hand on my belt. "It started happening after we got out of the elevator." Her other hand brushed over my cock, and I clamped my mouth shut so I wouldn't sink my fangs into her.

"Careful, Layla. You're not ready for me yet." The reality was that I wasn't ready for her.

Batting her long lashes, she gave me a sensual smile. "Maybe I am." She clutched onto my rock-hard cock through the fabric of my pants and moaned, a sound that drove the wild animal in me to pounce.

The hallway narrowed to just me and her. Gentle had never been in my vocabulary, and like the animal I was, I dove my tongue into the cavern of her mouth hard, fast, and rough. She tasted of freedom and home. That stabbing pain in my chest was history. In its place, butterflies took flight as happiness drenched my soul—a feeling that was foreign to me, and I wanted more, much more. I deepened the kiss, feeling her everywhere—physically and emotionally.

She was riding a high like me, squirming in my arms, breathing heavily, moaning, clutching onto my hair, and pulling me to her as though she couldn't get enough. As though I was the air she needed to breathe. *Fuck.* I needed her as badly as I needed blood to live.

I broke the kiss, both of us panting, and I licked my way to her ear. "I have to be inside you." I trailed kisses down to her carotid artery. Her blood pumped furiously through it, calling to me, tempting me.

As much as my entire being was primed to get my fill of her, I wanted that sweet spot on her thigh. I wanted her naked and laid out before me like the goddess I knew she was. I wanted to take my time, to feel her ecstasy as if it were my own.

She tilted her head, giving me permission to sink my sharp canines into her.

"Not yet," I whispered. "And not here."

She giggled like a teenager, and my balls tightened.

My phone blared through the long, cavernous space, and we both stiffened. For a brief second, I couldn't move and didn't want to. But the annoying piece of technology wouldn't stop.

Growling, I yanked the thing out of my pocket. "Yeah," I snapped.

"Where the fuck are you?" Ben asked.

"On my way." I hung up on him before he could say anything else.

Layla's cheeks were flushed, her lips swollen, and she was attempting to tame her hair.

"We're late." I started for the exit.

"For what?"

I laughed. "I have a surprise for you."

20

SAM

The command center was a flurry of activity as the tech team banged on keyboards and talked on phones while Harley wrote on the whiteboard.

The minute Layla stepped in, awe washed over her. "Are all these people vampires?"

I beelined it toward the interrogation room. "Of course. But don't worry. They won't bite." I chuckled. "I do, though."

She rolled her eyes. "You're all talk, if you ask me."

And we were right back to trading one barb for another. That intimate prelude we'd had in the hallway seemingly never happened.

"Need I remind you about the bet we have?" I

didn't have an ounce of doubt we would be naked and knotted together. What I wasn't sure of anymore was who would win. My resolve was solid, hardly penetrable, but Layla was chipping away at it with a sledgehammer.

She set her jaw. "By then, the city will be in my rearview mirror.

Not if I had any say in the matter. Layla Aberdeen was mine. She just didn't know it yet. And fuck my old man if he thought he could keep me from her. Fuck *anyone* who stood in my way. Besides, what better way to watch my enemy than to have her at my side and in my bed.

Sawyer's blond-streaked brown hair surfaced as he stood up from his cubicle. He homed in on Layla as we approached. Then his voice was in my head. *She's hot as fuck.*

I just grinned.

Layla studied Sawyer. "Your eyes. They're a myriad of colors."

"Mostly a greenish gold, according to my mother. You must be Layla Aberdeen." He held out his large hand.

She exchanged a handshake with him. "I guess everyone here knows who I am?"

"We're always on alert whenever we have an

enemy among us," I said in a sarcastic but serious tone.

While Layla scanned the room, her pulse creeping higher, Sawyer said to me telepathically, *The phone you gave me keeps ringing. I haven't answered it, but I am trying to get a location on the number. It's a burner phone, more than likely.*

Layla reached over Sawyer's desk. "Is that my phone?"

Sawyer snagged it before she could take it. "That's evidence, ma'am."

"I need that to call my sister Jordyn."

Sawyer cocked his head. "Where is your sister?"

She tried to take the phone from Sawyer. "I want it back."

A nervous energy filled the space between us all as she mashed her lips into a thin line. "That's my dagger." Her bravado was admirable as she attempted to collect her family heirloom from Sawyer's desk.

Those kaleidoscope eyes instantly turned vampire black. "Ma'am, don't touch anything on my desk. That is evidence as well."

She sent him a scathing look in return. "Put your fangs away. They don't scare me."

"They should," I said, enjoying the little show.

She flipped me off. "That's a family heirloom." Her cheeks flamed red.

Harley glided over with a clipboard in her hand. "What's going on? Is my brother giving you a hard time?"

"Brother," Layla said. "He's more of a—" She swallowed before she clamped her mouth shut.

"He can be quite the hard-ass, but he's only doing his job." She smiled warmly at Layla. "Are you feeling better?"

Layla lowered her shoulders, the tension vanishing. "I am. Thank you." Her tone was sweet and friendly.

Ben sauntered out of the interrogation room, his attention fixed on Harley. "Am I missing the party?" He swiped a large hand over his cinnamon-colored hair, as Jo had once described it. "Hey, are we still on for dinner later?"

I cocked an eyebrow. "He's your date?"

"You sound jealous, Sam," Layla was quick to say as the smooth skin around her mouth tightened.

"Yeah, man." Ben agreed with Layla.

"Okay," Harley piped in. "I need to run and so do you, Ben. Webb is waiting for you in his office." She gave him a gentle nudge in the ribs. "Come on." They had started for the exit when

Harley glanced over her shoulder. "Layla, if you're still around here tomorrow, maybe we can hang out."

A nervous laugh escaped Layla. "Thanks, but my sisters and I are leaving the city."

Over my dead body. Then again, with the snow piling up, I doubted she would be leaving anytime soon.

"Well, if things change, you know where to find me." The door squeaked open and then closed with a thud behind Harley and Ben.

Tripp poked his head out from the interrogation room. "Mason, get in here." His tone was stony.

I placed my hand on Layla's back, and electrical pulses shot up my arm. "Time for your surprise."

She shuddered but didn't budge.

My eyes flashed silver as her anger and lust consumed me. "Don't worry. You'll come out alive."

She puffed out air and stomped ahead of me like a child who hadn't gotten her way. "Fine. I want my dagger and phone when I come out."

She was smoking some serious dope if she thought we would give a vampire hunter a weapon while in the company of vampires. Not that she stood a chance in doing any damage with that dagger.

"You must be Layla Aberdeen." Tripp tried to greet her, but she brushed past him and into the interrogation room like she owned the place.

Tripp's face twisted as his bronze-colored eyes bugged out.

I laughed. Layla Aberdeen was something else. She tried to put up a wall of toughness, when inside, she was scared shitless. But I wasn't complaining. I was digging all her personalities.

"What are you doing here?" Her tone rose in pitch.

I strutted in. "Surprise."

Wyman smiled, showing a crooked bottom tooth. "Nice to see you again, Layla."

"Do you know this man?" Tripp asked Layla as he came in.

A crease dented her smooth forehead. "He's the Uber driver who dropped my sisters and me off at the club. I don't understand."

Tripp pulled out a chair. "I would like you to meet Dowell. His real name is Agent Wyman, former CIA. Please, have a seat."

She reared back. "CIA? Why would you hire us, then? You have the skills to capture a vampire. Although it now makes sense how you know so much about Sam and vampires. The CIA must know lots about them and how to deal with them." She sat on the edge of the chair, pursing her lips.

A chill swept up my arms at the mere thought that the CIA could get wind of us.

"The CIA doesn't know about them," he said. His pulse was steady, which indicated he was telling the truth.

He'd mentioned in his apartment that he'd planned on turning me in to his former employer. But I had to be sure. "You never approached the CIA since you left?"

He twined his fingers together on the table. We didn't have him handcuffed. He would be a fool to try anything with us. "I told you my memory is spotty, and I needed proof anyway. Otherwise, they wouldn't believe me." He sighed as he returned his attention to Layla. "To continue, I couldn't risk Sam recognizing me, and what better way to lure him out than with a beautiful woman. Besides, your father told me you were the best at what you do."

She gaped. "You knew my father? He never mentioned you."

"He didn't want anyone to know he was working with me. His brothers didn't believe in keeping vampires alive, and he had to be careful.

He knew Sam's father, who tried to recruit him. But he was lured by the money. He thought he could use it to start a better life than hunting vampires. He wanted that for you and your sisters." Wyman swung his gaze to me. "Maybe your father killed hers."

I grunted. "Careful, Wyman. You might find yourself walking around not knowing who you are. And I guarantee whatever I do will last forever this time."

"Did he? Did your father kill mine?" Layla asked me. "My uncles told me that my father had to know the vampire who drained the life out of him. There was no struggle, no signs of a fight, and in fact, his body was laid out in such a way to indicate that the vampire cared about him. Your father seemed saddened when I told him my dad was dead."

"Maybe he died at the hand of his vampire lover," I said in a serious tone. That was quite possible.

She gulped down air. "Nonsense. My dad would never." She lowered her gaze to her fingers, where she absently picked at a nail. "Do you think that's true?" she asked Wyman.

He shrugged with one shoulder. "I wouldn't know. The only personal information he ever mentioned was how much he cared about getting you and your sisters out of the family business."

Tripp cleared his throat. "Let's focus back on why we're here."

Layla's gaze was riveted to Wyman. She completely ignored Tripp. "Why did you want Sam alive? You didn't give us much information about the job."

I leaned against the wall. "To hand me over to the CIA so they could lock me in a cage and study my DNA like every other fucker out there."

Wyman leaned forward as if he was about to tell her a secret. "I feel like I should warn you about him." He tipped his chin at me.

She batted her blue eyes my way, shy yet patronizing. "I know what he's capable of."

I couldn't wait to see her begging me to fuck her over and over again. "I doubt that," I uttered with a grin.

Tripp, who was across from me, cleared his throat loudly as irritation washed over him. "Tell us about Roman, Wyman. Otherwise, I will be tempted to have Sam do more than take your memories."

"Roman?" Layla's voice hitched.

Tripp's gaze jumped to Layla. "Before Wyman shares his knowledge, I want to be clear. We have a lot of power on this naval base, and I'm not just talking about the damage Sam can do. As much as we don't want to harm a human, we will go to great lengths to get the truth." He tucked his hands in the pockets of his cargo pants as some of his anger subsided. "Therefore, before we leave this room, you and Wyman will lay everything out on the table. Is that understood?"

She was breathing heavily as her rage hit me harder than Tripp's had a moment ago. "Anything to get the fuck out of here. I'm tired of being around your kind."

Wyman sat back. "You'll let me go too. Right? No funny shit like toying with my brain?"

Tripp looked at me as if he wanted my permission. I wasn't sure if we could let him go. With our luck, Wyman would end up working for Roman or any of our enemies. Or he might have proof of us. Granted we had his notebook, laptop, and files, but I didn't think he was a complete idiot. He had to have a backup of his info somewhere.

I think we should keep him here until we can learn more from his notebook or make sure he doesn't have any video or pictures of us on some backup drive, I relayed to Tripp telepathically. *I would hate to have the CIA breathing down our necks. Plus, he says his memory is spotty—let's make sure it is.*

"That's up to you," Tripp said to Wyman. "We still have a lot to discuss."

For real. Like whether he has had contact with his former partner, finding out if he was really working alone, and what, specifically, he remembered.

A muscle ticked in Wyman's jaw until he sighed. "Fair enough. I wouldn't give you a firm answer either." He seemed to be thinking back to when he was an agent and in a similar situation and role as Tripp. "I'll cooperate."

We didn't need him to since my father and Jo could read his mind if we asked. However, reading minds knocked the wind out of them, and according to Jo, it was a terrible ability to have. She hated experiencing others' thoughts.

"Layla, you need to tell them that you're working with Roman."

"I am not," she rushed out as she dripped with shock that Wyman had outed her. "The vampire wants my sisters and me dead."

"And that's why you're here," Wyman added. "Though I haven't figured that part out. All I can tell you is that Roman and a woman are holding Jordyn hostage."

Layla scurried to the door faster than the speed of light.

I had her by the arm before she could storm out. "Wait one second."

She bared her teeth at me. "Get those disgusting fingers off me."

I smiled, showing my fangs. "You will come clean." I was growing tired of her defiance.

"Please. You don't scare me." Her heartbeat was slower than ever, indicating she wasn't frightened of me at all.

The door burst open, and she stumbled back into me.

Webb stalked in. His glare was epically frightening as his blue eyes churned to molten black. Even Wyman gasped.

"The way I see this going, Layla, is either you tell us the truth, or I will be tempted to lock you in one of our prisons around the world," Webb delivered without any sign that he was ready to shred her. "We have them especially for humans who have teamed up with a criminal vampire whose sole purpose is to benefit off the innocent." His fangs were longer than most other vampires', and his fists were closed tightly.

She pressed her back into me as her body shook. "What are you talking about?"

"Layla, meet my commanding officer, Webb London, and Jo's husband."

The empty chair rattled and skidded along the floor as Webb's rage was all-consuming. He had the power to manipulate three of the four elements. All the SEAL team members had more powers than the average vampire, but none could control all four—earth, water, air, and fire—like the Mason family.

Layla started breathing erratically.

"I suggest you answer him," I said. "Otherwise, this room will crumble."

"Wyman is right. Roman has my sister." Her voice quaked so hard I was afraid she was a second from passing out.

Webb took one measured step toward her. "And you're here to do what exactly? Get information for Roman?"

She pressed her body into me as though she was hoping I would swallow her up. Of course I wouldn't mind, but I wanted the truth. I wanted her to stop dicking around. Maybe then we could resume our efforts to take down Roman.

"Then what?" Webb asked. "Speak," he roared.

Normally, I wouldn't question or interrupt him when he was trying to get answers, but Layla's emotions began to fuck up my insides again. *Webb, can you take it down a notch?* I asked telepathically.

Webb gave me one of his blank expressions.

The fuck I will. And let's not forget what your anger did to her sister. We've been as patient as we can with her. And Sawyer tracked that number that keeps pinging her phone to a large piece of property on the Indian Reservation. Need I remind you the last time we were in the middle of a war, you and Jo were bound and gagged and used as Edmund's test subjects on the Reservation?

I regarded Webb. *Then let's use that to get her to talk. If you're right, then her sister is in danger.* Not that Roman wanted her sister's DNA. He was using Jordyn as a bargaining chip.

Sighing, Webb retreated a few steps, retracting his fangs. "We can help you get your sister, but you need to tell us what Roman wants."

I guided Layla to her seat.

She wiped a tear that had trickled down her face. "The drug Wyman had left for us in a locker at the city airport was supposed to not only attack the muscles but knock out a vampire. Wyman told us it wouldn't kill any vampire—" She sighed. "—but Roman's girlfriend was a shifter. Apparently, the drug kills shifters."

Silence ensued as Wyman gaped.

"So, you're telling us that you killed a shifter?" Webb rubbed the back of his neck. "Do you know who the shifter was?"

Layla scrunched her nose. "Of course not. But the Sasquatch of a woman who claims to be this dead shifter's sister now wants to murder mine. The only reason Jordyn isn't dead is because of Roman."

We all stared at Layla.

"What does he want?" I asked. Roman's type wanted money and power. Nothing came free or without something in return.

She picked at the skin around a nail. "I had planned on coming here to ask Sam to help Rianne, and Roman knew that. He must've followed me home, because out of nowhere, he showed up with the shifter. He wants me to confirm that you"—she wagged her finger at Tripp, Webb, and me—"are protecting a little human girl. He has a source who told him about Abbey. If I don't come through, then Jordyn is dead."

"Fuck me," I said. "Roman was referring to Abbey when he said someone is worth more than me." All of us suspected that, but hearing Layla confirm it made my blood boil. Shit just got real. "You said a source told him. I take it he didn't tell you who?" Anyone who knew Abbey existed had died five years ago, unless...

Fuck!

I'd wiped memories from Agent Thomas, a

former soldier of Edmund named Nicki who was in a vampire prison, and Dr. Case, the human who had been one of the moles.

I shoved my fingers through my hair and again opened up a telepathic line to Webb. *I'm sorry. This is all my fault. My powers back then weren't as strong. The only thing that makes sense is that the source has to be Wyman, Nicki, Agent Thomas, or Dr. Case. One of them probably got his or her memory back.*

My stomach knotted.

Webb deadpanned and addressed Layla. "Did Roman tell you who, or anything else about Abbey?"

"He knows she's special and has vampire powers. I'm supposed to report back to him when he calls me."

"And he's been trying to call for the last few hours," Webb said.

I was surprised Webb wasn't breaking shit or snapping necks, knowing Roman wanted Abbey. I was ready to do both of those things, as guilt rode me hard.

Webb grabbed the base of his neck. "Roman isn't going to stop at just information. He'll ask you to do more."

She sagged in her seat. "I don't want any harm to come to Abbey. Without even knowing her, I'd already planned not to give Roman any information. You might not believe me, but it's the truth. I came here for Rianne, but I have to find a way to save our sister. What would you do in my shoes?"

"Why haven't you called your uncles for help?" Webb asked. "I understand your family doesn't do jobs alone."

"Too long a story to get into, but the short version is that we don't get along. Not since my father passed. And we needed the money." She turned to Wyman. "I guess I won't be getting the rest of that two hundred grand."

"That's all I'm worth? I asked sarcastically.

"That was my life savings," he said as though that would make me feel better.

Layla tucked her hands in her lap. "What do we do now?"

"We do what we do best," I said. "We go hunting."

21

LAYLA

The vampires left the room, and the scary beast, Webb, barked orders to someone.

I shivered and gnawed on a nail. Usually, I wasn't that frightened of vampires, but Webb had a certain demonic vibe. Maybe that chill running through me stemmed from the fact that his fangs appeared longer than most vampires' I'd come in contact with.

A stiff shot of whiskey would be good right about now. Everything that had happened since I'd met Sam was overloading my brain. How I was feeling about the vampire wasn't making any sense. I had been trained to kill his kind, yet when it came to Sam, I wanted to do anything but hurt him.

In fact, on our trek down to the control room, I could feel what he'd been feeling. How? I had no freaking clue. I felt the need to take away his pain. Maybe his blood had not only made me sick but had connected me to him on some supernatural plane. I wasn't making any sense.

"Webb is the lethal one from what I remember, although Sam's dad isn't far off," Wyman muttered, tearing me from the hell I was in.

It didn't matter who was scarier than who. I'd just sealed Jordyn's death. Roman would know I told Sam. He would hear it in my voice. Vampires were that astute even over the phone. I agreed with Webb. Roman would want more out of me if I confirmed his intel, and if I didn't, then Jordyn was as good as dead.

She is, anyway. You know that. The shifter isn't going to let her go without taking revenge for what Jordyn did, my inner voice supplied.

I was ready to bawl my eyes out. I wanted to scream and run and get the heck out of there and far away from any supernatural. But I was in deeper than ever before, and the ship I was on was sinking fast. Even my uncles wouldn't be able to help me. Vampires and shifters joining forces would only end in the death of every Aberdeen on the planet.

"I'm sorry," Wyman said in a low voice. "This is all my fault."

I wanted to blame him, but I couldn't. "My sisters and I agreed to do the job."

"Layla, look at me."

I dashed away an errant tear.

"As much as I despise their kind, they are the best at what they do. Well, maybe not in the tech department." He mumbled the last line.

"How do you know?" It was more a question to settle my mind. I knew he was right. After all, a vampire Navy SEAL team with supernatural powers had to rival any human military force out there.

"I've been studying this team." He pointed to the door. "They know how to handle their people better than us. You might think you know vampires, but not these ones, particularly the Mason family."

Maybe that was one reason my family had never targeted the Masons. They knew they didn't stand a chance. "What did Sam do to you?"

"He wiped a few of my memories, so I can't recall much."

I chewed on another nail. "Where did you meet my father?"

He leaned his elbows on the table. "After Sam

compelled me to leave the city, I packed up my family. My wife has a sister in Montana. Anyway, I met your father at a local bar in Big Timber. Actually, I'd overheard him and his brothers talking about vampires and in particular, Steven Mason."

I smiled. "You met him at the Deer and Elk?" My dad and his brothers loved that joint—warm beer, peanut shells on the floor, and deer and elk heads hanging from the walls.

Wyman nodded. "He kept coming in. Sometimes alone. Other times with his brothers. But the night I met him he was with a young woman."

My head jerked. "A woman? How long ago was this?" My mom had been dead for four years, and my sisters and I had encouraged my dad to move on. Maybe he had, but he'd never told me or my sisters. I was beginning to realize Dad had kept a lot of secrets.

"Maybe two years now," Wyman said. "Your father died not long after we'd met."

I scrambled to think if my dad had given us any signals about a woman he'd been seeing, but nothing came to mind. Not long before he'd died, my dad's relationship with my uncles started to become strained and weird. They'd had a few big fights over things like finances. Apparently, Uncle Ray had gambled away a good portion of the family's money, which prevented them from purchasing weapons and other items needed to keep the business going.

Sam's woodsy scent gave him away before he sauntered in. "Your phone has been ringing nonstop. We suspect it's Roman because of the local number. We want you to answer it if he calls again, but I caution you—until we devise a game plan, you need to do as he says and not let on that you told us."

I snagged the phone from him. "I'm not a moron."

He grinned, showing his dimples. "That's debatable."

I rolled my eyes, wanting nothing more than to tell him to fuck off. But it wasn't the time, and my stomach was doing some backflips over the enticing sight of him—broad chest, narrow waist, thick thighs, and those daggers strapped to his legs. I imagined he was a sight to behold in battle.

Wyman laughed. "You two have chemistry."

Sam growled at Wyman.

I snorted. "Is that all you can do is growl like the animal you are?" It was more of a statement than a question.

He leaned down and whispered in my ear. "Soon enough, Layla, you'll see what I can do, and

I know without a doubt you'll be begging me to do it over and over again."

His sexual innuendo wasn't lost on me. In fact, my damn pussy throbbed, and heat blanketed my body. He'd spoken quietly enough that I doubted Wyman could hear, but I was still blushing like a damn schoolgirl. *Again, what the fuck is wrong with me?*

Asshole.

Wyman cleared his throat. "I gave you what you want, Sam. I want to leave now."

Sam straightened to his six-five height. "I'm afraid you can't."

"Why the fuck not? You are not messing with my brain." Wyman's face deepened to a dark red.

"We still have questions, and until we can trust you to walk out of here and not go running to the CIA, you'll be our guest," Sam delivered with venom.

"Guest or prisoner?" Wyman asked.

My phone chirped, and I jumped in my seat. The caller ID indicated a local number. I inhaled deeply through my nose and blew out through my mouth.

Sam shut the door. "One word out of you, Wyman, and you'll wish you'd never returned to this city."

I ignored the egos flying around the room. "Hello." My voice cracked.

"Where the fuck have you been?" Roman shouted. "I swear if you so much as said one word about our agreement, the shifter will rip your sister's insides out."

I laughed, hoping I didn't sound nervous. "Why would I do that when you have my sister?" I prayed he believed me.

"Why haven't you answered your phone?" Roman asked.

I stared at Sam, who had a blank expression. "Coverage is spotty here. I want to talk to my sister."

"In due time. Where are you? Have you left the base? Did you find out anything?" Roman's gravelly voice was grating on my nerves.

A shaky laugh escaped me. "I can't just come out and ask. Besides, you said to get in bed with Sam, so I'm waiting for him. He's not here." *Please believe me.*

Sam sported one of his downright irritating yet cheeky smirks, causing my belly to twist in a delicious way.

Roman chuckled. "Sleeping with the enemy is the only way to get information."

Maybe with a moron, but Sam was far from a

moron, and no matter how much I flirted with him or fucked him, he wouldn't spill his deepest secrets to me. I sure wouldn't if the tables were turned.

"I want to talk to Jordyn." I infused as much sweetness in my tone as I could. I always believed everyone had a soft side. Maybe I shouldn't lump vampires in with "everyone."

"Vera is having a great time with Jordyn." Roman had too much giddiness in his voice for me.

I fisted my free hand. "I swear, I—"

"Now, now," he said innocently. "Careful. Your threats will only seal your sister's demise."

I captured a nail between my teeth. "If your sources are right, then what?"

Sam glared daggers at the phone in my hand, or maybe his hard look was directed at me.

"Then I'll take it from here," Roman said. "You have twenty-four hours to bring me information, or say goodbye to your sister." Then he was gone.

I threw my phone against the wall, narrowly missing Sam's head. I was at my wit's end. "I don't know how *one* job turned into a nightmare."

I was waiting for him to volley back a retort or something snarky. Instead, he picked up my phone and handed me the irritating piece of technology that now had a cracked screen.

A tattooed hulk of a vampire breezed in with a goofy smile. "Sam, you got a fighter on your hands." His dark mahogany eyes swept over me as he beelined for Wyman. "All right, Wyman. Up on your feet."

Wyman leaned away from him. "Where are you taking me?"

The hulking vampire grasped his arm. "To the Taj Mahal."

"No!" Wyman's voice rose in pitch. "Mason, I can help you."

Sam tipped his chin at the hulking vampire. "Kraft, get him out of here."

Kraft started to haul a squirming Wyman across the room.

I jumped up. "Wait. Let him speak."

"I'll make you a deal," Wyman said to Sam.

"We don't make deals with humans," Kraft fired back. "Not ones who want to turn us over to the CIA."

"That was just a threat," Wyman squeaked out.

I inched closer to Wyman, who was about three inches taller than me, and I remembered something that gave me hope. "You followed me here. You have been following my sisters and me." It wasn't a question. "Does that mean you know where Roman is holding Jordyn?"

"I know where they went, but I'm not sure if they're still there," he said.

"On the Indian Reservation?" Sam asked, eagerness dripping in his question.

Wyman shrugged out of Kraft's hold, or rather Kraft let him go. Wyman rubbed his arm. "They're at the house next door to Layla's."

My jaw hit the floor. "No way. Which neighbor?" I didn't have to ask but needed confirmation.

"His name is Gerald Becker," Wyman said. "Single, thirty-five, family died in a fire when he was fifteen, and he's employed by the port authority. Oh, and he's human. I saw Roman pull the car around the back of Gerald's property, behind a shed."

I continued to chomp on a nail. "The man gives me the willies."

"Did he try something with you?" Sam's nostrils flared as though he was ready to tear off Gerald's head.

It was admirable that he wanted to protect me, but I could protect myself. I started for the door. "I'm going to get my sister. And I want my dagger."

Sam was in front of me before I took one step. "Not so fast. We can't just go storming in. We need to get eyes on the house and confirm if what

Wyman says is true. If we know Roman, he's not going to make it that easy to find him."

"He's right, Layla," Wyman piped in. "Listen to them for your sister's sake."

I hated that they both were right.

Sam moved a strand of my hair off my face.

The small gentle act made me swallow a moan.

"You haven't eaten. Rianne is asking for you, and you should get some rest."

"Careful, Sam," I said. "You're beginning to sound like you care."

He dropped his hand as quick as lightning. "Get Wyman to a holding cell," Sam barked at Kraft, a stark contrast to the softer tone he'd just used on me.

"Let me help," Wyman pleaded. "I feel responsible."

Sam's features pinched. "Now you're getting a conscience?"

"I knew her father. I feel like I owe it to him to watch out for Layla and her sisters," Wyman pleaded.

I understood his reasoning about why he didn't want my sisters and me to know who he was in the event we gave him up, and I had. Still, if he'd been upfront with us, we might not be in this predicament. But again, I couldn't lay all the blame on him.

I touched Sam's muscular bicep. "Let Wyman help. If he screws anything up, then do whatever it is you have planned for him." As a former CIA agent, he had to have skills that would prove useful for capturing a criminal. "I'm not saying you vampires don't know what you're doing, but take the additional help. Maybe then we can find Jordyn faster." I believed Wyman was only trying to find his way back to some type of normalcy after the ordeal Sam had put him through years ago.

Sam nodded at Kraft, who in turn hauled Wyman out of the room as Wyman mumbled swear words.

I stuck my hands on my hips. "Why are you being stubborn? He can help."

"It's not up to me," he said.

"Then why are we standing here? Go do whatever it is you do to find my sister, or else I will."

He didn't argue as he escorted me out just as Harley was walking toward us.

Her blinding white teeth sparkled beneath the lights from above. I couldn't tell if she was all smiles for Sam or if she was happy to see me. The former made my muscles tense as a knot formed in my stomach. I'd never been jealous of another woman for liking a guy. Maybe since I'd never dated a guy long enough to get attached.

Oh hell. I discarded my jealous notions. I couldn't fault Harley for liking Sam. After all, he was out-of-this-world handsome. *But he's an ass*, that realistic voice in my head reminded me. Besides, it was impossible to fall for a vampire—that was a recipe for a meltdown or death.

Harley snapped her fingers. "Layla."

I swallowed thickly, and when I blinked, Harley and Sam were staring at me.

Voices droned in the vast space of computers and technology along with the clicking sounds of vampires typing on keyboards.

"She's hungry," Sam said, "and could use some rest."

The food could wait, although my stomach said otherwise. I had to help in some way.

Harley hooked her arm in mine. "Come on. Let the team do their job. I'll get you settled in the women's barracks and get you some food."

My stomach growled, and my mouth watered for a juicy hamburger. Also, I wouldn't mind closing my eyes for a few minutes. Maybe all the craziness wouldn't look so bad once my head was clear. Somehow, though, my Spidey sense was screaming that things were about to get worse.

22

LAYLA

I dropped down on one of two twin beds in a modest room that reminded me of a studio apartment. In addition to the beds, the room was designed with a small kitchen nook, two dressers, two nightstands, two cushioned chairs near the beds, a high bistro table with barstools, and a closet tucked in the corner off the kitchen nook.

I sighed, feeling like a heavy weight had been lifted off my chest when in fact nothing had been resolved. "Where's Rianne? Has she woken up yet?" She'd been sleepy when I'd left her in the infirmary.

Harley tapped out a quick text. Then her phone pinged. "A guard is escorting her down here. I've asked them to stop at the cafeteria and get some food for both of you." She stuck her strawberry-blond head in the closet then pulled out sheets and blankets.

I clutched my stomach as it screamed for food. "So, tell me about Webb." When I'd been talking to Harley in the lobby while Sam had been with his father, Harley had mentioned she worked for the commander of the SEAL team. "He's scary to me."

She giggled, light and airy. "Webb London is one of the most respected and revered vampires in the military other than Steven Mason. He's also Jo's husband. And he'll murder anyone who dares to threaten his family."

My dad would have done the same, and he had done it many times when vampires stirred up trouble as they passed through our sleepy ranch town in Montana.

She set the bedding down on the mattress next to me. "You'll need these."

I yawned. The adrenaline was slowly seeping from my veins. "I'm not staying the night." Blizzard or not, Rianne and I should leave, even if we had to stay in a hotel. The idea of sleeping among vampires caused a chill to creep down my spine. Besides, if the vampire Navy SEALs were as good as

Wyman had said, they could find Jordyn in a matter of hours.

She smoothed a hand down her pencil skirt. "It's best if you do. You're well protected here until the team can figure out what their next move is and get Jordyn back. The fridge is stocked with beverages. The bathroom is down the hall. I'll drum up some clothes for you and Rianne. You both seem to be similar sizes, yes?"

We were about the same height at five-eight. Jordyn was the short one who took after our mom at five-four.

I nodded. "I appreciate you helping us, but I would rather wear my own clothes."

"I'll check with Webb and see if we can send someone over to your house to collect your things."

I let out a shaky laugh. "You sound like I might be living here." That was not happening.

"I've learned a long time ago to prepare for the long haul. It's snowing, it could take a while for the team to locate Roman, and you should relax."

The latter would be a monumental task while knowing Jordyn was in the clutches of animals, but I was tired. "This shit with Roman should be over within twenty-four hours." At least I kept telling myself that.

"Maybe," she said. "Settle in. I'll check on Rianne." Her black flats clicked along the wood floor as she started to leave.

"Harley, how much do you know about Abbey's visions? I mean, do they come true?" I hadn't forgotten about Abbey. How could I? She was the star of Roman's twisted plan, whatever that might be.

She backtracked and gave me a sad smile.

My heart dipped. "So, they do come true?"

She rubbed her hands together as if trying to warm them up. "I can only go by what I've heard, which is that she's usually correct. But don't listen to me. I'm just Webb's administrative assistant."

Dr. Vieira had tried to sugarcoat Abbey's vision, and Sam had tried to brush it off the first time I asked as if it was no big deal. But he'd been more truthful when I asked him the second time.

"Abbey says that Rianne will kill me."

Harley's pink lips parted as she sat down in the cushioned chair next to my bed. "Oh." She straightened her spine. "For what it's worth, and I don't know how true this is, I've heard Abbey has been struggling with what she sees in the future."

That piece of information did nothing to erase the trepidation coursing through my veins. I blew out a breath as a cold shiver danced down my spine. I needed to change the subject. If I kept worrying about that, then with my luck, my own mind would manifest my sister killing me. "You don't come off as a vampire. The ones I've known have been cold and calculating, much like Roman."

She reached over and placed a hand on my knee, which was bouncing to the beat of my heart, fast and furious. "There are many of our kind who are nice, sweet, and normal. But I get what you mean. Look, I'm here for you."

I inhaled deeply. "Thank you."

The more I was around Harley, the more I felt a connection to her. I'd never had a bestie in high school. It had been hard to latch on to a whole best-friend relationship, given that my family held secrets mere humans would piss their pants over.

I could see Harley and me as besties. On top of that, I was desperate for someone other than my sisters to talk to, someone who was unbiased and could give me advice.

"I promise you, you're in good hands with the SEAL team. As much as Sam can be quite over-powering, he's got a huge heart. He loves hard, and if I were in battle, I would want him to have my back."

"You sound like you have a thing for him." A pang of jealousy came out of nowhere.

Withdrawing her hand, she half smiled. "Sam and I have screwed around."

My head lolled backward, not expecting her to be such a straight shooter. "Okay." An uncomfortable feeling washed over me, and I giggled.

She did too. "Sorry, I don't beat around bushes."

"I see that. And I like it. If you are laying things out on the table, is he...?" Fire singed a path straight to my clit. "Actually, don't answer that." I wasn't going to screw him, and if I knew he was as good as her smile said he was, I would be tempted to go one round with him. Then that would lead to another and then another, and before long, I would be addicted.

"I do tell it like it is, but what happens between a couple in the bedroom is where I draw the line. However, Sam does have a thing for you. And I can see why. You're stunning."

My cheeks flushed. Aside from my parents, no one had ever told me that with so much emotion. "Ditto." Her thick, shiny waves of blond hair draped down over her shoulders. Her navy-blue eyes sparkled as if someone had sprinkled gold dust in them, and her curves were carved out in the right places. "But as far as Sam goes, I'm guessing he's drawn to my blood."

She raised a sweater-clad shoulder. "True. But it's more than that. As a vampire, I can detect these things. Look, Layla, I can see the war going on in your head. I get that vampires aren't your cup of tea, but we have emotions too. Sadly, though, some of our kind can be evil. Just like some humans can be as well."

She had a point, and one I hadn't thought about in quite some time. Uncle Jack's wife, Tab, had said something along those lines in a conversation several years ago. She had a soft spot for anyone with a beating heart, but her opinions about vampires were quickly silenced by Uncle Jack.

Harley pressed on. "We really do try to protect humanity. If it weren't for Jo, humanity would look a lot different today."

"Jo?" *How could one person shape humanity?*

She crossed one ankle over the other. "Yeah. She and Sam have been targeted ever since they became vampires. Their DNA is in high demand. But five years ago, she stopped Edmund Rain— Abbey's dad, of all people—from building an army of vampires out of humans. Ben was caught in the craziness, and now he's a half-breed. We know of one other human who made it through the experiments, and he ended up becoming a full-fledged vampire."

"Abbey's dad? Wow! What happened to him?"

"Edmund is now dead. So is Jo's uncle Patrick, a well-known geneticist who turned on his brother, Steven Mason. The crazy thing, too, is that Edmund and Steven had been best friends at one time. Anyway, back to Patrick. He'd been the mastermind behind the experiments. Jo and Sam suffered greatly, almost dying in the process."

My mouth was hanging open. I sat there, thinking of my own family drama, but it was nothing of that magnitude. "Speaking of Ben, who probably wants revenge on me for holding a dagger to his throat, he's your date tonight?"

She hopped up. "Crap, I need to go. I have a few things to take care of before then."

I didn't want her to leave. Harley was a wealth of information, and I was right. She *was* super nice and would be a great friend. I laughed.

She twirled her phone in her hand. "What is it?"

My stomach gurgled. "My family would be horrified if they knew I was here among vampires, but more than that, talking to a vampire like we're best buds."

"We can be. I could use a friend around here. Hanging with my brother, Sawyer, gets boring. And just to put you at ease around me and others here, we keep our bloodthirst sated pretty well. You don't have to worry about a vampire attacking you."

That was debatable, given how Sam wanted to sink his fangs into me.

"I've got to run," she said.

"Harley, one more question. Where does Sam sleep?" I had to be sure he wouldn't or couldn't sneak into my room.

She pinched her perfectly manicured eyebrows together. "He won't attack you if that's what you're worried about. Or maybe you don't trust yourself." Her red lips split into a slow smile.

Truth be told, my resolve to stay away from Sam was weakening by the minute. I was sure he would win our bet if I couldn't get him out of my head. "It's not what you think." *Liar.*

She snorted. "Does it matter what I think?"

I lifted a shoulder. "I wouldn't mind your advice."

She clasped her hands in front of her. "I'm listening."

I rubbed my lips together. "He bet me I would end up in his bed within two days." Our heated encounter had happened several hours ago. That meant the clock was ticking down. I was hoping he would cave before me, and I would win, which meant I could do whatever I wanted to him. My first choice had been to drive a cobalt dagger through his heart, but the more I was around him, the more I was seeing a different side of him, namely his tender touch in the interrogation room and his caring attitude, though that had been fleeting. Maybe Harley was right. Maybe Sam had a big heart. Despite it all, I felt an overwhelming desire to bare my soul to him.

I sighed heavily. I was tired, my brain was overloaded, and I wasn't thinking clearly. That was it. That was my excuse.

She hadn't lost her blinding smile. "Interesting. He does love a game of cat and mouse. And before you ask, no, he and I never made a bet like that. So, knowing where he sleeps would do what for you?"

"If his room is next door, then I want another room."

She shook her head. "Liar."

I busted out laughing. "You got me. There's a pull to him I can't explain." I sighed. "It's more than sexual." I was tempted to spill my guts and tell her I could feel what he was feeling. But then I would sound like a crazy lady, and she had a date with Ben.

"I heard you bit him."

Heat pinched my cheeks. "Does the whole building know?"

She shrugged. "I only do because I work for Webb. Anyway, I suspect what you're feeling is from his blood. It will pass. The Mason blood packs a punch."

Come to think of it, I hadn't had a vision or felt dizzy or sick since I'd left the infirmary, which, if I was keeping track of time, had been maybe two hours before. "Thank you for sharing all that."

She pointed to the door. "I should run. I'll check on you tomorrow. Oh, and Sam has an apartment on the fourth floor of this building." She held back a laugh. "Don't do anything I wouldn't do."

As she walked out, Rianne came in, carrying a tray of food. "Hungry, sis?"

"Starving." I pushed to my feet, and as I crossed the room, the greasy aroma of the hamburgers wafted up my nostrils. I groaned. "Yummy."

She set the tray on the bistro table. "The cafeteria had burgers and subs, but I thought you would prefer a burger."

"You know me well." I threw my arms around her. "Thank you."

She hugged me back. "I've missed you too."

We stood holding each other for the longest minute before I eased away. "How are you feeling?" I slid onto a barstool.

"Still a little out of it but hungry as a dog." She sat on the stool across from me.

Once we prepared our burgers with pickles, mayo, and ketchup, we dove in, taking huge bites. I moaned as I chewed. We kept eating as though we hadn't had food in over a week.

After she swallowed her last bite, she wiped her mouth with a napkin. "I'm ready to leave. But have you seen the snow outside?"

I dipped a fry into ketchup. "Since I left the infirmary, I haven't been in a room with windows." Even on the way to the room, Harley and I hadn't passed any windows. "The SEALs are—" Shit, I hadn't told her about Jordyn. I opened one of the bottles of water and took a long drink.

She perked up even though she looked as tired as I felt. "The SEALs are what? Did you help them? Did they find Dowell?"

It was time to break the bad news. "Roman is holding Jordyn until I can get him information on Abbey."

She reared back. "What the fuck?"

My stomach soured. "I couldn't tell you in the infirmary. I wasn't ready to share that with Sam, and you know how sharp vampire hearing is." I went on to explain what had happened at the house, the shifter, what Roman wanted me to do, everything, including the events since I'd first arrived on base. I left out the intimate parts between Sam and me for now. "I'm sorry I didn't tell you sooner. Sam and his team are devising a plan. Dowell, whose name is really Wyman, had been following our every move. And it just so happens he tracked Roman to our neighbor's house. We think that's where he's keeping Jordyn."

She scrunched her nose. "You mean that creep Gerald?"

I blinked once.

She stared at something behind me. "I don't think Roman is stupid enough to keep Jordyn that close to our house."

"True. But it might be kind of smart. From what I know, the SEALs had tracked Roman to a warehouse. If not for Wyman following us, the SEALs would be looking elsewhere."

"Do you really trust these vampires to help us? Because I don't. We need to rescue our sister."

I waved a hand to get her attention. "We're fish

out of water here. That shifter, Vera, is massive and scary as fuck. We might know vampires, but we're not prepared for a shifter or her pack." I blew out a breath. "Roman gave me twenty-four hours to get the intel he wants to confirm Abbey is under the SEALs' protection."

She picked up a fry. "Then what?"

"No clue." I took another swig of water. "He told me he would take it from there. Let's see what Sam and his team can do."

She huffed. "Fine. But if they don't make any headway, then you and I are out of here."

"Agreed. In the meantime, I could use a couple of hours of sleep." I reached over the table and grasped her hand. "We'll get through this." I didn't know if I was reassuring myself or her.

She gave me a weak smile. "After this is all over, let's discuss our future. I've had time to think while I was in the infirmary. I want to see if I can get into the military."

I squeezed her hand. "For sure." I wanted nothing more than to see her and Jordyn happy. But I had a feeling that discussion wouldn't happen anytime soon.

23

SAM

Tripp, Webb, Sawyer, and I sat around the conference table in the war room, waiting on intel from Ben and Kraft. We'd sent them out to Gerald Becker's home right about the time Layla had gone up to the women's barracks with Harley, which was about four hours ago. Ben and Kraft had been checking in every hour but had no activity to report yet.

We'd learned that our lead on the Indian Reservation didn't pan out. The warehouse had been empty, but we suspected Roman had been there given the human blood our team found.

Webb leaned back in the leather chair at the head of the table. "Let's run through the items we have on our list and make sure we have everything covered."

Tripp stopped typing on his laptop.

Sawyer looked up from his computer screen.

And I was ready to snap the pen in my hand in two. Since the club last night, we hadn't had a chance to breathe, and it seemed every piece of crap was flying at us at breakneck speed. Truth be told, I was thinking about Layla in between everything else. I couldn't get the auburn-haired beauty out of my head.

"We have Layla and Rianne Aberdeen here," Webb began. "The other sister, Jordyn, is in the hands of Roman. We have a drug that kills shifters. Wyman has resurfaced. His former partner, Agent Thomas, could be lurking somewhere nearby." Webb's blue eyes shifted to black as his jaw hardened. "Sawyer, any word from your contact at the Puerto Rico prison?"

Since Wyman's surprise appearance, we were checking on Nicki and Dyson, who both had worked for Edmund Rain. We needed to be sure they hadn't had any visitors or contact with the outside world, which was against prison policy. If Wyman didn't have any recollection of the memories I'd erased, I felt confident that Nicki and Dyson wouldn't recall what part they'd played while working for Edmund Rain, nor would they remember Abbey, for that matter.

Sawyer pecked at the keys on his laptop. "Let me check to see if I got a response back from the warden." After a second, he added, "Not yet, but I'll stay on it."

"Now, the humans Dr. Case and Agent Thomas." Webb turned his attention to Tripp. "Has the tech team been successful in tracking them down?"

"They're still working on it," Tripp responded.

I grabbed the back of my neck, rubbing a knot the size of Texas. "I'm sorry about all this. It's my fault Wyman remembered us."

Webb roughed his fingers through his shoulder-length brown hair, looking tired and stressed. "Sam, you were a young vampire. If it's anyone's fault, it's mine. I gave you the order. The good news is he doesn't have any recollection of Edmund or anything about his role in Edmund's organization. But just to be sure, I'll have Jo read his mind." Webb jotted something down on the legal pad in front of him.

"We haven't discussed Jonah," Sawyer said. "He'd worked for Edmund and is very well aware of Abbey."

I'd been so consumed with the events so far that I didn't think of Jonah. He had been one of Edmund's right-hand men until Edmund had murdered the love of his life. Then he'd joined us on my father's request right before we'd taken down Edmund. In fact, he'd helped Jo save Abbey's life. Since then, he'd been working for my father as a guardian at vampire headquarters. Guardians were equivalent to the human police and hand-picked to work at vampire headquarters by the Council of Elders.

"He's clean," Webb said with certainty. "Steven read his mind. Besides, he adores Abbey. It's been five years since he joined us, and I can say without a doubt that he would massacre anyone who would hurt her."

"Just wanted to be sure," Sawyer said. "Also, should we get Layla's phone in case Roman calls again?"

Tripp checked the diver's watch on his wrist. "He gave her twenty-four hours. Considering he called her around six p.m., that means we have until roughly six p.m. tomorrow. Let's hope we find him before then."

"Tripp, did you get a hold of Crysta?" Webb asked.

Crysta was Tripp's cousin and a shifter herself,

and we wanted to talk to her about what shifter packs were in the area.

"I have a message in to her. She's on some job in Washington for the vampire government," he said. "I'm sure she'll respond when she gets a minute."

Webb made a few more notes on his legal pad. "Let's get Doc down to the holding cell to talk to Wyman about that drug he gave Layla to use. I want to be ready in the event we have a run-in with the shifters."

Tripp opened Wyman's notebook. "I thought he would have something in here, but there's nothing about the drug." He skimmed the pages.

"Anything of importance in that book?" I asked. Wyman had been quite irritated when Tripp took the journal.

"Not really. Dates, places." Tripp stopped and read. "Huh. Wyman wrote, 'The Aberdeen brothers hate each other. It seems the feud between Jack, Ray, and Wayne is over a woman. They don't agree with Wayne's choice, and Jack and Ray insist that Wayne get rid of her.'"

"Which one is Layla's father?" Webb asked.

We sounded like a gaggle of women gossiping. "We know Jack isn't," I said.

Tripp turned the page and pulled out a sticky note. "Coordinates. Interesting."

Sawyer held out his hand. "Let's find out where they lead."

"With our luck, they lead to a warehouse of humans who've been turned into vampires." An undercurrent of sarcasm lay beneath the seriousness in Webb's tone.

It felt like icy fingers scraping down my spine as that cold, bleary day in Alaska came roaring back.

The minute I had entered the cavernous room embedded in a mountain, I'd almost choked on the stench. Bodies upon bodies were piled high—dead humans who were part of an experiment gone wrong. Horribly wrong. My uncle Patrick and Edmund were sick fucks, and all because they wanted power. It was a better world without them in it. I just hated that my sister had been the one to battle Edmund to the death, but she did it with strength, fortitude, determination, and a desperate urge to protect humanity. I would never forget seeing Edmund's head on the pile of bodies or when my old man flung Edmund's head over the edge of the cliff in that cavern. Elation and a sense of peace had washed over Jo, Webb, my dad, and me.

Webb's phone rang, drawing me out of that hellish memory.

He tapped his phone screen. "Steven, you're on speaker."

"Good," Dad said. "Any word on if your lead has panned out with Layla's neighbor?"

Webb had been keeping my father up-to-date every hour.

Webb chewed on his pen. "Nothing yet."

My father blew out a heavy breath. "I'm going to be in Boston for at least another day. I'm still trying to get a hold of Jack Aberdeen. The council wants to meet with him. Has Layla spoken to him?"

"Not that I know of, Pops," I said. "I'll let you know if she has."

"Son, I take it that things have calmed down between you and her."

Sawyer, Tripp, and Webb watched me intently.

I wasn't about to go into detail about Layla and me or tell him I urgently needed to be close to her, protect her, and that I wanted to fuck her. "She's sleeping." Harley had checked on Layla before she'd gone home. Her date with Ben had been canceled since he was on a recon mission.

"Steven," Webb said, "do you think Jack will meet with the council?"

"Not at all," my father said rather quickly, "but we have to try. And we need Jordyn in our custody. If he does return my call, I would like to be able to tell him that his nieces are all safe."

"I don't think Layla will say a word to him if she does speak to him," I said. "There's some strong animosity in that family. Even Wyman details that in his notebook."

"Speaking of the former agent," Dad said, "where are we with him? Has he given us anything to go on?"

"No, sir," Tripp responded. "He doesn't even remember Edmund."

"Abbey?" Dad asked.

A muscle ticked in Webb's jaw. "We didn't bring up Abbey. It's best if we don't. But I'm planning on having Jo read his mind."

"Good call," Dad said. "I have to run."

"Steven, I'll update you again later." Then Webb ended the call.

Sawyer pecked on his keyboard. "Um... those coordinates." He pinched his unshaven chin. "Looks like a house in Montana."

"It's probably where Wyman's family is," I said. "Or Layla's family." Which didn't matter in the grand scheme of what we were battling at the moment.

Tripp's phone pinged. "It's Kraft." He tapped the screen. "Go."

"Sir, everything is quiet still. There isn't any activity in the house. Ben is doing a sweep of the back of the property."

"Did you check the house Layla's staying in next door?" I asked.

"Dark. No vampires or humans."

"We're going to comb the woods and the other homes nearby."

"Keep us posted. I'm sure the neighbor will show himself. Maybe not until the morning," Webb said to Kraft.

Tripp hung up. "Not much to do until we can get eyes on Roman, Jordyn, or the shifter."

I rose. I needed to stretch my legs, take a shower, sleep, and drink—anything to take my mind off of what we were up against, and above that, Layla. Still, I had to mention, "We haven't discussed Roman. He told Layla that once she confirmed we had Abbey, he would take the lead. We need to prepare."

"Once Jo reads Wyman's mind, I'm taking her and Abbey up to our house in Maine," Webb said. "Tripp, let's get extra guards around the perimeter of the base just in case." Webb stood. "I need to talk to Dr. Vieira, and then I'll send him down to the prison to meet you. I'll also send Jo down."

"Tripp, do you need me for anything?" I asked.

Sawyer was absorbed in his computer. The tech team was working on tracking Dr. Case and Agent Thomas. If I had to question Wyman, I might tear off his head, but since Jo was about to read his mind, there was no need to question him until we were blue in the face.

Tripp tucked his laptop under his arm. "No. I'll let you know if I hear anything from Kraft and Ben."

"I'll be up in my apartment," I said to Tripp. "Webb, can I talk to you for a minute?"

Webb started to leave. "Walk with me."

Once Webb and I were out in the hall, I said, "I want to apologize again. I keep racking my brain about what I did wrong with Wyman.

He clutched my shoulder. "Again, it's not your fault. I should've known not to put pressure on you back then. You were still learning."

The knot that had formed in my stomach loosened. "I promise it won't happen again."

He released my shoulder. "I know. Your abilities are much stronger."

I had a ton of respect for Webb as a soldier, vampire, and my brother-in-law. He was a true leader and a great man. "I'll die before I let anyone touch Abbey," I said with a sigh.

"I know, but you'll have to get behind me, because if anyone dares to fuck with my family, heads will come off."

The image of Edmund's head soaring over that cliff danced before me. I was ten thousand percent sure the next person to fuck with our family would suffer the same fate.

He shoved his hand through his light-brown hair. "I need to go if I want to take Jo and Abbey to our house in Maine and return by the morning."

"The weather sucks." When I last looked outside, which was maybe three hours ago, it was still snowing.

He nodded. "I'm sure the highways are clear. The weather forecast says the snow should be stopping in the next few hours. If I don't make it back by morning, Tripp can handle the team. I can't risk having Abbey here, and Jo isn't driving up alone."

I didn't blame him. Besides, Roman's deadline was six tomorrow night. I stabbed my thumb behind me. "I'm going to take a shower. Kiss Abbey for me."

We went in opposite directions. I took the stairs up to my apartment on the fourth floor, but when I reached the third floor, I came to a hard stop.

The temptation to check on Layla was searing my veins and burning my groin. I refused to break down and lose the bet. I wanted her to come to me. I might be a lot of things, but I wasn't the type to force myself on any woman.

I continued on to the fourth floor, and when I grabbed the door handle, I hesitated.

I should make sure she was okay, and she would probably want an update.

Dude, don't do it. Let her sleep. You'll see her soon enough.

I gritted my teeth and stormed through the door and down to my apartment, cursing the entire way.

24

LAYLA

I meandered through the darkness, looking over my shoulder as though someone was pushing me toward something. I couldn't see five feet in front of me. I could barely see my feet. I tried to backtrack but was only met with a crushing force of what felt like a wall.

I wiped the sweat from my forehead as the heat surrounding me became unbearable. Nerves jabbed my stomach. I had no choice but to move forward.

"Hello," I called to the darkness before me. "Is anyone there?"

As if someone heard me, a glow of light spilled out from a room up ahead. My pulse sped up as I took a tentative step forward. Then another.

The sound of running water tickled my ears, and beneath it, a soft drumbeat. Or maybe that was my *heart punching my ribs. The closer I got to the light, my anxiety began to wane. In its place was a sense of euphoria. I felt as though I'd walked into a field of flowers on a warm summer day, where happiness ruled and peace reigned.*

A smile emerged on my face as I peered into the room. Candlelight flickered around the cavernous space. Water filled a bathtub that was tucked in an alcove, while a massive bed fit for six sat centerstage.

I stepped into the room, my bare feet sinking into the plush brown carpet. "Hello." My voice was low and shaky.

The door snicked shut behind me, and that sudden euphoria was replaced with icy fear. My breathing became labored. My palms clammy. My legs weak and trembling. I ran for the door. Large, strong hands grabbed me out of nowhere. I screamed, but nothing came out.

"No need to be afraid," the husky masculine voice said as he licked a path from my neck to my ear. "This is your fantasy." He lifted me up and carried me to the bed.

I blinked several times, and when I did, I was completely naked. I oriented my vision, struggling to see who the voice belonged to, but he wasn't there. I frantically searched around, and when my gaze landed on the virile man near the bathtub, I gasped.

A solid wall of muscle stood there, naked, built as if the gods themselves had carved him out of stone. Thick thighs, narrow waist, broad back, hair almost down to his shoulders. He turned the water off, and when he pivoted on his heel, my eyes went wide.

I couldn't breathe. I couldn't form words. I couldn't even move.

Silver eyes glistened in the candlelight. Canines, sharp and deadly, seemed to drip with hunger.

My gaze traveled down his torso, tracking every breath he took, every dip and valley on his abs. I was prepared to go lower, but I couldn't look away. He stood like a Viking, every inch of him hard and ready to do battle.

My tongue darted out to moisten my lips.

He closed the distance between us, eyelids hooded, chest rising and falling, and his erection... I swallowed the dryness in my throat. He was huge, thick, long— and he was ready to show me a world I'd never set foot in.

He grinned, and his dimples emerged, giving him an even sexier look that had my pussy dying to feel him inside me.

"Layla." His voice was gravelly and caused goose bumps to blanket my body and my clit to throb.

I crawled to the edge of the bed, his voice pulling

me, his body exciting me, and I wanted nothing more than for him to sink his fangs into me.

"Sam." I said his name like it was a prayer, pleading and desperate, and as though it was the most natural thing in the world, I closed my hand around his shaft.

His eyes rolled back in his head as he groaned. The sound was glorious and sent excited shivers to swirl in my belly. I felt powerful to have this man, this vampire, who could end me in a nanosecond, become putty in my hands.

He thrust his hips toward me, urging me to take control and to do as I pleased. I lowered my head, pumping him up then down, and when I lightly licked the tip of his cock, he grunted so loud the walls shook.

Before I could track his next move, he repositioned me so my butt was seated on the edge of the mattress, my legs were splayed wide open, and he was on his knees.

I was dizzy, excited, feeling like I could fly as I bared my body to the one creature I despised in all the world. Yet there was no other place I wanted to be. I was aching for his touch, his tongue, his cock, his hands, his lips, anything he could give me.

He kissed his way up one leg then the other, groaning, growling, and dragging his fangs along the sensitive flesh of my inner thighs.

My pussy was on fire. Hell, my body was burning with a desperate need for him to pound endlessly inside me.

But suddenly, the candles snuffed out, the room darkened, and the air was hotter than a blistering summer day. I felt around for Sam, but he was gone.

I sat up in the darkness, blinking several times as the light sound of someone snoring made its way to my ears.

Sweat dripped down my back, my hair was drenched, and my clothes clung to me.

Mother hell. My clit was swollen hard, pulsing, dying for relief.

Damn vampire. I couldn't even get away from him in my dreams, yet I pouted at the fact that I'd woken up. I took a few calming breaths, scolding myself for fantasizing about a vampire. I was going to hell.

I wiped the sleep from my eyes and swung my legs over the bed, throwing my head in my hands as my body ached for Sam.

Not going to happen.

Instead, I could easily take care of myself, but not there.

Rianne was sound asleep in her bed on the other side of the room. I decided a shower would cool me off until I glanced at the clock on the wall.

Eleven p.m. *Shit!*

I hopped up quickly. My sexual needs dissipated as my brain kicked into gear. Jordyn? Did the SEAL team find her?

I spotted a pile of clothes on the cushioned chair.

Harley must've dropped them off. I picked through the stack—dark jeans, a white camisole top, a thick blue V-neck sweater that was soft to the touch, and brand-new undergarments. I smiled as I examined the matching pink lace bra and panties.

She had good taste. The sweater alone looked expensive. Underneath the pile was a note: *Hope these fit. Also, no news yet on your sister. The team is still surveilling your neighbor's home. See you in the morning. Harley.*

I had no idea when she'd left the note, but maybe they'd found where Roman was keeping Jordyn.

First, I needed a quick shower, then I could find my way down to the control room.

I grabbed the clothes and was ready to hit the shower when I stilled. I needed something to protect me. After all, I was in a building full of vampires. At that realization, I shivered as I quietly picked up the butter knife that had been on the food tray. It would barely harm a vampire, but it would at least do some damage and give me time to run.

I proceeded to tiptoe out, careful not to wake Rianne. Once in the hall, I looked to my left and then right. I didn't see any signs for a restroom. Harley had said it was down the hall, but I didn't know which way.

The exit sign glowed up ahead, and suddenly my mind was right back in my dream. The dark hallway, the candlelit bedroom, Sam naked and ready to screw my brains out.

My feet were on the move toward the exit. My legs scurried along like I was heading toward something exciting and thrilling like an amusement park I'd loved to frequent as a kid.

I was ten feet from the exit when my brain finally fired on all cylinders, and I stopped.

No, I'm not going up. I'm not giving in.

Icy fingers tiptoed down my spine. Suddenly, I felt as though Sam were next to me, breathing on my ear, touching me lightly as he dragged his fingers along the swell of my breasts.

No. No. No. I was not about to have another vision. I shook my head and pivoted on my heel when the squeak of the door echoed in the hall. My blood instantly froze. My limbs were locked tight. His spicy scent drifted in. I didn't have to turn around to know Sam was behind me as his footsteps pounded on the tiled floor.

I should move but couldn't and didn't want to. I gripped the knife tighter as I held the bundle of clothes to me as though they would protect me. That crushing force in my dream wasn't a wall in real life—it was Sam's solid wall of muscle pressing into me. His hands shaped my hips. His mouth was on my ear, his damp hair tickling my neck.

"Were you coming to see me?" His voice sounded sexy and sleepy and full of desperation.

Yes. No. "I was looking for the bathroom."

"Yeah, I bet." He licked my neck, eliciting a string of goose bumps.

Damn vampire. The pulsing in my core was too much, and if I didn't do something about it soon, I would definitely give in to him.

"You're on the wrong side of the hall." I could feel his grin against my sensitive flesh behind my ear.

"I'm lost," I whispered in a breathy tone.

"So am I."

I choked on a laugh. "Bull. You can't stay away from me."

He palmed my swollen breasts as I pressed my ass into his erection.

"I feel your lust, Layla. You're dripping wet, and I don't even need to slip my hands into your panties to know."

"Asshole."

I could feel him grinning against my neck. "How was that dream you had?"

The lust coursing through me vanished, and I stiffened. "What the fuck?" I darted away, spinning on my heel, my eyes bugging out of my head. "How do you know about that?"

Sam raked both hands through his hair. "I don't know." He let out a frustrated breath.

We stared at each other beneath the dim lights overhead. Human against vampire. Hunter against the hunted. A force beyond our control was drawing us to each other.

I swallowed, the sound reverberating off the picture-covered walls. "You had the same dream?" I asked reluctantly, not sure I was ready to hear his answer.

He bobbed his head, and for the first time since I'd met him, I saw a hint of apprehension, almost like he was freaking out more than me. "The feel of your hand around my shaft. The taste of your skin on my tongue." He gripped his groin with his own hand, adjusting his bulging dick, which was molded in the fabric of his sweatpants.

I whimpered. I freaking whimpered like a woman who had never been laid. I was ready to strip naked before him. "So, you saw me naked?" Butterflies took flight inside of me and flapped their wings wild and crazy.

He licked his lips, his hand still seated on his cock, and I wanted to be that hand. "Beautiful." His voice was pained. "You glistened with need." He lowered his gaze as if he could see my pussy in the flesh.

"Erase me from your memory then—because you'll only see me in your dreams." Boy, didn't that cliche ring true?

He threw his head back and laughed. "Dreams, real life, whatever. There's no denying you want me." He came toward me with a sense of purpose that would only lead to one thing—hot, steamy, and fiery sex.

I let the clothes fall to the floor and whipped out my hand, ready to gut him with the butter knife if he so much as touched me.

Again, he laughed. "Your dagger didn't kill me, and you think that dull blade will?"

I aimed it at his dick. "I can try."

"Tsk, tsk, tsk, Layla. "You don't want to cut my

cock off—you want to suck it so bad, your mouth is watering."

Shivering, I backed up a step, then another, debating whether to run or give in. Fight or flight. *Who am I kidding?* I was ready for him to bend me over and fuck me from behind. I was ready to ride him, wild and fast and free. I was ready to do anything as long as he was inside me.

He held out his arms as he settled inches from me. "Do your worst. When it comes to my turn, I'll make sure you never forget what it feels like to have sex with a vampire."

I didn't know if his cocksure attitude was irritating or turning me on. I dragged the butter knife along his erection, my pulse off the charts, my mouth dry.

He didn't move as he watched me, moaning, breathing heavy.

I put pressure on the knife as I continued to swipe it up and down his massive erection, the tip almost peeking out of the waistband of his pants. *Holy hell.* He was commando.

I held back a whimper as I craned my neck up to meet the most brilliant silver eyes. It was as if the hornier he got, the brighter the hue of his eyes became.

"You have five seconds to decide what your

next move is." He sounded ready to rip off my clothes.

I tipped my head to one side, trying to give him the shyest look I could. "Or what?" My cheeks burned as he scrutinized me.

"You want me, Layla." He traced circles around my nipples, which were swollen and poking against my bra. "And I'm not afraid to say I want you." He pinched one nipple lightly. "We're connected for better or worse. Not sure how, and frankly I don't care how. You're mine, Layla Aberdeen, and it's time you come to terms with that."

I'd only known him for a day, yet I felt as though I'd known him my entire life. I couldn't deny that we were connected, sharing dreams and feelings. Hell, I wondered if he was also having visions like me.

"I can't," I said weakly, my shoulders slumping, the knife falling from my hand with a clang. "I don't understand any of it."

He leaned in, sniffing my hair before he threaded his fingers through it. "Maybe if you just went with what you feel, you might find the answers you seek."

I shook my head and shrugged away. "I don't do vampires." I walked backward, and with each step, the pain in my gut increased. I felt like I was losing part of my soul.

What the fuck is happening?

A tear slid down my cheek out of nowhere.

Sam stood godlike as he watched me, his features tightening as lines dented his forehead. I didn't have any powers, but at that moment, I swore I did. I swore I felt his sadness and pain as I got farther and farther away from him.

At that moment, I came to the realization that I had to get rid of the feeling like I was going to die if I didn't have his arms around me.

He sensed my indecision. I knew he did. How? I wasn't sure.

His long legs ate up the space between us, his gaze glued to mine. His fangs still present. His silver eyes were brighter than before.

I should be scared, but I wasn't. I gave in and went with what I felt, and I felt him. I wanted him. We could figure out our issues another time. But right now, I had to have him.

He scooped me up in his arms, and at lightning speed, he was climbing the stairs to the fourth floor.

25

LAYLA

My arms were locked around his neck, my mind empty, my heart racing as fast as his was as he carried me through his apartment in hurried strides. Before I could take in my surroundings, we were in a dark room that smelled like him: musky, soapy, and clean.

He kicked the door shut and growled. "Last chance to run."

My chest heaved, and I shuddered as I tamped down the nerves that were doing a number on my stomach. Excitement, trepidation, elation, and desperation were mingling together. "I'm not running." My voice didn't sound like my own.

He lifted my hands up above my head and pinned my wrists to the cold steel door. "After tonight, you're mine. And if you run, I'll catch you." His tone was husky, deep, and commanding as he glued his gaze to mine. "Say it, Layla. You're mine."

Any other time, I would kick a man in the balls who thought he could own me. But I couldn't. Not with Sam. I wanted to be his. Maybe it was the lust. Maybe it was some magical spell he had over me. It didn't matter. What did, though, was sating the need I had for him to kiss me, fuck me, and do whatever the hell he pleased. I felt what he felt. I felt his desire like it was my own. I felt his heart beating in time with mine.

I swallowed the knots clogging my throat as I searched his eyes. Something far more than lust swirled in them, and I sucked in air.

"You feel what I feel, don't you?" he asked in such a soft and loving tone.

I nodded slowly, afraid to admit that whatever was happening to us or between wasn't just a one-time thing, and that freaked me the fuck out. But I would dwell on that later. He needed to stop talking. "Sam." His name fell from my lips on a whimper. "I'm dying here. I want you as badly as you want me. So shut up and do something, or I'll tear you to shreds."

He chuckled as he let me go and took a step back. "Do as you please, baby doll."

My eyes were finally adjusting to the darkness as a muted light spilled in from the window beside his bed, casting an ominous shadow over the room.

He ripped off his shirt, held out his arms, and stood there like a god as he waited for me to move, to do anything but stare. I prayed I could get my legs in gear without faltering, but as I took in the dips and valleys on his upper torso, sweat began to bead on my neck.

He tore off his sweatpants, and his cock sprang free—hard, thick, long—and like in my dream, I hungered to taste him.

I pushed off the door, stepped toward him, slowly at first to be sure I wouldn't collapse. He watched me watch him. He grabbed his erection and stroked it once, his eyes hooded, his fangs free.

I moaned as I reached him, replacing his hand with mine.

He groaned his approval.

His skin was velvety and felt like pure silk as I squeezed his shaft. He moaned, pushing his fingers through my hair.

I wasted no time in dropping to my knees and

sucking him into my mouth. He roared as he thrust his hips forward. I sucked once, pumping him hard and steady as I licked the tip of his cock —but he wasn't having any of the light teases.

He lifted me to my feet and ripped off my shirt, literally tearing the fabric from me before helping me undress until I was completely naked. It was his turn to take in the view. Slow and sensual, he hiked his gaze down my naked body, lingering on my tits, which were heavy and needy.

I rolled a swollen nipple between my fingers as I played with my clit.

He pumped his cock, his silver eyes cemented to mine.

I swallowed thickly, hoping the next words out of my mouth were intelligible. "I"—a breath escaped me—"need you inside me."

It had been way too long since I'd been with a man and felt that fullness with friction I urgently needed. But Sam wasn't just any man. He was built from stone—formidable, powerful, strong, otherworldly. And I knew that sex with him would not compare to any other lover.

In one smooth move, he lifted me up onto a tall dresser so we were eye to eye. I wanted to ask him why not the bed, but frankly, I didn't care, and nothing between Sam and me was conventional.

He splayed open my legs, his hungry gaze never wavering from my pussy or maybe my inner thigh. I hadn't forgotten what he'd told me in that elevator. My pulse blasted out of the room at the thought that he would sink his fangs into that one spot he'd marked.

He pulled me to the edge of the dresser top, his big body wedged in between my legs. Then as if the world had moved at warp speed, Sam dove in, feasting on my body like it was his last meal. He bit one nipple, then the other.

I latched on to his hair as I pressed his face into my tits. "Harder." The word came out strangled.

He did as I commanded. The painful pleasure was too much yet not enough. I squirmed on the wooden dresser, holding on to his black silky locks, tugging and mashing his head down, raising my hips up, hoping he got the signal that I needed him to sate the throbbing between my legs

Before I took a breath, he yanked me almost off the edge of the dresser, his hands on the lower half of my ass cheeks as he bent down slightly and swiped his tongue over my clit. When he did, I bucked. He sucked. I squirmed, moaned, and begged him. "More. Harder."

He kept up his assault on my pussy, sucking and sucking and sucking.

I threw my head back, stuck out my chest, opened my legs wider, and just when I was about to crest over that blissful edge, he stopped.

I righted my head, my eyes wide.

In a flash, he tossed me on the bed, crawled up my body, and kissed me like a man possessed. We rolled around—him on top, me on top, hands everywhere, tongues tangoing, bodies sweating.

I pressed a hand into his chest and grabbed his cock with my other. I positioned it at my entrance, ready to ride him hard and fast, when he flipped us.

I squealed as he leaned down and licked that sensitive spot behind my ear. "Your scent is driving me mad, and if I don't taste a drop of your blood, I swear I will die."

The word "die" should've thrilled me. After all, I was a vampire hunter. Yet at that moment, I would bawl my eyes out if Sam died. Crazy shit right there.

My pulse was erratic, my body on fire, and my mind at ease with the thought of him sinking his fangs into me. For some weird reason, I trusted he wouldn't drain me.

"Then taste me, Sam."

He grinned against my neck. "Are you sure?" His voice was husky and sexy and held so much pain.

"Bite me then fuck me. If you don't, I will kill you."

He laughed hard as he jumped into action, and once again he pressed his face between my legs.

I barely took a breath before he bit, quick and fast.

I screamed, arching my back as the instant sting of his canines sank into my inner thigh. Then pleasure seeped in as he sucked my life force into him. If I felt Sam before, it was nothing like I was feeling him now. Every emotion coursing through him was in me: happiness, elation, satisfaction—and the list went on.

I clutched the blanket, breathing heavily, giving in to the vampire as he continued to draw life from me.

My eyelids became sleepy, my head dizzy as my belly twisted and knotted. I was ready to close my eyes when the bed dipped, and he was hovering over me. Blood dripped from his fangs as he ran his tongue over one of his canines. "So fucking sweet."

I gasped once at the sheer sexiness of how he looked—sated and happy. Then I gasped a second time when he thrust his long, thick cock inside me.

"Holy fuck," dropped from his lips. "So tight and wet." He grinned like a man who'd won a million dollars. "You're mine, Layla. I want you to say it."

I pinched his nipples, rolling my hips in time with his. "No. No one owns me."

He stopped moving.

I snarled. "Really?"

"Say it," he commanded, leaning down until his mouth was an inch from mine.

I squeezed around his dick tightly, hoping that would energize him, but the vampire was stubborn even though his eyes rolled back in his head. And as much as I hated to give in to the bullheaded vampire, I had to orgasm or else I would die.

"I'm *yours*, Sam Mason. Now *please fuck me*." I put as much feeling into those two statements as I could.

He began fucking me like a wild man.

I matched him thrust for thrust. Then he stopped again.

I growled like an animal. *Not again.*

But he had other plans. "On your knees."

I smiled wide and gladly obeyed. I think my

compliance threw him off his game because he tilted his head. Once I was on all fours with my ass facing him, he gripped my hip with one hand and guided his cock into my pussy with the other.

I pushed back into him, urging him to hurry the hell up. Then he wrapped my long locks around one hand, gripped my hip with his other, and fucked me hard and fast.

Skin slapped on skin. Sweat poured off my body as we fucked like rabbits. Moans, groans, and grunts peppered the air.

"Sit on me," he commanded.

We adjusted ourselves so I was seated on his dick with my legs around him. He dug his fingers into my waist, helping me move up and down. The friction was glorious as my tits bounced with every thrust.

I held on to his head, helping him move from one breast to the other, never losing speed as we rocked and rolled. Then, taking a play out of his book, I pulled on his hair, his head lolling backward. I kissed his chin, his mouth, and his jaw as I reached the precipice of my orgasm.

"Fuck me harder, Sam. I'm almost there."

He obeyed me and flipped me over, not breaking our connection, and kept pounding into me.

I whimpered, squealed, and got caught up in a world I never wanted to leave. I was lost in him and what he was doing to me. I knew I would never be the same. I knew he was mine, and I dared any woman, human or vampire, to touch the one man who ripped my soul from me and pieced it back together.

"You're mine, Sam Mason," I said in a breathy tone. "Say it." I sounded like a different person.

His fangs grazed my chin. "I'm yours for eternity, Layla. You can count on that."

I didn't comprehend the eternity part but didn't give a damn at the moment. My orgasm hit me, and I shot up and sunk my teeth into his shoulder, holding on to him as a small amount of his blood exploded on my tongue.

He roared like a lion as he thrust hard one last time, pulsing, throbbing as we rode out our orgasms in sync.

We stayed tethered to each other for maybe seconds or minutes—I wasn't sure. What I was sure of, though, was I would never be the same when I walked out of his room. In what way? I wasn't certain.

SAM

I untangled my body from hers and went into the bathroom to get a washcloth. When I returned, Layla was fast asleep.

I grinned at the sleeping beauty. She was curled up with one hand beneath the pillow and the other tucked under her chin. I thought of waking her. My dick was still rock hard and ready to go a few more rounds or all night, and I was too amped up to sleep, but she looked peaceful, and I wanted to check in to see if Kraft and Ben had eyes on Roman.

I pulled the blankets over her then kissed her on the head. "Sleep well."

She moaned, wiggling into the pillow.

"Dream of me," I whispered in her ear.

I gathered a clean uniform and left, closing the soundproofed steel door softly. No one could hear us, and no one was getting through unless they came in through the window. Even then, my enemy would have a difficult time with the thick bulletproof glass.

As I showered and dressed, I replayed the last hour between Layla and me. The sex had been intense as fuck, and every one of her emotions had been mine and mine hers. The orgasm was out-of-this-world. I felt both of ours at the same time. Maybe I should thank the gods for giving me my empath ability.

But something far greater was happening between us. I'd screwed other women and had never felt as connected to them as I had with Layla. Maybe because those women, like Harley, were vampires.

My heart tripped at the thought that Jo could be right, that I could be falling for Layla. That was impossible, though. Or maybe it wasn't. I just didn't know. I believed my dick was in control. My bloodthirst was coming in a close second, and the two were messing with my head.

I discarded any notion that love came into play. I was still riding my sexual high, as evidenced by my erection that wasn't going down anytime soon, at least not when Layla was naked in my bed. Besides, a relationship with a human would never last.

Your mom was human.

I froze as I began to brush my teeth. I'd never asked my old man any intimate details about his relationship with my mom, such as his feelings for her. *What drew him to her? Did he feel what she felt? If she hadn't died of leukemia, would she still be alive?*

I switched the light off in the bathroom then wound my way down the hall. The moonlight spilled in through the wall of windows directly ahead, casting a glow into the open living space where the kitchen flowed into the family room.

I went over to glance out and into the night. The snow-covered ground below glistened. The building across the courtyard was dark with the exception of one room on the first floor. Tripp, Doc, and Jo were probably talking to Wyman since the prison cells were located in the basement of the building.

I checked my phone. The time was shortly after midnight, and I had no messages. I skirted around the two plush couches, and the island separating the kitchen from the family room and grabbed a container of blood from the fridge.

The minute I took a swig, I almost spit it out in

the sink. It tasted like shit since I'd had my fill of Layla's blood. I was screwed from here on out. I downed the contents, nonetheless. I needed to keep my bloodthirst sated as much as I could while close to the auburn-haired goddess.

Once the container was empty, I threw it in the trash. Then I pulled out my stash of the mind-blocking potion I had tucked in one of the kitchen cabinets. I should've taken it the minute my old man had read my mind in the war room, but with all the craziness going on, I hadn't had a chance.

Regardless, I needed it now. Sure, I could erect my mental shields between me and him and Jo, but the potion was better. I didn't care if they knew I'd slept with Layla. However, I didn't want them to see a play-by-play. My bedroom antics were private.

Images of Layla's beautiful naked body flashed before me. Her sensuality. How she was comfortable in her own skin. I shook my head hard. I couldn't be thinking of her all day. Hell, my dick was rock solid and would stay that way if I couldn't shake her. Maybe someone should take my memories away, at least the ones of Layla. That way I could function. I inhaled deeply, unscrewed the cap on the bottle, then downed the four ounces of bitter liquid.

As I set the small vial onto the marble counter, a text came in.

Tripp: *Rianne is roaming the halls, freaking out that Layla isn't in their room. Where the fuck is she?*

I could see the tall brunette checking every nook and cranny in the building, probably ready to stab vampires to find her sister.

I tapped out: *Sleeping.* I couldn't lie.

Tripp: *What did you do?*

Me: *She's fine.*

Tripp: *SAM MASON!*

Me: *Don't worry. I didn't do anything she didn't want me to.*

Tripp called me.

"Stop flipping out," I said before he could yell.

"Are you insane!" Tripp shouted.

"Why are you acting like my father?"

"Did you use protection?"

I laughed. "Why would I?"

"You realize that you could get a human pregnant?"

"Only if she has the right blood type, and she doesn't." I didn't know that for sure. In the heat of the moment, my brain hadn't been interested in anything but her.

"Do you know that for sure?" he asked.

"No. But seriously, those human females with

Vel-negative blood are rare, and if she did have that blood type, she wouldn't have slept with me." I was sure Layla knew all about our kind and the ways we made babies.

"Okay," he said in a less strident tone. "I'll give you that. But if her family finds out about you two, we'll have more than a fucking war on our hands."

I loved Tripp and respected him as much as Webb and my father, but they needed to take things down a notch. "Her family will never find out." At least I wasn't about to tell them. I doubted she would either.

"Get her out of bed and down to the barracks. I'm tired of consoling Rianne. This human is about to test my resolve."

"Welcome to my world," I teased. "Did Jo find anything useful from Wyman?" I asked.

"Nothing about Edmund, his partner, or Abbey. He was telling us the truth. He doesn't remember."

I sighed loudly. "That's great news. Ben or Kraft get eyes on Roman?"

"No," he said.

"Tripp, did Webb leave with Jo and Abbey yet?" Maybe I had time to see Abbey and Jo before they left. For some reason, I had this dire need to hug them both.

"No. Given the weather, Jo wants to wait a few hours. Look, once you get Layla down to the barracks, I need you down in the control room." Then he hung up.

Well, that went well. Tripp hardly ever let his temper show. He was usually the calm one on the team.

Nevertheless, I obeyed his order. Layla stirred the minute I entered my bedroom. She threw the blanket off her and exposed her voluptuous tits as she flopped on her back. The sheen of sweat covering her body sparkled in the muted light. I wondered if she was dreaming.

I was kicking myself because I hadn't tried to sleep. Her last dream had me jerking off. It was a mystery how I was even in it. I shouldn't have been surprised, since I knew Jo saw the future through her dreams. In my world, anything was possible.

I adjusted my dick once again as my erection took shape. An intense debate erupted in my head as to whether I should go for round two. I snapped mental picture after mental picture and added it to my memory bank along with the collection of replays I had from our earlier session.

I sat on the edge of the bed, reached over, and tweaked one of her nipples.

She let out the softest moan.

Before I could stop myself, I was sucking on her nipple as I slid my hand down her toned body to settle in between her legs. Fuck, she was soaking wet.

I suckled on her tit, circling her clit as she squirmed, arching her back as her legs fell open. I dipped two fingers inside her channel, and she grabbed my hair then pushed, signaling me to go down.

"Mouth, please," she said in a sleepy voice.

I lifted up as I continued to fuck her with my fingers. "What else, baby doll? What else do you need?" I adjusted her body so my mouth had full access to her pussy.

She dragged her nails through my hair. "Your cock."

I groaned as I flattened my tongue against her clit, staving off the need to drive inside her. As much as I wanted to feel her wrapped around my dick, I was getting off on her sensual sounds, gorgeous body, and the way she reacted to my touch.

I sucked and licked and dove into a groove as she wiggled and squirmed.

"Sam." My name on her lips was pure fucking heaven. "Bite me."

I stopped cold, looking up at her, not sure if I should. I was becoming addicted to her. The more

I tasted her blood, the harder it would be to stay away. As it was, things were going at warp speed with us, and I wasn't sure if that was a good thing.

She nodded with the sexiest look I had yet to see on her. "I trust you."

My brow arched. Those three words were like a balm to my dark soul.

"Please," she whimpered.

My fangs shot out at her plea. I couldn't deny the one woman who was changing me in a way that was both thrilling and frightening at the same time. I knew Tripp was right. I knew my old man was too. Maybe even Jo when she'd said I was falling for Layla. Nothing good could come out of a relationship with Layla. At that moment, I didn't fucking care. I had this desperate need to please her. It was almost as if she had control over me.

As though she saw the war going on in my head, she said, "I'm sure."

I didn't move. My throat burned with longing to have her blood sliding down my throat, probably more so than to drive my cock into her.

She sat up, moved my hair out of my face, and studied me. "What's wrong?"

So many things. "You're beautiful. Fucking stunning." Her hair was wild around her face. Her cheeks were rosy, and she had a glow about her that I hadn't seen before.

She smiled, giving me a shy look as she traced a finger over one of my canines. "I can't decide if you're more handsome with these or when you're normal."

I chuckled. "There's nothing normal about me."

She giggled. "True."

I sat on my haunches, keeping my hands on her legs. "We need to talk."

She lost her smile. "Is this where you tell me that what happened tonight will never happen again?"

I was kicking myself in the ass that I'd ruined the mood. "Fuck no. You're mine, Layla. I didn't just say that in the throes of sex or because I wanted to get inside you. I was serious."

She shuddered, and her shoulders sagged. "I can't explain it, but I feel the same way. I feel this strong connection to you. I feel what you feel. I'm trying to fight it."

I rubbed her calves. "Don't."

"Isn't it unnatural to feel like I want to spend eternity with you when we just met, like, what, a day or two ago? I know it's your blood making me feel you, want you. Maybe when I leave, the spell will break."

I gritted my molars at the thought that I wouldn't see her again. But I wasn't about to argue with her. Not yet anyway. "We didn't use protection."

Her blue eyes glinted. "I know. You can't get me pregnant. I don't carry that rare blood type."

I sighed heavily.

"Was that what you were worried about?"

I wasn't sure how I felt about having kids. I'd never thought that far into the future. I was a vampire who had never set his sights on a long-term relationship, especially with a human woman. She would grow old. I wouldn't.

"Not at all. I figured you wouldn't have slept with me if you had that rare blood type, but the bigger issue is your family. Given that you're from a long line of vampire hunters, some here are concerned that we could spark a war between humans and vampires."

"My uncles don't care about my sisters and me."

"Have you spoken to your uncle Jack? I have."

Her mouth dropped open. "You spoke to him? I assumed it was your father who had."

"He called your phone while I had it. He told

me he would string us up like pigs and roast us or something to that effect."

"He would because you're a vampire, not because he cares about me," she said seriously.

I pushed to my feet and extended my arm. "He's never met a Mason." I closed my hand over hers. "You should take a shower. You smell like sex and me."

"The sun isn't up yet." She glanced out the window that faced a brick building with no windows in it. "We could continue where you left off." She rubbed her free hand along my dick.

"Baby doll, I would like nothing more, but Rianne is looking for you."

"What!" She jumped up and ran around the room, searching for her clothes. "I can't tell her about us. Don't you dare tell anyone, Sam." She plucked clothes off the floor.

"About that...."

She stomped her foot. "No, you didn't."

"Kind of hard not to when vampires have that sixth sense." I wrapped my arm around her waist and tugged her to me. "Tripp won't say a word."

"We can't be seen together. And no one else can know about us."

I tipped her chin up. "Agreed, for now." I

pecked her on the lips and was about to release her when she smashed her mouth into mine.

"I want a proper kiss, Sam Mason. Kiss me like you mean it."

It was the least I could do. I had to embed her essence into my psyche, or maybe that was the wrong thing to do. If I couldn't get her out of my system, it would be hard to stay away from her. *Who am I kidding?* No matter if I kissed her or not, Layla Aberdeen was a part of me now.

Our tongues fought for dominance as I gave her everything I had in that kiss until my phone rang, and just like that, the heated passion burst.

She jumped back. "Shit! Jordyn! I'm such an idiot. Did you find her?"

I held up my finger as I answered.

"We have eyes on Roman," Tripp said. "Get your ass down here now! And make sure Layla is in the barracks in ten minutes, or else I'll throw you in the brig." Then he was gone.

At least he didn't threaten me with my old man. In my mind, that would be a worse punishment.

27

LAYLA

After I took a quick shower, Sam escorted me down to the barracks. The sound of silence between his apartment and the women's barracks was deafening.

I felt a whole lot different now that I'd slept with a vampire. Several emotions overwhelmed me—equal parts embarrassment, happiness, dread at what my sisters would think, fear that my uncles would find out, and confusion over how I really felt about Sam and me. But beneath all that, a boulder sat heavy in my stomach as I scolded myself for not asking him sooner about Jordyn. I should've been out there searching for her, tearing shit up to find her—not sleeping with a vampire.

"Here we are." Sam's voice pulled me from my thoughts.

I blinked to find us outside my room. I glanced both ways. The images of Sam and me in this hallway only hours before sent a wave of flutters through my stomach, replacing the boulder that had been there a minute before.

"I meant to ask up in my apartment," Sam said. "Any dizzy spells from drinking my blood?"

That was the furthest thing from my thoughts, although now that he'd brought it up, I didn't feel queasy or dizzy. Then again, right after sex, I'd slept. Maybe that had quelled the aftereffects of drinking several drops of his blood.

I cleared my throat, hoping I could speak. "No on the dizzy spells. Any news about Jordyn?" I craned my neck up, swallowing the dryness in my throat.

He was looking at me as though he was trying to decide whether to kiss me or not. "No. Just on Roman. I'll find out what's going on." He continued to study me. "I feel regret dripping off you."

I opened my mouth to speak when the door to my room flung open.

Horror etched lines in Rianne's smooth forehead. "What the heck?" She swung her angry brown-eyed gaze from me to Sam and back to me.

"You were with him?" Her disgust was clearly evident in her tone.

Sam didn't acknowledge Rianne. Instead, he pulled out his phone and read something on it. "I'll send word once I talk to Tripp," he said, and then he swaggered away.

Rianne jerked on my arm as she pulled me into the room and slammed the door. "I've been worried sick that you'd been compelled or... argh! At least leave me a freaking note. When I saw the heap of clothes on the floor in the hall, I thought the worst." She stabbed a finger at my bed. "They are over there if you want to change."

I'd never planned to disappear with a vampire. "Calm down," I told her as I started to undress. It would be nice to put on fresh underwear. "I'm sorry. You were asleep, and I was only going to the bathroom."

I glanced at the clock on the wall, not sure how long I'd been gone. I'd woken up at eleven p.m., and it was now one thirty in the morning.

She glued her hands to her hips. "So, what? You got lost and ended up in Sam's bed?" She sized me up. "It looks to me like you two showered together. Does that mean you fucked him?"

Taking in a deep breath, I closed my eyes briefly. I didn't think she would judge me. After all, my sisters and I had all fantasized about having sex with a vampire, although Rianne had never been as into sex with a vampire as Jordyn and me. I wasn't ready to admit out loud that I'd slept with one. That would make it more real, and then I would have to deal with my actions.

I quickly changed before I grabbed a bottle of water out of the fridge.

"Well, answer me," she demanded.

I guzzled the water as fast as I could to ease the sandpapery feeling coating my throat. Maybe it was the need to taste Sam's blood again? No, I couldn't possibly want Sam's blood. If I were being honest though, I liked the taste of his blood. It was irony but sweet. Weird as fuck. None of what was happening to me with Sam was making any sense.

"Do you really want to know?"

She combed her fingers through her wet brown hair. "He's evil, sis." She smoothed her hands down her dark jeans. She'd changed into the clothes Harley had left—a white camisole underneath a red cardigan that hung over dark jeans, almost meeting her over-the-knee boots. "It's not that I'm weirded out by you sleeping with a vampire since you, me, and Jordyn have always had that on our bucket list, but Sam Mason? After what he did to me?"

"I get it, okay? But I can't help who I'm attracted to. Can we talk about this later?"

Someone knocked on the door before it opened. "It's me, Harley." She breezed in with a big smile and a tray of coffee and pastries in her hands.

I let out a soft sigh, thankful for the distraction. "It's only one thirty in the morning. Do you vamps not sleep?"

She set the tray on the bistro table. "I heard you two were awake, and no, I couldn't sleep. My date with Ben was a no-go. He's out watching your neighbor's house, and I've been keeping tabs on the situation."

"Did they find Jordyn?" I rushed out.

Rianne snagged one of the cups of coffee. "I'm going to need a full pot to calm my nerves, or maybe whiskey."

I could use some of the amber liquid myself.

Harley raised an eyebrow my way. Upon further inspection, she was dressed rather casually in crisp cotton pants instead of a skirt, a mint green button-up blouse that was tailored to her waist, and her blond hair was twisted into a bun on top of her head. I could see why Sam liked her. She was pretty, especially with the beauty mark right above her upper lip.

"Do your eyes change colors?" I asked her. "Yesterday they were blue."

She slid onto a stool and commandeered a cup of coffee. "Yeah. It depends on what I'm wearing. Today, they're green. My brother, Sawyer's, eyes do the same." She sipped on her beverage. "Did you both sleep well?"

Rianne finally sat on the remaining stool and regarded me. "Yeah, Layla, did *you* sleep well?"

I glared daggers at her. "We are not talking about this now."

Harley gave me a cheeky grin. "It's written all over your face. You slept with Sam."

"Did he tell you?" I widened my eyes in shock, and I was sure I was white as a ghost. Then again, I shouldn't be surprised. Sam had just mentioned vampires had a sixth sense.

"I know his scent," Harley said matter-of-factly.

Of course she did. I threw my hands up in the air then dragged the cushioned armchair from near my bed closer to them and sat down.

Harley smiled as she handed me the remaining cup of coffee.

The three of us sipped our drinks.

"Well, no questions, comebacks, or third degree?" I asked no one in particular. Harley didn't care what I did with Sam. "Rianne?"

"You don't want to kill Sam anymore?" Rianne asked.

I shrugged. "Ask me tomorrow." I honestly didn't know how I felt except he and I had a bond that was tying us together in more ways than I cared to count.

Harley's phone chimed, and again, I was relieved that the focus wasn't on me as Rianne and I studied the phone.

Please let it be good news about Jordyn.

"Yes, sir," Harley answered. "I will. We'll be right down." She lowered her phone. "Webb wants you two down in the war room. I think they've found your sister."

Rianne was on her feet before I could take a breath. "Alive I hope."

Harley's shoulders lifted. "Not sure."

Rianne deposited her cup on the table. "She better be." She hurried out before Harley and I had a chance to get out of our chairs.

"Are you okay?" Harley examined my neck as concern flitted across her rosy cheeks.

"That's not where he...." I couldn't bring myself to say "where he bit me."

Rianne poked her head in. "Come on."

"I'm good," I assured Harley.

Harley hooked her arm in mine. "I'm here if you ever need me."

"I'll keep that in mind. Right now, I need my other sister alive."

In less than five minutes, Harley was ushering Rianne and me into the war room, which looked like a movie theater.

Webb was leaning against a long conference table in front of a movie screen. His brows were pinched over his blue eyes, his brown hair was pulled back into a low ponytail, and his jaw was clean-shaven. He waved his hand at the empty row of chairs. "Please have a seat."

I wondered where Sam was as I lowered myself into a cushioned theater-style chair. Rianne did the same while Harley went up to Webb.

The two whispered about something, then Harley hurried out.

After Webb introduced himself to Rianne, he studied both of us for the longest time.

"Well," Rianne said. "Why are we here?" Her tone was snarky, yet I could hear the shakiness underneath.

Webb was calm, a stark contrast to when he'd about taken off my head in that interrogation room.

The side door squeaked open, and Sam and

Tripp waltzed in. Both were dressed in a black cargo uniforms, seemingly ready for battle with daggers strapped to their legs. My heart went pitter-patter at the sheer sight of Sam. I thought I was attracted to his green eyes, black hair, strong jaw, and many other physical attributes, but I was mistaken. A man in uniform with weapons clinging to him shot heat straight to my clit.

Rianne emitted a low noise as if she was ready to snap at Sam. She was probably even more irate now that she knew I'd slept with him. "The sandy-blond one is even more of a dick than Sam."

Tripp grinned. "You know I can hear you."

Rianne flipped him off.

I gave her a sidelong glance, but considering we weren't there to discuss our hatred or love for vampires, I made a mental note to ask her about Tripp later.

"Enough," Webb barked at Rianne. "You're our guest here. Don't give me a reason to treat you like you're not."

And the scary Webb was back.

Rianne sat up straighter and huffed.

Sam and Tripp took up posts off to the side of Webb, hands behind their backs, shoulders tight, spines straight, and focused on their leader.

"Why did you want to see us?" I asked, hoping to take the tension in the room down a few levels.

"We need you to look through some pictures to identify if one of the dead bodies we found at your neighbor's house is your sister."

I sucked in air as pain spread through my chest. I couldn't lose another loved one. I wasn't sure if I would survive. The loss of Mom and Dad was still gut-wrenching.

Rianne slapped a hand over her mouth.

Sam regarded me with sad eyes.

No. No. No. My stomach churned like a violent storm at sea.

I gripped Rianne's thigh. "Easy. We don't know anything yet." I should take my own advice, but that storm brewing in my stomach was getting worse the longer we waited for Webb to speak.

Webb ambled off to the side and pointed a presentation clicker at the computer sitting on the table.

A picture of our neighbor's house brightened the screen.

"Kraft and Ben have been surveilling this house all night, and they've finally gotten eyes on Roman coming and going."

Wyman *was* right. Damn. I definitely would thank him the first chance I had.

The next slide showed Roman coming out of the basement door from the back of the house with Vera on his tail.

"That's the shifter," I said. "Vera." I shivered at the mere sight of Sasquatch.

Webb nodded at me. "We did some digging, and we still don't have all the info on her, but if our research is correct, then she's part of the Gray Pack that has been all but extinct in New England for the past three centuries. She could pose a bigger problem than Roman Brown, but I'll table that for the moment. Roman hasn't returned to the house since midnight, so our team was able to get in, and I'm sorry to say we've found two dead bodies. One of them is your neighbor, and another is a human female."

I refused to believe it was Jordyn.

Rianne started to get up, but I swung out my arm. "Sit," I said in a voice that sounded much like our mom when she was mad at one of us.

She reluctantly obeyed, fisting her hands in her lap. She could be a ticking time bomb and react without thought sometimes, much like she had at the club when she'd threatened Sam. She'd backed us into a corner when hunting a few times too. And she was the crux of some of the problems we'd had with our uncles.

"I take it you have a picture to show us," I said.

Webb nodded and clicked the device. "Sam tells me Jordyn looks more like Rianne, but he can't be certain that the woman in this picture is your sister."

The image was grainy, and I couldn't tell either, at least not from where I sat. I went over to the screen and examined the young woman who had to be about the same age as Jordyn. I traced a circle around the girl's lower neck almost where it met the collarbone. "Jordyn has a birthmark here. I don't see any except the vampire bite."

Rianne sighed loudly. "Who is she? And where is our sister, then?"

"We don't know who the woman in this photo is," Webb said, "and we still don't have eyes on your sister. We tracked Roman through the woods that butt up against the property, but with the snow falling, we lost sight of him. We still have a team combing the area."

I was tired of sitting around. I needed to be out there looking too. Then a thought sideswiped me. "I might know how to find Roman." It was an insane idea, but since I'd met Sam, arrived on base, and drank Sam's blood, insane was becoming my new normal.

All heads jerked my way.

"You do?" Sam asked with his mouth partly open.

Rianne's face was twisted. "What are you, psychic?"

My sister might blow a gasket when I explained my plan. And even if it didn't work, then at least I'd done something to save Jordyn.

I opened and closed my fingers as the four of them watched me intently. "I need to drink Sam's blood." The violent storm in my stomach became an F5 tornado as nerves and nausea spun out of control. Yet no sooner than I dropped that bomb, I realized it probably wouldn't work. I'd had more of Sam's blood during my mind-blowing orgasm, but I hadn't had a vision at all.

The silence in the room was maddening.

Rianne was frozen except for her eyes, which bugged out.

Webb and Tripp didn't seem shocked, but I could tell they were thinking hard. Sam, on the other hand, just grinned. I would bet my life he was thinking about us naked.

Webb pinched his chin with between his thumb and forefinger. "Are you saying Sam's blood causes you to have visions?" He sounded like he'd experienced something similar.

I nodded. "Don't ask me to explain it. All I

know is that I saw Dr. Vieira jabbing a needle in Rianne before it happened, and other minor things."

Rianne winced. "Wait one second. You're saying you, Layla, a human, bit a vampire like a vampire would bite you? And since you did, you're seeing into the future? Nonsense."

When she articulated it that way, it sounded ludicrous. "I know it's hard to believe. I'm having all kinds of issues with it too, but I swear on our parents' souls I'm not lying."

Sam gnawed on the inside of his cheek. "Since we've swapped blood, we're connected. I feel what she feels so strongly that it knocks me off my feet sometimes."

"You're an empath," Tripp said. "Of course you would feel what she feels."

"Man, I thought that too," Sam said. "But I can feel her when she's not close by."

"You can?" I asked.

"Our father would be flipping out if he were alive," Rianne said in a low tone. "Our uncles too."

Tripp, Sam, and Webb swapped a concerned look.

I went over to Rianne and sat down. "Sis, you cannot tell our uncles." I didn't think she would. She had issues with them too. Still, if they got wind of what I'd been through, they would flip out, and we couldn't afford for them to get in the middle. Otherwise, I was afraid we would never see Jordyn again.

"Like I would," she said. "Let's find our sister."

I couldn't have agreed more.

"Layla, if you're going to drink my blood to spark a vision, you're probably going to need more than a handful of drops," Sam said.

"Which means we need Dr. Vieira to monitor you," Webb added. "Sam's blood is potent, and you're human. The side effects could be life-threatening if you drink too much at once."

I was willing to try anything to save my sister, no matter the consequences.

28

SAM

The woman was flat-out fucking nuts, but I loved her thinking. I loved her bravado and was beginning to love everything about her, right down to her soul.

She sat in the bed in the infirmary with her legs kicked out. Her auburn hair framed her face and blended with the smattering of freckles that brought out her beauty even more. Her electric-blue eyes were bright beneath her long lashes, and her bottom lip was plumper than the top as she nibbled on it.

"Are you listening to their conversation?" she asked.

I gripped the footboard. "Yep. It's not going well."

Dr. Vieira, Webb, and Tripp were talking privately in Dr. Vieira's office.

"Are you guys out of your minds?" Dr. Vieira said in a tone that bordered on a screech. "If Steven finds out about this, he's going to sever your heads. I cannot give vampire blood to a human. The Council of Elders will take my license. Layla biting Sam was one thing. That was out of my control."

"Damon." Webb's tone was placid. "There's something much bigger at play here."

"Yeah," Doc said. "We could have a dead human on our hands. She passed out once from Sam's blood, and that was from a few drops. Are you forgetting what the Mason blood can do?"

"Let's all take a breather," Tripp piped in.

Silence ensued for a beat.

"This is nuts," Dr. Vieira said.

"We get it," Tripp said calmly. "But it's not just about getting Layla's sister out alive. We also have Abbey to think about. We need to find Roman. We need to strike before he shows up here. We have a base full of people to consider too."

"Who's winning?" Layla's sultry voice drew my attention back to her.

"No one yet. Are you sure you want to do this?" The thought that Layla could die from my blood stirred an anxious feeling in my gut. The last time I felt like that was when Jo had been on her deathbed. But Layla wasn't my sister or even family.

"I have to do something, Sam. Maybe I shouldn't have said anything and just took matters into my own hands. I'm sure you wouldn't have protested." She crossed one ankle over the other, smug and playful.

I waltzed up to the side of the bed, leaned in, and touched my nose to hers. "You're dripping with lust, Layla."

Her cheeks flushed. "So, what?"

I brushed my lips over hers. "You want to fuck me so bad, you can't stand it."

She stuck out her tits. "What we did was just a one-time thing."

I snarled as my fangs lowered. "I told you, you're mine, which means nothing between us is a one-time thing."

She shivered. "You're such a caveman."

"You love it. So stop denying it."

"It's not natural for us to be together, Sam." She sounded sad and worried all of a sudden.

I pinched her chin. "Stop analyzing shit," I said, although I couldn't disagree with her.

"My family isn't going to accept you and me."

"I don't give a fuck about your family. Do you?" She gave me the impression she didn't but seemed to be looking for an excuse not to accept what was happening between us. I trailed my fangs over to her carotid artery. "Well, do you?"

She angled her neck, giving me access.

"What the heck are you doing?" Rianne screeched, sounding like nails on a chalkboard.

I didn't wince often, but Rianne was getting on my last nerve. "Don't make me compel you again."

She puffed out her average-size tits. "I dare you."

"Rianne," Layla warned.

She skirted the bed to stand on the other side, folding her arms, almost pouting. "I'm not putting up with his shit. And I don't like this. You can't drink his blood. You heard Webb. It's life-threatening. I'm not going to lose another sister."

Layla grabbed her hand. "I'll be fine. I'm doing this for Jordyn."

Rianne pursed her thick lips, her brown eyes narrowing. "Let's get out of here. Let's join the search."

"We will once I can locate Roman or Jordyn," Layla said through gritted teeth. "It shouldn't take long. The last vision I had came immediately, and that was after I walked out of the elevator."

"You didn't have any after we f—"

"No, Sam!" Layla blurted out.

Rianne gave me a disgusted snarl. "I'm out of here." She stormed off.

"I should go after her," Layla said. "She can be quite the hothead when she doesn't get her way." She started to swing her legs over the bed when Dr. Vieira strutted in, frustration emanating from him.

I guessed he'd lost the argument.

He settled alongside me with his lips mashed into a thin line. "Layla, I want to prepare you for what could go wrong in this process. Humans cannot tolerate ingesting human blood, let alone vampire blood." He pinned soft brown eyes on Layla. "But more than that, the Mason blood has a powerful kick that could have some deadly side effects."

Layla swung her pensive gaze to me then back to Doc. "Is there a cutoff amount that would put me in danger? I don't think I need a lot. And whether I get sick or not, or die or not, I have to do this. I won't be able to live with myself if something happens to Jordyn."

Dr. Vieira was about to speak when Layla's phone rang. She paled as she lifted it off her lap. "I think it's Roman." Her pulse increased. "It's not time for him to call."

The phone kept ringing.

She blew out a breath. "Hello."

"Layla," Roman said. "I'm disappointed in you."

Doc and I had no problem hearing him.

She locked eyes with me. "What are you talking about?"

Telepathically, I said to Doc, *Can you get Tripp or Webb?*

He rushed out of the room, and Webb came in a flash.

"You gave me up to Mason. You told him what I wanted."

"What?" Her mouth was ajar. "I've done no such thing."

"Put me on speaker. I know one of the vampires is with you, or if you're in bed with Sam, then put him on."

Her knuckles were white as she gripped the phone like she was trying to squeeze Roman out of it.

I plucked it from her and put it on speaker. "Get to the point, asshole."

Webb listened intently.

"Mason, glad you could join us." Roman's

cocksure attitude was making me dig my nails into the palms of my hands. "Now that we are out in the open, I'm pleased to inform you that you'll never see your half-breed again, nor will Layla see her sister. Oh, and Vera is over the moon about that too, Layla. You know how she's been salivating to have Jordyn as her next meal."

Layla screamed bloody murder. "I will gut you, vampire, and feed your insides to the crows.!"

Roman roared with laughter. "Tsk. Tsk. Tsk. You stand no chance in doing so. Neither do the brave men of the vampire military. I don't say that to be cocky. I'm stating a fact. The vampire government is going to shit their pants when they learn what I have in my back pocket."

Webb and I exchanged a questioning look. We knew that Ben wasn't exactly something to get the vampire government up in arms. They already knew about him, anyway.

"Seems to me you're gloating," I said. "And is that last statement supposed to scare us?"

Roman got off on threats. He was the type that lived for them. I only knew that because in a way, we were alike. Others' fears and threats were two catalysts that drove me into action.

"It should," Roman said.

"Surely, you didn't call just to dangle a threat," I said. "You want something."

Roman let out a breath. "Smart man. Oh, I want Abbey, and I'll get her—but I've decided I want you too. I have a separate plan for you."

Webb was about to crush the footboard of the bed at the mention of Abbey.

"Who's your source? Who told you about Abbey?" I knew he wouldn't tell me, but I had to ask.

"I thought my source was giving me a line of bullshit when I heard about this little girl who had these mind-blowing powers, and she isn't even a vampire yet," he said. "But Mason, you should know I won't give up my source. However, I will tell you, your half-breed confirmed Abbey is under your protection. Such a shame he talked so easily."

Webb growled.

"What do you want with me?" I asked. I was furious, but showing my anger wouldn't solve anything.

"That's a surprise," Roman said. "I will let Jordyn and your half-breed go if you walk over to my side freely. No team of Navy SEALs. No sinister plot to storm in and save the day. You come into my camp of your own free will. If you do, I promise I'll let them go."

Webb shook his head and mouthed, "No way."

It seemed too easy. Roman was up to something. But I wasn't confident in Layla's plan. I was also worried something would happen to her. Besides, if he wasn't blowing smoke up my ass and really wanted me in his camp, I could find out more about his plans.

"On one condition. Let Jordyn go before I even walk over to your side."

The clanging of metal hitting metal sounded in the background. "Not a chance in hell."

I itched to punch a wall or something since I couldn't carve out Roman's heart. Not yet, anyway. "Name the time and place."

He belted out a laugh. "I knew you would see it my way. Meet me at Layla's house in four hours." Then the line went dead as Layla's phone screen returned to the picture of her and her sisters.

I held up my hand at Webb. "I'm doing this. Besides, it's a trap."

Layla knitted her eyebrows. "It is? I don't believe it is. Roman told me you were worth a lot of money."

"Whether it is or isn't, we need to prepare as if it is a trap," Webb said. "Our window has just been reduced from eight hours to four. I need to call Steven."

"Webb," I said. "I think it's time you take Abbey and Jo to Maine."

"About that. We've changed plans. Your father wants them at vampire headquarters in Boston. Jo and I agree that it's the best place for her and Abbey. I need to be here anyway." He stormed out.

"It's time I drink your blood," Layla said. "I had a vision with a tiny amount. Maybe that could happen again without me drinking a boatload. If we can find Roman in the next two hours, then you have the advantage, and you wouldn't have to become his prisoner."

She had a point. Plus, she'd drunk from me during sex, and she hadn't had a reaction like she had the first time. Maybe her system was getting acclimated to my blood.

Before I could respond, she snagged one of the daggers from my leg. "Give me your wrist. This is my decision, and I don't care what Dr. Vieira or anyone says." Her demanding tone was turning me on.

Like a smitten fool, I extended my arm.

The minute she slit my wrist, her eyes dilated with a hunger I'd only seen in vampires. For a split second, my heart stopped. How could a human be thirsty for vampire blood?

But that question went out the window when she dropped the dagger and clamped her mouth down over the cut. I lost track of where I was. The mere act of her taking my blood was more erotic than her sucking my dick.

I stroked her hair with my free hand. "Take it slow, baby doll." I trailed my tongue down her neck, my gums pounding, my bloodthirst strong.

She continued to suck as the need to taste her was driving me mad. But it wasn't about me.

She swirled her tongue around my wrist before she eased up and smiled.

The sight of my blood smeared on her lips made my heart skip a beat. She looked even more beautiful. "What?" she asked innocently.

I wanted to ask her if she felt queasy or dizzy, but the only thing on my mind was kissing her. I mashed my mouth to hers and dove in until Tripp cleared his throat.

"We have a problem. Rianne sped off base in Layla's car."

Layla stiffened as she pulled away. "We need to go after her. It's snowing and the middle of the night."

"How did Rianne get off base? We have guards everywhere," I said.

Tripp clenched his jaw. "She wanted fresh air. I had a guard take her outside. Next thing, she's driving off."

Layla snapped her spine straight. "She probably hotwired the car. But we have a bigger problem. She's probably heading to our house, which means she could walk right into Roman's hands."

I was ready to fill Tripp in on Roman's call when he held up his hand. "Webb updated your father and me about Roman's call."

Layla paled. "Please take me to my house. We have to stop her."

I was tempted to tell her no, chain her up, and keep her safe, but I was finding that the Aberdeen sisters were stubborn. And if the tables were turned, and someone told me to stay put when my sister's life could be in danger, I would tell them to fuck off.

Tripp rubbed his jaw. "Kraft and Olivia are combing the woods behind Layla's house for any signs of Ben, Jordyn, Roman, and his men. So far nothing. But since he's given us four hours, we still have time to stop Rianne. Suit her up," he said to me. "The last thing we need is three Aberdeens dead or missing."

Layla winced on the last part of his statement.

"Oh, one more thing, Sam," Tripp said. "Check in with me when you get there. And watch your six out there."

"Always do." I grabbed Layla's hand as we followed Tripp out.

SAM

An hour later, I was navigating the snow-covered streets with Layla fidgeting in her seat. Her sweet fragrance infused the inside of the Hummer, driving me to want to pull over and strip her naked. How sexy she looked with weapons strapped to her legs and waist didn't help. Before we left, she'd insisted on having her family heirloom dagger, which we'd given her. I was confident I could trust her not to stab me. If she did try, she wouldn't succeed, and I believed she knew that.

Nevertheless, I was beginning to realize it was more than her physical appearance that was doing a number on my psyche. Her very essence was cracking through the walls I'd built, and before long she would have a tight grip on not only my heart, but my soul. She was becoming the yin to my yang, the woman who I could see myself spending eternity with.

She glanced out the passenger window as we passed storefronts and office buildings. "The snow hasn't let up. I wonder if Rianne even made it to the house in that crap car of ours."

Forecasters predicted blizzard conditions, but the plows were out and doing a decent job of clearing the streets. However, the roads leading out of the city might be a different story.

Layla puffed out her cheeks. "Sam, I have a craving for more of your blood."

I jerked my head at her. "Explain." No way was she morphing into a vampire, though I couldn't help but remember when Jo had craved blood as a human. At first, I'd thought my sister was nuts. We didn't know it at the time, but that had been a sign she'd carried the vampire gene.

Layla's blue eyes met mine. "I want more blood. Yours. I don't know why." She sucked in air. "This is insane. Crazy. Fucked up. I'm losing my mind."

I felt her face. "Do you have a fever?" I remember Jo telling me she had a high fever during the change. Then again, Layla couldn't become a vampire even if she did carry the vampire gene. The process to turn involved her drinking her father's blood, and that couldn't happen for two reasons. One, he was dead, and two, if he were alive, he had to be a vampire. She was warm to the touch, but not feverish. "Do your gums hurt?"

"No. I can't explain it except that it's like your blood is a drug or something."

"Not surprised. That's one reason people like Roman run blood cartels. They sell blood like mine."

"But you and your family are one of a kind when it comes to your abilities and power. Are there other vampires that fit the bill like you?"

"Every vampire on the SEAL team has potent blood—not as strong as mine, but strong just the same. That's one of the reasons the Council of Elders recruited them into the military."

I turned down a dark road as the Hummer's headlights lit the way. "Are you sure you don't have vampire DNA in you?"

"Absolutely not. My parents would've told me." She sounded horrified.

"Maybe your parents didn't want to tell you."

Her luscious lips parted. "They wouldn't lie about that. We hunt vampires."

A mile down the winding road, the dense trees that created a tunnel gave way to open ground with three homes on the right that had several acres of land in between them.

She pointed to the middle house. "Rianne is here."

I wheeled into the gravel driveway as snow crunched beneath the tires. I threw the Hummer in park behind the Nissan and scanned the eerily quiet area as far as I could in between the snowfall.

"Which house is Gerald's?"

She flicked her thumb to her right. "That one."

I glanced at the other house on the left. "Who lives there?"

"An elderly couple. They're at their vacation home in Florida." She winced.

"What is it?"

"My head is hurting all of a sudden."

I felt her face once again. "You're sweating like a pig." *Fuck.*

She whipped out her dagger with her family's crest on it from the sheath on her leg. "Blood, Sam."

I could feel my forehead creasing. I would swear she was turning into a vampire. "You realize too much of my blood might harm you."

She ignored me, pushed up the sleeve on my jacket, and slit my wrist open. Within a nanosecond, she was sucking away like a baby on a bottle.

I pressed on my earpiece. "Kraft, come in." Tripp had said he and Olivia were scouring the woods.

"Go," Kraft's voice said in my ear.

"I'm at Layla's house. Where are you?"

"Olivia and I are deep into the forest but heading your way." Then he clicked off.

I scanned the area as well as I could with Layla suckling on me. We had two hours left before our official four-hour deadline. Between Layla suiting up and listening to Webb outline the plan to combat Roman in the event he showed up on base, we'd lost more time than I had wanted.

"Baby doll, enough." I pulled my wrist away, and she snarled. I definitely needed to talk to Doc about her need to drink vampire blood. "We need to move."

The plan was for Kraft and me to hang around there while Olivia took the sisters back to base before the party started.

Layla regarded me with a faraway glint in her eyes.

I waved my hand in front of her. "Layla."

She blinked, glanced at the house, and then was out of the Hummer before I could stop her.

I bolted after her as she ran like a lion chasing a gazelle and into the house when a blood-curdling scream tore through the early morning hours, practically shattering the windows.

I ran down a hall, and the scent of petroleum oil hit me like a brain freeze from eating ice cream too quickly. Another scream almost blew my eardrums out of my ears. I rushed down the stairs and into the basement.

"Layla," I called as I rounded the banister.

She stood with her shoulders up to her ears, her tension thick, her fear overpowering. She slid to one side as I approached.

Holy fuck.

Rianne was tied to a chair wrapped in C-4, eyes wide and red, panic pouring off her.

Layla went to rip the tape off her mouth.

"Don't touch her," I snapped hard. Any little movement could set it off or trip the wire attached to the timer. We had ten minutes to disengage the bomb.

My phone rang with an unknown number. I was keen on ignoring it, not sure if answering it would trigger something on the timer.

"We need to get her out of that," Layla said through clenched teeth. That faraway look in her eyes was still there. "The house is going to blow."

The ringing stopped only to start up again. "What!" I barked.

"Mason." Roman's tone was smug. "I see you arrived early."

My fangs slid out as I growled. "Your plan was to blow me up? That was your genius plan for me? You're more of an idiot than I thought. You know a bomb wouldn't do much to me."

"No shit," he said. "But it will slow you down. Too bad you didn't bring more of your team."

The fucker was planning on attacking the naval base. At least now we had confirmation.

"Oh, and what a nice surprise to have another Aberdeen sister walk right into our arms. You should thank me, Mason. I'm ridding the planet of vampire hunters," Roman said as though he was proud of himself. "But I sense you'll save them. Anyway, from my calculations, you have ten minutes to diffuse the timer. Then boom." Roman belted out an evil laugh.

Layla seemed to snap out of that other world she'd been in and flinched.

"See you soon." Roman said. The line went dead.

I squatted in front of Rianne and examined the wires leading into the timer.

"Tripp, come in," I said into my earpiece.

"Go," he said.

"This was all a diversion. But bad news. Rianne is strapped with C-4 in the basement of Layla's house. We have nine minutes. I'll try my darndest to diffuse it. Have Jo and Abbey left base?"

"She and Abbey left with two guards," Tripp said. "I'll have Sawyer walk you through disarming it."

"Sam," Sawyer said. "Send me a pic."

I snapped one with my phone and sent it to him. "Hurry the fuck up, man." I turned to Layla. "Get out of the house."

"I'm not leaving." Layla stared at Rianne. "She dies, I do too."

Admirable. But she was getting out if I had to drag her. "Baby doll. Please. I can probably survive an explosion of this magnitude, but you can't. I can't lose you."

Her jaw came unhinged. "Are you high on oil fumes, or are you just trying to coax me into leaving?"

"Whatever works," I said, although I couldn't lose her—that much was true.

She sneered and crossed her arms over her chest. "No."

Sawyer returned. "You need to cut both the green and red wires at the same time."

I pulled out a dagger. "Simple enough."

"No! Wait." Sawyer's voice was high-pitched.

"Man, we have eight minutes." I tried like a motherfucker to keep my voice calm. "Hurry up."

Rianne was sweating, crying, and pissing her pants.

I swallowed thickly. I felt more of her terror than my own. I wasn't frightened of much, but I didn't exactly want to get blown to smithereens even if I didn't die.

"Okay," Sawyer said. "I don't see a blue wire, which is supposed to diffuse the timer."

I didn't either. Before I could respond to him, Layla was cutting all the wires.

Rianne's eyebrows disappeared into her hairline.

Mine did too. "What the...? Are you nuts, woman?"

Layla ripped the tape off Rianne, ignoring me.

Rianne choked and gagged. "There's another bomb." She pointed to the oil tank.

I stalked over to it, my mind still reeling from

what Layla had done. Sure enough, Rianne was right. "One minute. Get out of the house now!"

I ripped Rianne from the chair. "Layla, run!"

Obeying, Layla sprinted up the stairs.

I rushed up as fast as I could. When I turned the corner, the last thing I saw was Layla running out the front door before *boom!*

30

LAYLA

The impact of the explosion threw me forward. I soared over the porch, bushes, and landscape lights. I stretched out my arms and hands, hoping I could break my fall, hoping the snow would cushion me too.

I landed with a thud on the cold, hard ground as another explosion rocked the earth.

My ears rang as pain pierced my body. I tried to get up, but my stomach had other plans. I puked for the umpteenth time it seemed. My head pounded as though someone had taken a sledge-hammer to it. Then tears shot out, hot and painful. I had no idea what was happening to me. I wasn't one to feel sorry for myself, but one bad thing after another had happened. It wasn't only the explosion or Jordyn getting kidnapped. My body was changing, my mind was a complete and utter mess, and I couldn't make sense as to why I craved Sam's blood, something fierce. That was fucked up on all levels.

Stop whining and get your ass up.

I crawled to my feet and stumbled. I opened and closed my mouth to clear the ringing, but it was no use. My hearing was probably damaged.

As I turned around, a muffled voice floated on the wind. Panic clutched my gut like someone had their hand in me, stealing every ounce of breath I had. I searched in all directions but couldn't see clearly enough with the snow falling, or maybe my vision was going.

I wanted to scream bloody murder. I wanted to rewind back to several weeks ago and tell Dowell or Wyman or whatever the heck his name was to shove the job up his small ass. If we'd never taken the job, Jordyn wouldn't be in the hands of a shifter who wanted to rip out her throat. Rianne wouldn't be buried under burning rubble, and I wouldn't feel like I was turning into the very creature I hated and wanted dead.

I swallowed the clump of sand in my throat as I continued to search all around me.

"If that's you, Roman, come and get me, asshole!" I shouted as loud as I could.

I stood for a beat as dead silence ensued. Another *pop, pop, pop* ripped through the air before flames shot up through the wreckage that used to be the house.

I ran toward the rubble when hands grabbed me from behind.

I whirled around, kicking and screaming.

"Easy," Kraft said as he held me to his big body.

"Sam and Rianne are in there," I cried. "I can't lose my sister." This was all my fault. I vowed if we got out of this mess alive, I would leave this city and never look back.

The lady guard, Brock, who had escorted me from the base gate that day, rushed up to Kraft and me just as a tall figure emerged like a phoenix rising out of the ashes.

My jaw hit the ground. How could it be? Sure, vampires didn't die easily, but no way could anyone have survived that explosion.

Sam's clothes were singed, his face covered in soot, his silver eyes a beacon in the waning night, and he was carrying Rianne's limp body.

I shrugged out of Kraft's hold.

"She's alive," Sam said.

I wanted to throw myself at him. Instead, I smoothed a hand over Rianne's head. "Sis."

Sam carried her over to the Hummer, which surprisingly was in one piece. "She'll be fine."

"How?" The question was more for me than anyone.

After he set Rianne in the backseat, he came up to me, smelling like fire and brimstone. He pushed hair off my forehead before examining me from head to toe. "Are you okay?"

I nodded, blinking away tears. "Thank you for saving her."

He tugged me to him and banded his arms around me.

We stood like that for a beat, not saying a word until Kraft cleared his throat. "We should get moving."

Sam kissed my hair then edged back and went into soldier mode. "We need to return to base. This was all a ploy. He wanted to draw me out and thought our whole team would come." Sam touched his ear. "I lost my comm. Olivia, can you call Tripp?"

Olivia Brock. Her first name was pretty.

Olivia whipped out her phone. In two seconds, Tripp's voice came through the speaker. "Give me the rundown."

"There were two bombs," Sam said. "Layla managed to diffuse one, and the other... well, everyone is alive."

"Thank fuck. It's all quiet here," Tripp said. "Webb and I have the place ready. Jo and Abbey are on their way to vampire headquarters in Boston. We're ready if Roman shows up."

Sam threaded his hands through his ash-and-snow-covered hair, sighing. "We're on our way."

"Sam," Tripp said, "before you leave the area, do one last sweep of the homes. Let's be sure Ben or Jordyn are not tied up in one of them."

"Copy that," Sam said.

Tripp hung up, and Olivia pocketed her phone. The three of them scanned the property far and wide.

"We only found tracks and a blood trail deep in the woods that led to an empty shack," Olivia said. "We searched the homes along the road as well. Nothing."

"We know Roman was here because of the bombs," I said. "Maybe Tripp is onto something. Maybe Roman left Jordyn and Ben somewhere nearby while he fights his way into the naval base."

Sam growled. "Kraft and I will do a quick sweep of the homes. Olivia, can you take Layla and

Rianne back to base? Call Kraft if you run into problems."

I was tempted to stay and help, but I needed to make sure Rianne was okay.

As if Sam knew the debate raging in my head, he said, "We'll be right behind you. This won't take long."

Olivia headed over to the Hummer. "Layla, let's go. I want to make sure we're there before Roman."

Sam kissed me hard and fast on the lips before he stalked away. I watched him and Kraft fade into the darkness, then I hurried into the backseat beside Rianne.

Once Olivia was speeding down the road like a NASCAR driver, I felt along Rianne's carotid artery. I sighed when her pulse beat lightly against my fingers.

"Sam likes you a lot," Olivia announced.

"I think he likes my blood more," I muttered as I held Rianne's hand, staring out at the passing trees. That was the only thing that made sense to me. We'd only known each other for a mere twenty-four hours, and love didn't just spark in an instant—or maybe it did with vampires. *Love? Ha.* I'd never been in love before. I'd had a crush on a boy in my freshman year of high school until he transferred out. That had been the extent of falling for someone.

Olivia's dark eyes met my blue ones in the rearview mirror. "It's more than that, so I'm going to give you some unsolicited advice. Hurt him, and you'll have me to deal with."

I was more afraid of how I was feeling and the changes I felt my body going through than her idle threat. Visions. Blood cravings. Those weren't normal for a human. Maybe Sam was right. I could have vampire DNA. But I refused to believe that my lineage was born from vampires.

I shuddered. "Sam thinks I have vampire DNA."

"Are you craving blood?" Olivia asked.

"Yes."

Her worried gaze in the rearview mirror was like a punch to the gut, but my problems vanished when she slammed on the brakes and the Hummer fishtailed on the road leading into base. "We're too late. Tripp, come in," Olivia said into her comm.

I glanced out the windshield in between the front seats. A guard was lying on the ground.

"Tripp, come in." Olivia growled her frustration. *Shit.* "Kraft." A beat passed. "Roman's on base. Get back here now. We're under attack."

I was ninety percent sure it was Roman, but one man down didn't mean Roman was there. "How do you know it's Roman?" The military vampires could have other enemies too.

She drove into a parking lot of an army thrift store and parked around the building. "Maybe it's your uncles."

My limbs locked. That was a possibility. "If my uncles were here that guard would be burned to a crisp." Uncle Jack's weapon of choice was a flamethrower. He felt the easiest way to get rid of vampires was to set them on fire.

"I need to see what we're up against. Stay here." She got out of the Hummer and took off.

I was about to jump into the driver's seat when Rianne stirred. She sat up, holding her head. "Where's Sam? Is he alive?" She sounded concerned for the vampire.

The sigh that came out of me shook my body. I knew she had a pulse, but I didn't expect her to wake up as if nothing happened to her, although she looked like death, covered in soot and with a small amount of blood oozing from the cut on her forehead.

"I'm thrilled and shocked you made it out of that rubble."

"Sam saved my life." She glanced through the windshield. "Where are we?"

"We're outside the naval base. They're under attack. Sam is fine." I opened the door. "I'm taking you to a hospital to get checked out." It seemed like the best option since we probably couldn't get to Dr. Vieira.

She rubbed her head. "Don't. I'm good. And if they're under attack, then they need our help."

That sounded odd coming from her. Hell, it was weird that we were starting to grow close to the military vampires, or at least I was. "You can't fight."

She winced. "Maybe you're right. My head hurts. Did we find Jordyn?"

"Not yet. What happened at the house? Was Roman there?"

"Everything happened so fast. I didn't see him but heard Jordyn's voice before some big-ass woman grabbed me then knocked me out. When I came to, I was in the chair with C-4, and she was setting the timer on the bomb on the oil tank."

"That had to be the shifter Vera."

Olivia returned, her features pinched.

I climbed out. "What did you find?"

She hurried to the back of the Hummer and threw open the door, then began loading up on grenades and other weapons. "We have vampires roaming the woods and going through the homes. Roman does have an army."

I took comfort that it wasn't my uncles. "He's looking for Abbey," I said even though all of us knew that to be true. Thankfully, Jo had taken Abbey somewhere safe.

I reached into a duffel bag to grab a grenade or two when Olivia grasped my wrist. "I want to fight," I told her. "If Roman is here, then Jordyn is too." At least I hoped she was.

Olivia's expression was circumspect as her vampire black eyes glinted in the glow of the light from inside the Hummer.

"I know how to fight," I assured her. I was going in whether she liked it or not.

Rianne hopped out of the vehicle on wobbly legs. "What can I do? I would fight, but I don't think I'm in any shape to."

Olivia secured what looked to be a police baton to her belt. "Take the Hummer up to the top of the road and wait for Sam and Kraft. When they get here, tell them to use the west entrance. I tried to get them on the comm again, but they're not answering."

A small pang of worry pinched me at the thought that Sam could be dead. But that was impossible. The vampire had survived an explosion. "Do you think Roman's men got to them?"

Olivia strapped grenades to the belt I had around me that could hold several weapons. "Possibly." She picked up one of two crossbows and handed me one. "Do you know how to use one of these?"

I briefly regarded Rianne, who pouted, seemingly jealous that I was going to use one of her coveted weapons. "Rianne is better with a crossbow than me, but I know how to use it."

Once we were armed, Olivia handed her phone to Rianne and proceeded to give Rianne her password. "Find Steven Mason's number in my contacts and call him. Let him know what's happening just in case Webb or Tripp can't get word to him. Also ask if Jo and Abbey made it safely. Got it?"

Rianne nodded.

"Layla, you might be experienced at this, but I doubt you've fought with several vampires at one time, so I need you to follow my lead. Is that clear?" Olivia asked.

"Crystal," I said, even though in my experience, our family had battled a handful at one time, not several, and I would guess Roman had more than five vampires with him. Plus, if Vera was part of Roman's team, and I was sure she was, then the shifter brought a whole different dynamic to the fight—one I had no experience in fighting.

"Stay alive," Rianne said as she got behind the wheel.

I planned to as a surge of adrenaline zipped through me, and as soon as Olivia and I were on a narrow path leading into the dense woods that separated the naval base from human civilization, a ball of nerves tightened in my stomach.

Snow fluttered to the ground from the tree limbs above as I trailed behind Olivia with my crossbow in front of me, ready to fire at the first sign of a threat. Anxiety continued to mix with excitement as we trudged through the woods. It had been a while since I'd hunted vampires, and I couldn't help but think of Dad. But this wasn't the time to take a trip down memory lane.

Raising a fisted hand, Olivia came to an abrupt stop.

I swallowed down the nerves. I was ready to find a warm beach, soft sand, salt air, and a bar that would serve me whiskey around the clock.

We scanned the area, aiming our crossbows in all directions. I opened my senses—listening, sniffing as though I could scent a vampire, and sharpened my vision.

"Anything?" I whispered. Of course, her senses were a hundred times better than mine.

"No." She waved her hand forward as we pressed on.

I looked behind me, to my left, and to my right. When I craned my neck upward, snowflakes fell and landed on my face. I righted my head and blinked. When I did, Jordyn flashed before me.

I sucked in cold air.

Olivia spun on her heel, aiming the crossbow at me. "What is it?" Her gaze darted in all directions.

"Jordyn." I swallowed. "She's here."

Olivia didn't bat an eye or look surprised. "You had a vision. Where?"

It sounded odd to hear her say I had a vision, which I did, but I shook off the craziness. I had a vision when I'd been sucking on Sam's wrist too. I saw Rianne strapped to the chair. *Mind-blowing.* I would have plenty of time later to dissect what was happening to me. "Outside the main building, under the portico."

She kept scanning the woods up and down and far and wide with a mechanical precision. "What else do you see?"

I blinked again, and that time I kept my eyes closed for a brief moment. But I got nothing.

A branch snapped, and I spun on my heel, the bow ready to fire. All I saw were fangs before a burly vampire stalked toward us with daggers in both hands. Then another emerged and another.

Olivia dove into action, firing her crossbow. "Shoot to kill. These arrows are cobalt and laced with an endotoxin that will stop them until the cobalt burns through their hearts."

The vampire she shot went down. I'd counted three enemies. That meant two were left. I fired at the one who had to be seven feet or maybe as tall as the tree I was next to. Either way, I fired again, my pulse ramming against my ribs.

The brown-haired vampire laughed, baring his fangs. "You better run, human. Because when I sink my fangs into you, you'll be begging me to stop."

I backed away and loaded the bow as fast as I could then fired again, and that time I aimed for his groin. He fell to his knees and roared so loud the ground shook.

Grunts sounded as Olivia battled the remaining vampire, but then a fourth one emerged with a sword, the blade long, no doubt sharp and deadly.

I tried to load my crossbow, but I was too late. The fourth vamp got close enough to swing his sword, which was on a collision course with my neck. I might not have the advantage with weapons, but I was quick on my feet. I shifted to one side and ducked.

He growled, his fangs dripping with venom, his eyes liquid black.

I pulled a grenade from my belt, ready to pull the pin. He grinned as though he'd seen the funniest thing. Then he dropped his sword, sniffed the air, and grinned wider. "A treat I wasn't expecting."

"Not tonight, vampire."

I tried to dodge him again, but he was quicker. He lunged at me, tackling me to the ground, and the grenade fell out of my hands. I landed on my back with an oomph. The air was punched from my lungs, and it was all I could do to breathe. Before I could get my lungs working, he hovered over me with his fangs primed to tear my neck off.

I fumbled for the daggers in the sheaths on my legs, but I couldn't get my hands on either one before he sunk his fangs into me.

I screamed, the sound echoing through the dense landscape. "You motherfucker!"

He sucked on me like a starving creature. I had no doubt he was hungry for human blood. I took in a deep breath and managed to pull the dagger free.

The trees above started to fade. Dizziness set in the more he drank from me. Before he took another pull, I rammed the blade into his neck. He released me, startled, which gave me a small opening to push him off me.

I propelled to my feet, and before he had a chance to react, I drove the blade straight through his eye. He snarled as my blood dripped from his fangs, but I didn't give him any window to get revenge. With the remaining grenade strapped to my belt, I pulled the pin, stuffed it in his mouth, and ran just as Olivia severed off the head of her attacker with a sword.

A boom shook the earth.

Blood and brains shot out, covering the pristine white snow in red. Olivia was thrown a few feet past me, but then she was upright and running toward the muted light.

I ran like my life depended on it, not caring if another vampire jumped out at me. I had to save Jordyn. The trees began to thin, and the top of the main building emerged. When we finally reached where the woods ended and the open landscape began, my vision blurred.

I was not prepared for the scene before me.

31

LAYLA

I clenched my teeth as I surveyed the scene through a cluster of trees. A spotlight shone, highlighting the bodies scattered over the snowy open area that led up to the main building. A sickening feeling seized my stomach, and the vise-like grip grew tighter when I spotted Roman standing on top of an SUV. He was dressed in a sharp pin-striped suit, of all things, his blond hair was styled back as though he'd had it done just for the occasion, and he was holding a sword like he was some sort of sentinel, standing watch.

When my gaze bounced past him, I gulped in cold air.

Olivia tugged me down behind a wide tree trunk. "Do not engage."

I couldn't even if I wanted to. My limbs were locked tight.

Ever so slowly, I peered around the tree to make sure I wasn't imagining things. Jordyn was cloaked in a bomb, much like Rianne had been. Vera stood by Jordyn's side, her head moving in one direction then the other. Given she was a shifter, I was sure she could scent some fresh meat had arrived—meaning us.

"I smell you, Layla." Roman twirled like a ballerina on stage. Okay, he could too.

Movement caught my eye near the SUV before a guy decked out in all black, including a ski cap, strutted up and said something to Roman.

Olivia made a satisfied noise.

I plastered my back against the spiky bark of the tree. "What is it?"

"They came up empty on finding Abbey," she whispered.

"Oh, Layla," Roman singsonged. "I want Abbey. You're going to tell me where she is. If you don't, then I have no choice but to blow your sister to smithereens. That would make two sisters dead. I'm sure you don't want that."

Olivia and I exchanged a smug look. Roman had no clue Rianne was alive. I would do whatever it took to ensure Jordyn was breathing when the shitstorm was all over with.

"You see," Roman continued, "I have someone here you might want to say goodbye to before he suffers a brutal and agonizing death." Roman laughed, evil and ominous. "Oh, I'm going to have so much fun."

I balled my hands into fists and dug my nails into my palms. The vampire was maddening. "You don't think he has Sam?" Roman had to have someone he thought I cared about. Then again, he wouldn't know that applied to Sam. Maybe that I was attracted to him, but caring? No way. I swallowed the thought that I'd just admitted to myself that I cared for Sam Mason. I puffed out my cheeks, deciding I would deal with that feeling later.

Olivia shook her head once. "No. The only way anyone could capture Sam would be to knock him out or cage him in a shit ton of cobalt."

Or burn him. Uncle Jack's weapon could spit fire from a good distance. But we weren't dealing with my uncle. We were dealing with an extremely cunning vampire.

Once again, I stole a look at Roman.

He waved his sword at the man in black, who in turn opened the back door of the SUV. A tall figure with reddish-brown hair that curled at his nape stepped out of the SUV.

I swallowed a gasp.

Olivia took a quick peek. "Who is he?"

"My uncle Ray." Well, the situation just got interesting and worse, if I had to guess. If Uncle Ray was here, that meant Uncle Jack was too, and maybe even the rest of the clan—cousins, lots of cousins. Between my uncles, they had ten kids in total, mostly boys.

Uncle Ray didn't have a frightened bone in his body, not until a very large white-haired wolf with bright red eyes trotted up from around the SUV. I checked on Jordyn, who was as stiff as a board with Vera still standing guard. So that wolf wasn't Vera. Then again, in wolf form, Vera would have a dark coat of fur like her hair.

Olivia muttered, "Things are about to get messy. Where there is one wolf, there's an entire pack."

I wouldn't agree with her. When I met Vera, she'd been the lone wolf to my knowledge, unless her pack had been surrounding the house.

"The question is what are shifters doing with Roman?" she wondered.

"The Gray Pack, right?" I said, remembering that Webb had said they had been extinct for three centuries, and that Vera could be a bigger problem.

"Yeah. We're learning they take no prisoners," she said.

We needed to end this crap and save Jordyn.

I peered around the tree trunk.

Uncle Ray tracked the wolf until the beast sat on his haunches about a car length from the SUV and observed his surroundings. Roman's man in black said something to the vampire then took off down the road that led to the main gate.

Roman ran the blade over Uncle Ray's head. "Are you scared, human?"

"Fuck you," my uncle spat at Roman. "You have no idea who you're dealing with."

If I had never met Roman or Sam or any of the vampire Navy SEALs, I would've supported that statement. But Uncle Ray was in for a rude awakening. As long as my family had been hunting vampires, we'd never come face-to-face with a shifter or powerful vampires like Sam and his family.

Roman jumped down off the hood of the SUV, landing on his feet with ease. His fangs gleamed in the spray of light from the spotlight off the building, as he got nose to nose with Uncle Ray. "Humans don't scare me, not even ones who hunt vampires."

If my uncle pissed off Roman, he could give the order to blow up Jordyn. "I'm going out there."

Olivia caught my arm. "Not on my watch."

"I can't watch my sister die." I shrugged her off and was about to go blazing out when Sam said, "Do not walk out there."

I spun around, looking in all directions.

"What is it?" Olivia listened.

"Sam." I searched high up in the trees. "Did you hear him?"

"No." She checked her earpiece. "Crap, my comm must've fallen out when I was fighting."

Maybe I was hearing things. I wouldn't be surprised if I was, especially with the weird supernatural experiences I'd been having. Again, I started for my uncle.

"Layla, stay put." Sam's tone was deep and commanding.

"Fuck you," I said low but out loud.

"Baby doll, you'll have plenty of time to fuck me. But right now, I need you to work with me. I'm on top of the main building. Do not look over here."

Of course, I looked immediately, but I didn't see Sam. "How can I hear you?"

"We'll talk about that later. Can you do me a favor?"

I huffed as Olivia watched me intently. "What?" I asked Sam.

Olivia glanced into the woods and bobbed her head.

"Is he talking to you too?" I asked. I should've been paying attention to what Roman and the white-haired shifter were doing, but I was stymied that Sam was speaking to me telepathically.

I had no doubt in my mind that I was morphing into a vampire. I had to be.

You need to save your sister, my inner voice supplied.

"Oh, Layla." Roman had that patronizing tone again. "I'm waiting. If you don't come out in five seconds, your uncle will suffer a slow death."

I was tempted to laugh. If anyone in the family had balls, it was Uncle Ray. Oh, Uncle Jack certainly had them, but Ray was more twisted in his scheming. He'd been the one to roast vampires for dinner. Seriously, the man ate them after he fried them over a pit like pigs.

At that thought, I was ready to puke again.

"Layla," Olivia whispered. "Listen to Sam. I need to meet Tripp on the other side of the property. Whatever you do, do not engage." Then she took off in the same direction we'd come from.

Great. Was I supposed to stand there like a beacon in the night?

I inhaled. "If you have a plan, Sam, speak now, or I'm walking out." I eyed the roofline, but I couldn't see through the falling snow. "Damn vampire. You want me to listen to you? Where are you?" I ground my teeth together.

Fuck this. I raised my hands and was ready to give myself up to Roman when a venomous growl pierced my ears before bright red eyes lasered me to the tree. The shifter trotted up, baring his canines.

"Easy now," I said in a shaky tone. I wasn't afraid of much, but I'd never been up close and personal with a shifter the size of one of the horses on my uncle's ranch.

With his snout, he nudged me to move. I stumbled my way into an open clearing and climbed over a body as the shifter coaxed me forward.

Roman whipped his head in my direction, grinning like he'd found the Holy Grail. "Well, there you are. I know Mason is with you."

Uncle Ray glared at me as though the situation we were in was all my fault. He wasn't wrong, but I would never admit that to him. When we got out of this mess, I would speak my mind once and for all. Then again, anything I had to say would only fall on deaf ears.

"Sam isn't here." I inched closer.

Aiming the tip of his sword at Uncle Ray's stomach, Roman flicked his chin to the white wolf. "Comb the woods."

The shifter took off like he was going to find the juiciest prey for his meal that night.

My uncle lunged forward and grabbed the blade with his bare hands, but Roman was quicker. He angled the sword upward, slicing off Uncle Ray's thumb, laughing as the body part flew through the air.

I came to an abrupt halt near the flagpole, and I lost my breath.

If Uncle Ray was in any pain, he didn't show it. Instead, he advanced toward Roman once again. Roman continued to laugh as he dropped the sword and, faster than I could track, pinned Uncle Ray by the throat against the SUV.

I thought Roman would suck my uncle dry given that Uncle Ray had just lost a thumb and was bleeding. But Roman didn't. Instead, with his back to me, he growled. "Layla, try anything, and I will detonate the bomb. Now, here's how this is going to go."

An animal yelp ripped through the air, and Vera pushed Jordyn farther out from under the portico as she scanned the grounds.

"He'll heal," Roman bit out to Vera. "Your job is to make sure she doesn't run."

As if Jordyn would run with a bomb strapped to her.

"Let the human go," Sam said from somewhere nearby. "You wanted me. Well, here I am."

I spun around, looking for the gorgeous vampire, but I didn't see him until I turned toward Roman. Sam strutted around the SUV, hands up as if he were getting arrested and wearing an expression that could have a whole city of humans running in the opposite direction.

Call me nuts, but I was in awe of him, and dare I say turned on as hell in spite of our circumstances.

He stalked forward with a sense of purpose, his silver eyes seeming to glow. His fangs were front and center, and he gave me the impression he was ready to snap necks and drain the blood from humans or vampires.

At the thought of blood, I was licking my dry lips and salivating to taste Sam's blood.

What the fuck? I swallowed as shivers racked

my body. When this was all over, I seriously had to see a psychiatrist.

Layla. Sam's husky voice was in my head. *Don't move.*

I hadn't planned on it, although I wished I had a grenade right about now. I could throw it at Roman or somewhere close by so I wouldn't kill my uncle. Anything to create a distraction.

Roman flung my uncle to the side and faced Sam head-on.

Uncle Ray scrambled to his feet, rushed over to me, and grabbed my arm hard. "Let's go."

It wasn't the time to argue with him, but I wasn't about to leave without Jordyn. "We need to get Jordyn."

Uncle Ray ripped off part of his flannel shirt and wrapped it around his thumbless hand. "This isn't our fight."

I bared my teeth at him. "Oh, it certainly is. I'm not leaving my sister."

Suddenly, the earth began to shake. The SUV moved as though a stampede of bulls were running at us. Uncle Ray gaped. I did too. I'd witnessed Sam's powers but not of that magnitude. The wind whipped around like a category three hurricane. Swirls of dead leaves and snowflakes churned around us.

Sam raised his arms high above his head as Roman pushed forward, seemingly struggling to get closer to Sam.

"Remove the bomb from Jordyn!" Sam's voice boomed.

"Not a chance in hell," Roman replied. "Unless you want to turn over Abbey."

Sam lowered one arm and closed his hand into a fist. The SUV slid toward Roman.

"I could crush you," Sam announced, staring at Roman as he continued to hold his ground.

"This is impossible," Uncle Ray said. "No vampire can do shit like this."

I had no retort for him. Actions always spoke louder than words and made skeptics believe. "He's not your normal vampire, or at least not the ones we're used to hunting," I mumbled.

I understood why Sam was in high demand, and if he had powers like those, then Jo and his father did as well. I didn't even want to think about Abbey, and I wasn't about to dwell on her prediction of my future.

As Sam opened his fist, three things happened at once. A ring of fire surrounded Roman, who was clutching his throat, laboring for oxygen. The vampire military converged, seemingly coming out of the woodwork, and Uncle Ray took off in Jordyn's direction.

Then as if a switch was turned off, the wind died, the ground stopped shaking, and Sam had Roman in his grasp. "If it weren't for my superiors, I would burn you alive," Sam growled the words through clenched teeth. Then he threw him across the field.

Roman coasted past me and landed at Tripp's feet just as he ran out from the woods with Uncle Jack on his tail.

I took off to save Jordyn, but I didn't get very far when Sam grabbed me from behind. "Not so fast. The last time you were confronted with a bomb, you almost blew up your other sister."

"Back off, vampire," I bit out.

Bones cracked before Vera shifted into wolf form, ready to eat Uncle Ray for her nightly snack.

My jaw landed at my feet. Seeing her shift was cool but weird on so many levels.

But then she bared her canines at Uncle Ray.

As much as I didn't care about him, I didn't want him to die. "Help my uncle Ray," I said to Sam. "He's thickheaded, and he's about to do something stupid." He'd already lost a body part, and if he didn't back down from Vera, he was about to lose more.

Sam let go of me, and I ran up to Uncle Ray, who was maybe ten feet from Jordyn and Vera. Jordyn shook her head, tears running down her face and over the tape on her mouth.

I slid between Uncle Ray and Vera and addressed the shifter. "Look, I know you want revenge, but honestly, we're sorry about your sister. We had no idea about the drug and how it reacted with shifters." I didn't think my apology would get me far, but I had to try.

Her wolf ears perked up as she twisted her dark head from one side to the other. She was a pretty wolf with a thick coat of dark fur that almost matched her human hair. In wolf form, she had spots of gold speckled throughout, and unlike the red eyes on the other wolf, hers were a shimmering amber.

Sam sidled up to me, and Vera growled. He held up his hands. "Our fight isn't with you and your pack. I get the need for revenge, but we have a bigger problem."

I gave Sam a sidelong glance. "We do?" I couldn't see anything else other than Jordyn's predicament.

Ignoring me, Sam continued. "Don't you want to know what's in that drug that killed your sister?

If it kills shifters, then others of your kind will become a victim to it."

Bones began to crack as Vera returned to her human form, which was very tall, curvy, and naked. "Are you threatening us, vampire?" She poked out her breasts, her nipples stiff, her jaw equally as hard as her amber eyes practically glowed with fire.

Ray all but pushed Sam out of the way. "Where's the fucking timer for that vest?"

Vera pressed her lips into a thin line. "There is none. The detonator is embedded inside the vest, and Roman has the device to set it off."

I whirled around, searching frantically for Roman. Webb was about to shove him into a van.

"No!" I sprinted as hard as I could, pumping my legs. "Wait!"

32

SAM

As soon as Layla bolted, I ripped the vest off Jordyn.

"Run," I said to her and her uncle. "Now!"

As soon as I'd slung the vest, it exploded over the SUV.

Motherfucker.

Anger as hot as embers shot down my arms. I was tired of the bombs. Screw Roman going to a vampire prison. Screw the Council of Elders and their laws. Roman had to pay for the damage he'd done. Not in prison, but with his life. Right here. Right now.

I stormed in the direction of the van, the snowy wind at my face, and I was sure I wore an expression that would level a building. I tempered

377

my elemental powers, although I was on the precipice of unleashing more than making the ground shake. I was ready to suck all the oxygen out of Roman and watch him suffer until he couldn't breathe anymore.

One of our guards was about to jump into the driver's seat as he nodded at Webb. I hurried, blowing past Layla and Jordyn as the two embraced.

The area was chaos. Kraft, Olivia, and other SEAL team members were checking the bodies strewn over the ground. Rianne was running toward her sisters as though she was being chased by one of the shifters. Upon closer inspection, I didn't see Vera or the other wolf. Tripp was talking with the Aberdeen uncles, or rather arguing with them, and Webb was watching the van take off as he brought his phone to his ear.

I kicked my legs into high gear and broke out into a full-on run when someone tackled me from behind.

I fell into a pile of snow that had been plowed and shoved to the side of the road. Quick as a flash, I threw my attacker off me. The white wolf growled as he rolled over once then twice before righting himself on all four legs. His red eyes lasered me as his canines dripped with venom.

I roared like a lion as I stalked toward him. "Prepare to have your neck snapped, shifter."

He growled, lowering his head, ready to attack, when a deep female voice shouted, "Dane, don't."

Then Webb practically growled my name. "Sam!"

It took me a second to snap out of my fury.

Vera jogged up, wearing a long leather coat that fell to her ankles. "We need him." She threw Dane a pair of pants.

"'Need' is a strong word," I fired back just as Webb approached, looking like one pissed off vampire.

Well, get in line.

The white wolf reshaped into his human form—tall, broad, and with hair as white as his wolf fur, yet the dude didn't look a day over thirty.

Vera's gaze bounced between Webb and me. "What do you know about the drug that killed my sister?"

Dane slipped into his pants.

Retracting his fangs, his eyes returning to blue, Webb clutched the phone in his hand. "We don't know much, but we can help."

Dane advanced a step, piercing Webb and me with his reddish-brown eyes. "I don't like him." He pointed at me.

Anger, hot and swift, caused my shoulders to lift and my gut to tighten. The feeling was mutual, but I kept my mouth shut.

Vera shot in between Dane and me. "Ease up, Dane."

Webb stiffened but extended his hand to Dane. "I'm Commander London. I'm in charge here. We don't want trouble."

Dane debated whether to shake or not. "Dane Gray, alpha for the Gray Pack."

The two exchanged a quick handshake.

The four of us settled in a circle as tension strung us together.

"Why are you working with Roman?" Webb asked.

The shifters exchanged a knowing look before Dane tipped his head at Vera.

She licked her lips. "It's a long story, but I'll give you the short version for now. About a year ago, Roman saved one of our own. We owed him a favor."

"Roman saved someone?" Shock laced my tone.

"Believe it or not," Vera said.

"Considering he used to work for a pharmaceutical company, he also promised he would help us find a solution to the drug that killed Vera's sister," Dane added.

A lightbulb flashed in my head. Roman had been the only one not to pass out from the drug-filled darts, which led me to conclude that maybe he had armed himself with some type of antidote. It wasn't unheard of. Dr. Vieira had formulated an antidote for the SEAL team to protect us from sedative-type drugs that our former enemy had used as weapons to slow us down.

"You conspired with him to kidnap my niece and Webb's daughter," I snarled at them. "And you're okay with murdering humans?"

Vera glanced over her shoulder at the Aberdeens, then pursed her lips. "They killed my sister. What would you do in my shoes?"

I couldn't exactly fault her for wanting revenge. I'd been ready to gut Rianne for threatening Jo.

Dane glowered, his eyes flashing bright red. "If there's a drug out there that could wipe out our entire species, I will do what it takes to protect my pack and other packs as well. Are you going to help us or not?"

Webb dragged a hand along his rock-solid jaw. "On one condition, and this is non-negotiable. You leave the Aberdeens alone. And before you protest, I understand that you want revenge, but we have bigger things at play here. We don't want a war on our hands with the Aberdeens or with you. Our role is to keep the peace. We're here to protect humans from your kind, our kind, and any supernatural. Do we have a deal?" Webb stared at Dane.

Dane considered Vera then Webb. "As long as you can uncover what the drug is and how to protect us against it, you have my pack behind you."

"Very well," Webb said. "We have a mess to clean up here. I have vampire hunters to deal with. Give us some time. I'll set up a meeting with our resident doctor who is skilled in finding and developing antidotes."

The tension clearly left Dane as he lowered his shoulders. Then Webb and Dane exchanged phone numbers before the shifters left.

I rubbed the back of my neck. "One problem down for now. So when did the uncles show up?" I asked Webb.

"They flew into Boston last night. I guess they had a hard time renting a car, given that most of the rental car companies closed due to the weather."

I was surprised the airport hadn't cancelled flights in and out. "And they knew where we were?"

"Apparently, the scout we have in Montana

told them, or Jack threatened it out of him," Webb said.

Tripp strode toward us as the uncles joined their nieces under the portico. Once he reached us, he flicked his head at the Aberdeens. "I'm going to take Ray up to the infirmary so Dr. Vieira can stitch up his hand. After that, the Aberdeens have a plane to catch."

"Steven wanted to talk to Jack," Webb said.

Tripp dragged a hand along his stubbled jaw. "There is no talking to those men, Webb. They need to leave. At the moment, their issue is their nieces. Let them get their family shit under control. Then Steven might have a better chance at Jack listening to him."

Webb nodded. "You're probably right. We have a ton to do here, anyway."

"Layla's leaving too?" I asked as I checked on Layla. She was absorbed in listening to Jack who appeared to be furious.

"It's best if she does," Webb and Tripp said in unison.

I wasn't ready to let Layla go, but I wasn't in charge. Besides, I had to choose my battles, and Webb was right. We had our hands full with shifters and many unanswered questions about Roman.

"Did we find Ben?" I searched the grounds but didn't see him.

"No," Webb said. "Sawyer has been trying consistently to get a ping on his phone's tracker."

"Everything secure with Roman's transport?" Tripp asked Webb.

Webb nodded. "He's on his way to our holding facility at the city airport. His fate now lies in the hands of the Council of Elders. I need to call Steven and Jo." He tapped on his phone as he walked away.

The million-dollar question was how Roman knew about Abbey? With my old man on the council, I shouldn't be worried. After all, he had mind-reading abilities.

"Sam, head in and find out where Sawyer is with pinging Ben's phone," Tripp ordered. "I'll handle the Aberdeens."

He was better at keeping the peace than I was, especially given that Jack Aberdeen was a hothead.

"By the way, how did Roman snag Ray?" I asked.

Tripp shook his sandy-blond head of hair, which was pulled back into a low ponytail. "He went out for a smoke just as Roman stormed the base. Then one thing led to another, and when

Ray saw Jordyn, he went apeshit. Roman learned who Ray was and decided to use him as a bargaining chip. He knew we wouldn't let the humans die." He took a breath. "We were prepared for Roman, but the minute we saw Jordyn with C-4, our plan came apart. Then it was chaos."

I stabbed my thumb at the building. "I'll find out where we are with Ben." The fact that he wasn't anywhere in sight made me worry. "I just want to talk to Layla for a minute."

"Make it quick," he returned as we made our way toward Layla and her family.

Jack wagged a finger at each of the sisters. "You've really started a shitstorm here. It's time you head home with us."

"We don't want to go home with you," Rianne said.

Layla was quiet, but her rapid pulse and the rage pouring off her were telling a different story. "You came all this way to rescue us? Why? Since our father died, you've wanted nothing to do with us."

"I promised your father I would watch over you three." Jack crossed bulky arms over his chest. "Up until now, I had no reason to come to your rescue."

Where Ray was muscled but lanky, Jack was

wide and burly. There was no mistaking the two were brothers. The Aberdeen men were gingers in different shades of red.

Tripp and I were about twenty feet from the Aberdeens when Rianne ran up to us.

Tripp muttered a swear word, and I held back a laugh. He'd had a rough time pacifying Rianne when she'd found that Layla hadn't been in her bed in the women's barracks.

At first, I thought Rianne would say something to Tripp, but instead she threw her arms around me. "Thank you."

I stiffened. "For what?" The woman hated me.

She playfully swatted at my arm. "Oh, don't be coy. You saved my life."

Jack's face was deepening to red as he watched Rianne.

"You know your uncle is not happy," I said.

She waved off Jack. "I couldn't give two shits. If it weren't for you, I wouldn't be alive."

"Does that mean you like vampires now?" I teased.

Tripp left Rianne and me to join Jack and his clan.

She rolled her brown eyes. "I wouldn't go that far."

I stole a glance at Layla, who was watching us intently. I was curious why she hadn't come over, when Ray asked, "Is there something going on between them?" The fire spitting from his gaze was epic.

Tripp opened the door into the main building. "Ray, Jack, shall we?"

Jordyn helped to usher her uncles into the building. "Sam saved Rianne's life. She's only thanking him."

Satisfied for the moment, Jack and Ray went inside, followed by Jordyn and Tripp.

As I strutted up to Layla, I opened a telepathic connection. I mainly wanted to confirm that I was still able to communicate with her that way. I'd almost fallen off the roof when her voice entered my head. I would still bet my life that she had some sort of vampire DNA or supernatural blood running through her veins. But that theory and the questions I had about how Layla and I had such a strong metaphysical connection weren't about to be answered anytime soon.

Hey, baby doll.

Her blue eyes widened at me as Rianne and I approached.

"I'm going to catch up to Jordyn," Rianne said before she hurried inside.

"I don't know how I can hear your voice in my head," she said.

I sized her up, taking in my fill of her curvy, gorgeous body. "It's a mystery to me, too." But I planned on talking to my father or even Dr. Vieira about that. "Are you staying or going home with your uncles?" *Please stay.*

She craned her neck up at me, giving me a sad smile. "If I don't, I'm afraid my uncles will make things difficult for all of us."

I kind of knew that would be her answer, but hearing her say it felt like she'd carved out my heart. Whoa! Maybe Jo and Abbey were right. Maybe I was falling for Layla. I didn't have the right to tell her what to do, but I sure as hell wasn't about to keep my mouth shut. "Your uncles don't own you, and we can handle them." Tripp and Webb would have my ass on a silver platter if they heard me now.

Layla slid her hands up my chest, giving me a sexy smile. "I know you can, but it's more than that. We have no house, no car, and little money. And my sisters and I need to chill for a while. The best place for us to do that is at my uncle's ranch."

I was tempted to kiss her, but then I wouldn't stop, and in a nanosecond I would have her naked.

I wrapped her in my arms, and my heart fluttered. "I don't want you to leave." Then I pressed my forehead to hers. "Stay?"

"Sam." My name from her lips sounded like a desperate plea. "I need to get my head clear." She lifted up on her toes and pecked me on the lips. "A lot has happened, and I don't know what's up or down anymore."

Man, I wasn't a beggar. Never had been and never would be. But in the heat of the moment, I was tempted. "You're mine, Layla. That wasn't a line to get you into bed." She needed to know I was serious. Deep down in the recesses of my soul, I knew she was the one for me.

"Things between us are moving too fast," she said in a low tone. "And who are we kidding? Can you see us in a relationship?"

Maybe she was right. Maybe I was blinded by her beauty, by the sweetness of her blood, and maybe my dick was the one making me feel like I would die if she left me. As much as I knew I should just walk away then, I couldn't. I had to commit her scent to memory, to feel her lips on mine one more time.

But fate had other plans when my phone rang. I wanted to ignore it but couldn't. We were waiting on news of Ben's whereabouts. I growled as I answered. "Go."

"We finally found Ben," Tripp said. "It's not good. We've instructed the ambulance to bring him here. I need you to meet them at the main gate."

"Fuck. Is he alive?" I wanted to crush Roman.

"Barely," Tripp said. "Get up to the gate now."

I hung up and pecked Layla on the lips. Not exactly the kiss to remember, but Ben was a SEAL, a friend, and a brother, and we dropped what we were doing to help our brethren.

33

LAYLA

Seven days had passed since the showdown with Roman and the shifters. Seven days since I'd walked off base with my sisters in tow. Like I told Sam, we had no house, no car, and very little money to our names. As much as it had pained me to leave Sam, I needed distance between us. My sisters and I were in desperate need of relaxing and healing, both physically and emotionally. We also wanted to get as far away from vampires and shifters as we could, or rather Roman and Vera.

I'd had plenty of time to think, to clear my head, and to analyze what I wanted to do with my life, which was something other than hunting vampires or dating one. But I wasn't sure if my sisters and I would ever be free of supernaturals.

I worried that Vera would retaliate even though Webb had assured us that she and her pack wouldn't be a problem for us. The vampire Navy SEAL team, with the help of Dr. Vieira, would work with the Gray Pack to find out what was in the drug Wyman had given us to use on Sam. As far as Roman was concerned, he was in the custody of the vampire government.

Ben, on the other hand, was fighting for his life. At least he had been when we'd left the naval base. I'd never seen Sam so distraught.

I sighed and popped my head back against the cabinet in the modest en suite bathroom. I was sitting on the floor with the toilet dead ahead of me, hoping I didn't need to use it. But my stomach was saying otherwise. For the last two nights, I'd been waking up in cold sweats then running to the bathroom and puking my guts out. All I kept thinking was I needed Sam's blood, but up until two days ago, I'd been fine. I'd had no cravings for his blood, no visions, no supernatural anything. I was beginning to think Sam had me under a magic spell in his presence. Then again, I knew his blood had been the cause of my visions and cravings, and since I hadn't been around the vampire or ingested his blood, I'd felt normal again—human.

I rushed over to the toilet and hugged it tightly as acid shot to my throat. It had to be something I'd eaten, but my sisters weren't sick, and neither was anyone else in the family. The only other conclusion was the flu.

Jordyn stumbled in, rubbing her eyes. "What's wrong? This is the second early morning hug fest with that toilet."

I grunted. "Maybe Uncle Jack is poisoning me for causing all that trouble in Massachusetts." I was kidding. My uncle might be an asshole, but he wouldn't hurt family. The most he'd done was yell, and boy, had he yelled.

I heaved again, the sound echoing in the bowl.

"I'm not a sympathy puker," Jordyn announced. "But I'm ready to join you for some reason."

Once I emptied what was left in my stomach, I flushed the toilet then splashed water on my face.

She sat on the bathtub. "Should we take you to a doctor?"

I wiped my face with a soft hand towel. "No." I proceeded to rinse my mouth out with a bottle of mouthwash. "I think it's the flu."

"Could you be pregnant?"

I snorted and choked on the wintergreen liquid. "Are you insane?" I snarled at her in the mirror. "There's no way I can get pregnant from Sam."

She crossed one pajama-clad leg over the other. "He's not your ordinary vampire. Maybe his sperm has magic in it." She was holding back a giggle. "Can you imagine if you had a vampire baby?"

I flipped her the bird. "You've lost some brain cells."

She sidled up to me and ran her hands through my bedhead hair. "Part of me is serious." Her sleepy brown eyes found my blue ones in the mirror. "You said yourself the connection you have with him is strong. You could even speak telepathically."

"Shh." I went over and closed the bathroom door. The bedroom my sisters and I shared at the ranch had an en suite, but still, I had to make sure my aunt didn't come in, which she had a habit of doing in the mornings to make sure we had enough towels.

I doubted she would be up at four a.m., but still, I had to be cautious. Uncle Jack would have our heads roasting over an open fire if he knew I'd slept with Sam. It had been bad enough when Uncle Ray and Uncle Jack almost lost their wits when Rianne had thrown her arms around Sam to thank him for saving her life.

"First, I haven't had any signs of supernatural crap since we've been here. Second, I'm not pregnant." I whispered every word.

"Maybe now that his blood is out of your system, you're having withdrawals."

That wasn't farfetched. Sam's blood was potent, and I had felt drunk or on some kick-ass, potent drug after I had had a few drops of his blood. On the other hand, I couldn't help but think that I had vampire DNA. I hadn't broached that subject with my sisters or anyone. There were too many ears in the house and on the property. I had been planning to ask my Uncle Jack about our family lineage, but I'd chickened out so many times, it wasn't funny. Mainly because Uncle Jack would see right through me, and then he would proceed to tell me I had been around vampires for too long. I guessed that was true.

"I honestly think it's just a stomach flu."

Jordyn felt my forehead. "You are a bit warm."

"If it doesn't ease up in a couple of days, then I'll go to urgent care in town." I closed the toilet lid and sat down. "I have an off-the-wall question."

She hopped up on the counter. "Shoot."

"Do you think we carry any vampire DNA or that there are vampires in our family history?"

She snorted. "No way. Mom and Dad would've told us. And I doubt we would be hunting them if we were descendants of vampires."

I yawned. "You're right. It was a stupid question."

"Let's get your mind off that topic. Is Sam still texting you?"

It was my turn to snort. "How is talking about Sam taking my mind off the topic?"

"He likes you a lot," she said.

"Does it matter? How in the world would or could we have a relationship? Human and vampire isn't exactly a match made in heaven, and let's not forget that our family is made up of vampire hunters. Us included."

"What if he shows up here?" Jordyn asked.

I laughed weakly. "He won't." Uncle Jack had spoken to Steven Mason on our way out of the city. Steven had wanted to meet, but Uncle Jack hadn't been in the mood. After our showdown with Roman, my uncles weren't ready to call a truce. They were ready to kill. "Steven doesn't want trouble. He'll make darn sure Sam doesn't start any. It's Uncle Ray we have to worry about, though." He was still furious that Roman had cut off his thumb.

"It's been kind of nice being here." Jordyn kept her voice low. "But I'm ready to leave. Before long, we'll be cleaning horse stalls and other chores I don't care to take on." She twisted her brown hair up on her head and secured it with a clip that had been on the counter. "I vote to return to Massachusetts."

My eyebrows disappeared into my hairline.

"Hear me out. If we stay here, we'll never be any better than them." She pointed to the door. "We can make a difference in this world, Layla. Dad always thought ridding the planet of vampires would give us a brighter future. What if we did just that but with the help of the vampire military? They're fighting to protect humanity. Let's fight with them. Screw the family here. We've never been close to them, anyway."

"No way. I've felt normal again since we've been here. Well, up until recently. But if we return, not only am I afraid of losing myself to a vampire, but our family will hunt us down. Of course, I agree we haven't been close with our uncles." I paused to take a breath. "I don't want the headache of dealing with vampires or our uncles. I won't lie and say Sam hasn't been on my mind. But again, he and I would never work."

She scratched her face. "Why not? He's a hot-as-fuck vampire. You like him. He likes you. So live it up. Have kinky vampire sex, if only for a little while. I wouldn't mind giving one of them a go in the bedroom." Her cheeks reddened.

"Ah, there's the real story," I teased.

"They're cool, and if I'm being honest, I feel better around the military vampires than I do here."

There were many unanswered questions, including one big one that I hadn't forgotten. "Will Abbey's vision of Rianne killing me come true?"

"All the more reason to be close to the Masons. That way Abbey can warn us quickly. You said yourself, Abbey wasn't sure how or when. And she was struggling with her visions, right?"

I bobbed my head. I wanted Jordyn to be happy. Hell, I wanted Rianne to be as well. I couldn't see Rianne living among vampires. Granted, she'd changed her tune about Sam since he saved her life, but that didn't mean she was about to break bread with him or any of the vampire Navy SEALs. "If Rianne agrees, I might consider it." From a convo Rianne and I had in the women's barracks, I knew she wanted to discuss the future, which involved her looking into the military. "Let's talk to her when she wakes."

"You know one thing that has been bothering

me about Uncle Ray and Uncle Jack?" Jordyn asked. "They quit hunting vampires cold turkey right after Dad died with some excuse about lack of finances for weapons and building a better life for their family. Yet when you drill down to who they really are, revenge is in their nature. I mean, why didn't they go looking for the vampire who killed Dad?"

"Where did all that come from?" I didn't see the connection between what she'd said and what we'd been through recently. Then my stomach took the wheel and drove me to open the lid on the toilet as fast as I could. I heaved once again.

Our sad problems would have to wait.

Forty-eight hours later, I couldn't get out of bed. My stomach hurt, my head pounded like someone was beating on it with a club, my limbs felt like saltwater taffy, and I had a low-grade fever.

Rianne patted my face with a cool washcloth. "We should get you to a doctor."

I licked my dry, chapped lips. "I'll feel better in a day or two. Where's Jordyn?" I hadn't seen much of her since our convo in the bathroom two days prior. Then again, I hadn't seen hardly anyone since I'd been in bed and sleeping most of the time.

"She went to the store for something," Rianne said.

I pushed myself up. "Can you adjust my pillows?"

Once she propped me up, I grabbed the glass of water Aunt Tab had brought me. She'd been giving me water and chicken broth and nothing else.

Speaking of my aunt, she ambled in, carrying a tray of toast and what looked to be hot tea with a stick of rock candy in it. Her salt-and-pepper hair was piled on top of her head. She wore an apron around her waist, and her red V-neck sweater clung to her petite frame.

I smiled weakly. Mom had used that very remedy to break our fevers when anyone in our house had gotten sick.

Rianne moved to the foot of the bed.

Aunt Tab set the tray on the empty nightstand then handed me the cup of tea. "It has whiskey in it, which should help zap the fever."

I usually loved whiskey in my coffee, but the sound of alcohol made me want to throw up. I took the cup, anyway, and sipped. As soon as the hot liquid coupled with the burn of the whiskey went down my throat, I gagged.

She grabbed the cup as her dark eyes filled with worry. "We should get you to a doctor."

"No. The chicken broth is working. The whiskey, not so much."

She returned the cup to the tray. "If the fever doesn't break by the morning, I'm taking you to get checked." Her tone permitted no argument.

I wasn't in the mood to protest, so I just gave her a nod and plopped my head on the pillow.

She kissed me on my temple. "I'll come back later to check on you." She started to leave but turned around. "Layla, you know Jack loves you and cares about you." She regarded Rianne. "All three of you. He's still not over your father's death, and he won't come out and say this, but he gets spooked with vampires because of what happened to your father, which is one of the reasons he's not hunting them anymore."

"Why hasn't he told me that?" I asked.

She smiled sadly. "He's a big ogre and a man. He doesn't do feelings. If he didn't care, he wouldn't have gone to Massachusetts to make sure you were okay. He promised your dad he would look out for you girls."

"He has a funny way of showing it," I mumbled.

"I know. I'm glad you girls are here. And you

can stay as long as you like," Aunt Tab said. "Get some rest." Then she left.

Jordyn's voice peppered the air as she said hi to Aunt Tab before running in and locking the door behind her. She smiled from ear to ear, her rosy cheeks growing redder as she swung her brown gaze from Rianne to me.

Rianne climbed on the bed and crossed her legs underneath her. "What's with stealth mode?"

Jordyn placed her purse on the bed. "Don't freak out." She curled her hair around her ear as she dug into her purse.

I rolled my eyes. "What did you do?"

"Ooh, do you have a joint in there?" Rianne lit up like a Christmas tree.

"No." Jordyn pulled out a pregnancy test.

Rianne snagged it from her. "Layla's not pregnant."

Rianne and Jordyn had been arguing and analyzing my situation since yesterday morning when I started feeling worse. They had me explain everything I'd been through with Sam since arriving on base. I'd left out some of the sexy parts.

"If she's not, that test will tell us." Jordyn grabbed the box from Rianne. "Okay, you said your period is just about due. Right?"

I shrugged. "Yeah, in about five or six days maybe."

Rianne read the box. "It says here this test can detect a positive or negative reading six days before you start your period."

"It can also give a false positive," I said.

"And negative," Jordyn added, "but let's just see what we get." She held out her hand. "Come on. Once you take it, I'll dispose of the test so no one in this house finds it."

Leave it to my youngest sister to think of everything.

"And if I say no?" I asked.

Jordyn stuck her hands on her hips. "Layla Aberdeen, get your ass up now."

"What's the big deal?" Rianne asked me. "We know you're not. But if you are, then we have a problem." Worry washed over her.

I rolled my eyes. "I'm not. So stop with the ifs and take the scared look off your face."

Jordyn didn't seem to care if I was or wasn't. If I knew her, she would think me getting knocked up by a vampire would be the coolest thing.

I had to side with Rianne. If I was pregnant with a vampire baby, I had a colossal problem that would bring down the Aberdeen family in one second flat. But I wasn't worried. I didn't have the right blood type.

Heaving a sigh, I crawled out of bed and into the bathroom. After peeing on the stick, I set it on the counter and swayed as blackness crept in from my peripheral vision. Just as Jordyn rushed toward me, the world went dark.

To be continued...

Please check my website at https:// sbalexander.com for more information on *The Predator*

I bit a vampire—sunk my teeth right into his flesh and drew blood, and I liked it. Now, something is happening to me. I'm craving blood as if I'm a vampire, and I'm not. My family has been hunting and killing the bloodsuckers for centuries.

So it comes as a horrifying shock when my aunt catches me licking blood off a knife like its cake batter. Panicking, she goes behind my back and calls someone who she thinks can help me. Little does she know that dangling me like a carrot to Sam Mason would have consequences no one is prepared for, especially me.

I'm not ready to deal with the cocky vampire who rocked my world so hard, my brain is still recovering, and my body is still tingling.

But when I find the powerful Vampire Navy SEAL and my aunt chatting like besties, my heart almost stops beating. If my uncle finds Sam on his property, he'll burn him alive.

Little do I know it's not my uncle I have to worry about. One of my sisters decides that I would be better off not falling for a vampire. I assure her I'm not. But she knows me better than I know myself.

Now instead of killing vampires, I'm rushing to save one. I pray I can't get there in time. Otherwise, my family will suffer a fate worse than death.

Chapter 1
SAM

The scent of wet dog burned my nostrils as I stalked into the infirmary with one purpose in mind—tear out Dane Gray's canines with my bare hands. My eyes flashed from green to silver and my fangs lowered slow and deadly.

Dane was responsible for what happened to Ben. I couldn't exactly prove it, but Ben's wound was definitely from a large animal. Bears were a possibility, but they were rare in and around the city.

For the last eleven days since the ambulance brought Ben in, he'd been in and out of consciousness, and as the days passed, his condition wasn't improving.

It felt like a dagger kept stabbing my heart over and over again anytime I looked at my best friend. He'd been through hell and back since I'd become a vampire. He'd been the product of an experiment gone wrong, and as a result, he was half human and half vampire. The vampire in him should be healing him, which led us to believe he'd been bitten by a shifter. According to Doc, their venom could be poisonous to vampires. Not so much for humans. With Ben's half-human side,

I was curious if part of him would become a shifter.

Tripp had said no unless it was from an alpha. Despite the science, I was thankful a clerk at a gas station not far outside the state forest had found Ben behind his establishment and reacted quickly. Luckily, one of the paramedics on the scene knew Ben was a Navy SEAL stationed on the naval base. He'd gotten ahold of us, and we'd rerouted them here.

Tripp marched toward me, his bronze eyes pinpricks as he shook his head. "Back away. We don't know that Dane's pack is responsible for Ben."

I glowered at the alpha in the distance as he and a bald-headed dude gave Dr. Vieira their rapt attention.

I gritted my teeth. "He is. I feel it in my bones."

Tripp slapped a hand on my shoulder just as Dane sat in a chair and held out his arm. He was here to give Doc a sample of his blood for Doc's research. We'd agreed to help the Gray Pack uncover why one of their own died from a shot of a drug used by Layla Aberdeen and her sisters that night at the club.

Tripp guided me into an empty patient room. "We invited them in. We are not getting into a fight. Not here. Not now. Are we clear?"

Growling, my fangs clicked into place as rage boiled inside me. I was a second away from ramming my fists into the glass supply cabinet. "Who's the bald dude?"

Tripp swiped a hand over his sandy-blond hair that was tied into a ponytail at the nape of his neck. "Dane's beta, Ross. Look, after Doc pulls their blood, I have a plan."

I retracted my fangs. "Care to share?"

"Just follow my lead." He sounded as frustrated as I probably looked.

I tucked my fury away for the time being, stretched my neck one way then the other, and trailed behind Tripp. If he had a plan, I was sure it was a good one. Unlike me, Tripp had an uncanny way of extracting the truth without beating someone over the head.

Blood flowed from Dane's arm into a vial before Doc switched the filled one with an empty one. Ross was engrossed in something on his phone as he waited his turn near the stainless steel counter along the sidewall opposite Doc.

Dane lasered his dark eyes on me as though he was ready to leap over the black countertop and slice off my head.

That rage I held in tightly was about to burst as I approached.

Tripp pressed his hands into the edge of the counter. *Easy, Sam,* he said telepathically.

I sidled up to him. *I'm cool,* I lied.

Dane swung his gaze to Tripp. "Did you work out your issues with the vampire hunters?"

"Let's stay focused on why you're here," Tripp said.

Ross's bald head shot up from his phone, his hazel eyes glinting beneath the stark bright lights overhead. "The Aberdeen women need to atone for what they did to one of our own."

I tucked my fisted hands in the pockets of my cargo pants, staring him down. "Touch any of them," I barked, "and you'll deal with me." If he so much as said Layla's name, I might tear him to shreds.

Ross whistled. "Sounds to me like you have it bad for one of them."

It was hard not to. Layla Aberdeen was beautiful, wild, tough, sassy, feisty, and bold as fuck, and she was all mine.

Sam, take it down a notch. Tripp's caustic tone was blaring in my head.

Easier said than done. Layla was embedded in my psyche, my skin, my veins, my brain, my dreams, and every part of me. I hadn't been able to stop thinking about her since she left. The way she made me feel like a god among gods. Like she was my other half, which sounded fucked-up on so many levels. A relationship between a human and vampire wasn't unheard of. After all, my mom had been human. But my mom hadn't been a vampire hunter and had no desire to burn my father at the stake.

Regardless, eleven days had passed since Layla had left. Eleven days of hell, not being close to her. Eleven days of sleepless nights, thinking of her and every other screwed-up thing happening in my life. I'd been tempted to get my ass on a plane and pay her a visit. Maybe that would calm me down. Hell, I knew it would. But the auburn-haired goddess wanted some space to clear her head, and I wanted to be here for Ben.

However, if she kept ghosting me and not responding to my texts, then vampire hunters be damned. I would storm their Montana ranch.

"Okay, Dane," Dr. Vieira said. "Ross, it's your turn."

The two traded places.

"Sam, I would like you to meet my beta, Ross Gray," Dane said.

Ross and I exchanged a glare.

"I see you and my brother will get along great." Sarcasm dripped from Dane's tone as he smirked.

I envisioned my hands around their throats and snapping necks.

As if Doc knew what I wanted to do, he piped in, zapping the tension strung between Dane and me. "I would like to run an autopsy on your dead shifter." He inserted the needle into Ross's arm. "Is it possible to bring the body to me?"

"It isn't," Ross said. "But we did extract some of her blood before the burial."

Dane slid a box that was on the lab bench next to him over to Dr. Vieira. "We kept it refrigerated."

"Mmm," Doc said as he finished pulling Ross's blood. "Not as good as doing an autopsy, but I might be able to work with this."

"How long before you have any results?" Ross asked.

Doc tore off his nitrile gloves and deposited them into a trash bin near the sink. "I'm not sure. The blood samples will go to our lab to have a full toxicology workup. We have a small amount of the darts that were recovered from the club. I'm having the drug analyzed as well."

Wyman, who had hired Layla and her sisters to capture me, was still in our custody. He'd given the drug to Layla to knock me out so he could turn me over to his former employer—the CIA. Regardless, he learned about the drug from none other than

Layla's father. As far as Wyman knew, it was a highly concentrated human sedative that the Aberdeens had been testing out when Layla's father was killed. I was 100 percent certain Layla didn't know that tidbit. In fact, she'd given us the impression she had no clue what the drug could do.

But I wasn't about to divulge that part, not to the shifters who were salivating to seek revenge on the Aberdeens. I couldn't blame them. If the tables were turned, I would want the same. Still, we couldn't allow shifters to take out humans.

I zeroed in on the conversation at hand.

"You don't think there's wolfsbane in the drug?" Dane asked Doc. "That's the only thing I can think of that would kill us. Can it do the same to a vampire?"

"It hasn't been known to," Dr. Vieira responded. "But as a doctor, I won't say it's impossible. However, not one vampire died at the club that night. Your shifter had been the only death." Doc wiped his hands with a paper towel. "I might need more blood from you and your pack. Will that be a problem?"

"No," Dane said. "Just let me know what you need."

"Good. Now, if you'll excuse me, I would like to pack up these samples for the lab," Doc said.

Dane scrubbed a hand along his angular jaw. "I have one last question. Why didn't Roman Brown react the same way as the other vampires in the club? From what he told us, the drug paralyzed him, but he was still awake."

"It's highly possible Roman has access to an antidote to counteract sedative-type drugs," Doc informed Dane. "We have one handy for that very reason, and the SEAL team is given a dose when entering into combat or potential situations with our enemies."

The Council of Elders had interrogated Roman until they were blue in the face. According to my old man, who was an elder, Roman wasn't talking. My father had taken the next step to read Roman's mind, but the fucker was smart. He knew how to clear his head so my father couldn't get a damn thing from him. Either that, or Roman had his own mind-blocking potion like we had. After all, he'd worked for a pharmaceutical company, so it wouldn't be a shocker for Roman to have access to drugs.

Doc glanced up at the six-foot-five alpha. "I'll let Lieutenant Tripp know when I have some concrete results on your blood samples." Then he collected the tray of samples along with the box Dane had given him and headed in the direction of his office.

Silence descended before Tripp cleared his throat. "Dane, if you have a minute, I would like to show you something. Follow me." Tripp didn't wait for the shifters to answer. He pivoted on his heel and stalked toward the patient rooms that banked one wall in the infirmary.

Dane and Ross exchanged a suspicious look but followed Tripp just the same into Ben's room.

Once the four of us surrounded Ben's bed, Dane's eyebrows pinched together. "You want to show us a patient?" It sounded as if he had never seen Ben before now. Maybe I was wrong about him.

The heart monitor beeped as Ben's chest rose and fell.

Tripp pulled back the blanket, exposing the bandage on Ben's waist.

Dane's Adam's apple bobbed as a nervous energy floated in the air.

A muscle jumped along Ross's jaw.

Tripp lifted the taped gauze to expose Ben's massive wound.

I fisted my hands at my side.

Dane pointed a finger at Ben's mangled waist.

"What's this? Are you trying to say we did this?" His tone bordered on a growl.

I glowered at the shifters. "Did you?"

Dane's eyes flashed red as his canines clicked into place.

Tripp jutted out his chin, calm and reserved. "We're only asking. Obviously this is a shifter bite."

"That could very well be from another animal, like a bear," Ross said smugly.

Tension, thick and angry, dangled over Ben.

Now it was Tripp's turn to show his fangs. "Do you think we're idiots, beta? If it were a bear, I'm sure Ben wouldn't be here. That's a wolf bite. I should know. I've seen plenty of them. Wolf blood runs in my family."

If they were surprised at Tripp's news, they didn't show it.

I didn't detect any guilt or that they were hiding anything. Then again, they weren't exactly human, which meant they knew how to hide their true emotions.

Dane flared his nostrils. "So you're accusing me or my pack of what happened to your man?"

"One of your pack members, Vera, had been Roman's sidekick," I said. "She wanted revenge for her sister's death."

Tripp's eyes flashed from bronze to liquid black. "Let's not forget, Dane, you were taking orders from Roman that night. You were desperate to do his bidding because you owed him a favor."

Dane's claws grew from each fingernail, sharp and deadly, as his red eyes bore a hole into Tripp. "I ought to rip out your throat."

"For what? Asking a question?" Fury fueled my elemental powers, causing the metal rolling table Doc used to fly across the room. "Seems to me you are guilty."

Ross, who had been standing at the foot of the bed, stalked up to me. "I don't like you." His eyes morphed from hazel to shimmering blue.

I was beginning to learn that the alpha had red eyes. His second had a deep cerulean-blue, but Vera, if I remembered correctly, had amber eyes in wolf form. Interesting hierarchy of physical transformations. Then again, my family had different eye colors that aligned with how powerful we were.

Ross and I were nose to nose, chest to chest, and both of us were breathing fire. "Feeling's mutual, beta." I itched to do something other than stare at the jerk. "Who in your pack attacked Ben?"

A deep grumble shook the walls. In a flash,

Ross was pushed aside, and Dane dug his claws into my neck. "Back the fuck down, vampire."

I grinned as I gripped his balls. "I could crush your jewels in a flat second, so take your fucking paws off me."

"Sam," Tripp warned. "This room isn't the place."

Pain etched Dane's face as his canines dripped with venom.

I snarled, pushing Dane so hard he stumbled into the medical supply cabinet, almost breaking the glass doors.

He lunged at me, swiping his sharp claws down my face.

Motherfucker.

Ross and Tripp intervened.

Dane shrugged off Ross as his red eyes bored a hole in my forehead. "Touch me again, and I will rip out your throat." Then he brushed his hands down his jean-clad legs, retracting his canines as well as his claws. "Keep your man in line, lieutenant. Or I'll have to do it for you."

It was Tripp's turn to show a side of him not many see as he spit fire at Dane, standing toe to toe and eye to eye with the alpha. "Let's get something straight. I don't take orders from you, and if you want our help with the drug, I suggest you answer our question. Did you or did you not tear out Ben's flesh?"

Ross ran a hand over his bald head. "Just tell them, Dane. Then we can get the fuck out of here. These vampires are making me itch."

It was useless to even acknowledge the brazen barb Ross dropped. "Karma's a bitch, man. But you're right. The faster you dogs leave, the better we'll all be."

Dane backed away from Tripp, sighing. "We have a new pup in our pack who couldn't control himself. When your man escaped from Roman, we had one of ours chase after him. Things escalated. The two got into a fight. Our man went down and yours disappeared."

Kraft had mentioned that he and Olivia had found a trail of blood in the snow that night.

I rubbed my throat. "He dies, I'm coming for you." I pointed at Dane. Fuck his beta. I wanted to take down the big bad alpha.

Dane arched a thick dark brow, which was in stark contrast to his white hair. "You can try, vampire. But you'll fail."

Tripp pinned me with daggers. No doubt daring me to engage.

I bit my tongue for now and stalked out. I

needed to release some fury, and short of getting laid, I had something else in mind.

End of Sample

Please check my website at https:// sbalexander.com for more information on *The Predator*

ABOUT THE AUTHOR

Bestselling author **S.B. Alexander** is an independent author with over 25 titles to date. She writes paranormal, new adult, and sweet romances that feature hot heroes stealing hearts.

S.B. or Susan as she likes to be called is a navy veteran, former high school teacher, and former corporate sales executive. She's a lover of sports, especially baseball, although nowadays you can find her glued to the TV during football season.

When she's not writing, she's a full-time caregiver to her soul mate of twenty-three years who got a bad deal in life when he was diagnosed with ALS. Her motto: "Life is too short to waste. So live every moment like it's your last."

You can connect with S.B. Alexander in the following ways:

Reader Group: https://
sbalexander.com/beastsandbitches
Author Website: https://sbalexander.com
Newsletter: https://sbalexander.com/newsletter
Email: susan@sbalexander.com

NEVER MISS A NEW RELEASE:
Sign up for her Author App
iTunes: https://bit.ly/sbalexanderitunes
Android: https://bit.ly/sbalexanderandroid

facebook.com/sbalexander.authorpage

twitter.com/sbalex_author

instagram.com/sbalexanderauthor

amazon.com/author/sbalexander

bookbub.com/authors/s-b-alexander

ALSO BY S.B. ALEXANDER

MAXWELL SERIES

Upper Young Adult/New Adult Contemporary Romance

Dare to Kiss

Dare to Dream

Dare to Love

Dare to Dance

Dare to Live

Dare to Breathe

Dare to Embrace

THE MAXWELL FAMILY SAGA SERIES

Young Adult Sweet Romance

My Heart to Touch

My Heart to Hold

My Heart to Give

My Heart to Keep

THE VAMPIRE NAVY SEAL SERIES

Paranormal Romance

On the Edge of Humanity

On the Edge of Eternity

On the Edge of Destiny

On the Edge of Misery

On the Edge of Infinity

VAMPIRE NAVY SEAL: SAM & LAYLA SERIES

Paranormal Romance

The Hunted

*The Predator**

*The Union**

*The Dawning**

*The Prodigies**

STAND-ALONES

New Adult Contemporary Romance

Crazy For You

Unforgettable

Holding Onto Forever

Breaking Rules

Rescuing Riley

THE HART SERIES

New Adult Contemporary Romance

Hart of Darkness

Hart of Vengeance

*Visit https://sbalexander.com/all-books/ to learn more about S.B. Alexander books and future releases. Please note release dates are subject to change based on reader demand and the author's schedule. Subscribing to the author's newsletter or following her on Facebook is the best way to stay updated with planned new releases.

GLOSSARY OF TERMS

Natural-born vampire: A human born with the vampire gene that, when activated, will turn them into a vampire.

Activation process: Those who carry the vampire gene can only turn by drinking the blood of their vampire father at the age of sixteen years or older.

Council of Elders – A group of five vampires who set the laws.

Genetic engineering: Turning humans into vampires through a process of restructuring their DNA.

Cobalt – A vampire's kryptonite. The metal will kill a vampire if staked through the heart. It will also burn a vampire's skin if they come in contact with it.

Reproduction: A natural-born vampire is born by a male vampire and a human female with a rare blood type of Vel negative.

Council of Eternal Affairs: The legal department of the vampire government.

Vampire characteristics: Sunlight doesn't burn them. Their hearts beat at <5 bpm. Skin temperature is ten degrees cooler than a human. Eye color changes to black except for a few chosen ones.

Steven Mason: Vampire and father to twins Jo and Sam Mason. He's dubbed the most powerful of all vampires because of his many powers, including his mind-reading abilities. He can only read minds when touching someone except when it comes to his children. His normal eye color is green. His vampire eye color is silver.

Jo Mason: Turned at sixteen. Powers include seeing the future through her dreams, mind-reading without touching a person, telekinesis, and she's an elemental with the ability to manipulate water, air, earth, and fire. Her normal eye color is silver. Her vampire eye color is violet.

Sam Mason: Turned at sixteen. Powers include feeling what others feel (Empath), telekinesis, and he can compel a person using a series of numbers woven into a magical spell. He's also an elemental with the ability to manipulate water, air, earth, and fire. His normal eye color is green. His vampire eye color is silver.

Jupiter Sentinels: A secret and elite Navy SEAL Team within the military. Their role is to help the human military and guard the supernatural world.

Plutariums: A rogue team of vampires who want power and to engineer an army that would change humans into vampires.

Guardians: Vampires who are equivalent to the human police.